SHELTER

ALSO BY CATHERINE JINKS AND AVAILABLE FROM TEXT
Shepherd

Catherine Jinks has published more than forty books for adults and children. She has won many awards including the Victorian Premier's Literary Award, the Aurealis Award for science fiction, the Adelaide Festival Award and the Davitt Award for crime fiction. Catherine is a four-time winner of the Children's Book Council of Australia Book of the Year Award and in 2001 was presented with a Centenary Medal for her contribution to Australian children's literature. She lives in the Blue Mountains of New South Wales.

SHELTER

CATHERINE JINKS

TEXT PUBLISHING MELBOURNE AUSTRALIA

textpublishing.com.au

The Text Publishing Company
Swann House, 22 William Street, Melbourne Victoria 3000, Australia

The Text Publishing Company (UK) Ltd
130 Wood Street, London EC2V 6DL, United Kingdom

Published by The Text Publishing Company, 2021

Cover design by Text
Cover image by iStock
Page design by Imogen Stubbs
Typeset in Adobe Garamond Pro 13/18pt by J&M Typesetting

Printed and bound in Australia by Griffin Press, part of Ovato, an accredited ISO/ NZS 14001:2004 Environmental Management System printer.

ISBN: 9781922330468 (paperback)
ISBN: 9781925923759 (ebook)

A catalogue record for this book is available from the National Library of Australia.

To Rhonda Jinks (1939–2019)

ARRIVAL

I FIRST SAW her spotlit by headlights, a pink plush rabbit tucked under her arm. She had a patch of rough skin near her mouth and another high on her cheekbone. Her expression was stoic. Beneath the hem of a white net tutu, her skinny little legs were bare except for a Wiggles bandaid on her right knee.

She looked just like Emily, and it broke my heart.

'Megan.' Jill tossed me a packet of nappies. 'You'll need these.'

'I've stocked up already.'

'No. These are for Analiese. She still wets the bed.'

'Oh.'

'And she's got eczema. Don't tell me that's not stress-related.' Jill dragged a bulging suitcase from the back of her four-wheel drive. 'I bought some cream from the chemist, but I'm still a bit concerned. Nerine's run out of the prescription stuff.'

I could barely absorb what she was saying. Everything

had happened so fast, I still hadn't caught up. Five minutes earlier I'd been sitting alone in my silent car, worrying that Jill wouldn't be able to find me. Nights are always darker on country roads and the moon was masked by a thick veil of cloud. As for the church I'd chosen, it was set well back at the end of a long dirt driveway, and the sign on the front fence wasn't very obvious. Not to someone who didn't know the area. Not to someone who'd been driving for five hours with two kids and a nervous mother breathing down her neck.

I'd picked the church because it was quite remote—a little stone chapel in the middle of nowhere. Farmers had once come for miles to attend its Sunday services, but now it was just a wedding venue and a photo opportunity. There was no chance at all that anyone else would be there at midnight. *No* chance.

The only risk was passing traffic, though I'd parked well behind the building, away from the road. After an hour, finally, it happened. Tyres crunched. An engine purred. Two beams of light swept across the ragged clumps of sifton bush beyond the fence. Then Jill's gleaming car bumped into view—so big and fancy that I was alarmed at first. I'd been expecting an old clunker like mine. But the face behind the wheel reassured me, even though it had aged a lot. Ten hard years had frosted Jill's dark curls and carved deep lines around her mouth. Her glasses were new, though her hug was the same. Fierce and bony.

Unlike me, she'd never carried much weight.

Introductions took a few seconds; Jill seemed rushed and

slightly distracted. She headed straight for the rear of her car and I followed her.

'Is your boot open?' she asked. I grabbed another packet of nappies and scurried back to my own vehicle, where Nerine was wrestling with a booster seat. *She* wasn't what I'd expected, either. When you're told that someone is 'desperate and abused', you get a picture in your head—but this girl wasn't small and shuffling. She was tall, rangy and intense, with lots of pent-up energy. Her bleached hair was dark at the roots. With her bold jewellery, cropped jacket and slashed jeans, she looked confident. Forceful, even.

When she pulled her head out of the car, I saw the tension in her face. Her pale eyes were bloodshot.

'Could you strap Ana in?' she asked me. 'I need to do Colette.'

'Sure...yes...of course.'

I dropped the nappies into my open boot, then turned to the little girl with the pink rabbit. 'Hello, sweetie. I'm Meg. I'm so happy to meet you.'

She didn't reply. Instead she climbed into the booster seat and waited, staring blankly at the headrest in front of her. It was years since I'd buckled a kid into a car seat. I had to cast my mind back to when Emily was young and let muscle memory take over.

'You must be at least five years old if you're using a seat like this,' I said.

She nodded.

'When's your birthday?'

The answer was just a thread of sound. I didn't catch it even though I was leaning across her, buckling her up.

'Sorry, sweetheart, I missed that.'

She opened her mouth again. But then Nerine came bursting through the opposite door, wielding a car seat the size of a garden mulcher. 'That middle one—is it just a lap belt?' she demanded breathlessly.

'Uh—yeah.' I couldn't help feeling embarrassed. 'Sorry. It's a bit of an old bomb...'

'Don't worry,' she said. 'I can manage.'

Thump. The whole car rocked as Jill dumped a suitcase into the boot one-handed. She was holding a grizzly toddler on her left hip and obviously needed help, so I went back to her four-wheel drive and grabbed two overstuffed sports bags and a soiled baby's quilt. There wasn't much else to move: just a couple of pillows, a backpack and a big paper shopping bag from Marcs.

'Marcs? And a LandCruiser?' I said to Jill. 'Have you been promoted or something?'

'Work's going pretty well.' She was jingling her car keys at Colette, who had the silky blonde curls of a Renaissance cherub. The toddler wore only a nappy and a pyjama top smeared with snot and chocolate.

She looked underweight to me.

'Does she need a change?'

'I don't think so.' Jill sniffed at the nappy. 'How long before you get home?'

'Two hours. Maybe a bit less...'

Jill raised her voice. 'Do you want to change Collie, Nerine? It'll be another two hours yet.'

'She'll keep,' Nerine replied. 'Bring her over, will you? I'm nearly done here.'

Colette complained loudly about getting strapped in, though I couldn't make out what she was saying. I wondered if she could talk at all. On the phone Jill had told me that the younger kid was twenty-two months old.

Emily had been joining words together at that age.

'We got some pull-ups for Ana because she was scared to pee in the bush,' Jill informed me as we transferred the last of the luggage. 'Most of the public toilets we passed were shut. But she's usually okay in the daytime.'

'Right. Thanks.'

'No. Thank *you*.' Jill put her hands on my shoulders, looking down at me with a frown on her face. 'Are you all right with this? Is there anything else you need to know?'

'Um...' I tried to think. Diet? No—I'd already asked about diet. Jill had told me over the phone that neither kid had any obvious food allergies; Ana's eczema was linked to stress. I'd also been told that there was a history of violence, and that both girls were showing signs of trauma. 'The only thing we can do is provide a calm and nurturing environment,' Jill had said. 'Luckily my other contact is a counsellor, but she only had them for a week and it wasn't enough time.' After a moment's pause, she'd added, 'I probably shouldn't have mentioned that. Oh, well. Mea culpa.'

Huddled beside her, battling late-night fatigue, I racked

my brain for an intelligent question. Not diet. Not toilet training.

'Do you know how long they've been…' I didn't want to say 'at large'. 'On the move?'

'I'm not sure,' Jill admitted. 'About a month, I think. Their first contact was too close to home and had to push 'em on quickly.'

'They'll be here for a while.' I'd already warned Jill about the delay, but I thought it was worth repeating. 'My contact can't take them in for another month. Did you tell Nerine?'

Jill nodded. 'She's fine with that.'

'It's a family thing—'

'Shhh! Don't tell me!' Raising her hand, Jill smiled and said, 'Let's stick to the rules, eh?'

She'd already explained the rules. Every network member had two direct contacts: the friend who dispatched and the friend who received. So if anyone ran into trouble, the trouble wouldn't spread.

'Nerine's very anxious,' Jill went on. '*Very* anxious.'

'I'm not surprised.' I was feeling pretty anxious myself.

'Yes, but it can be hard to cope with. I'm just warning you. If you need any help, give me a call.' Before I could thank her, she added, 'Not with your own phone, obviously.'

'No.' I'd already been given the public phone drill. Jill had been very thorough. It was her third time, so she was an expert. 'And if one of the kids gets sick—' I began.

'Call the emergency number I gave you. Failing that, the jig's up. But warn me before you head for the hospital.'

'Hey!' Nerine called out suddenly. 'Are we going, or what?' She was standing by my open passenger door.

'Be right with you!' I was putting on a brave show, but my confidence was leaking away. I had a horrible feeling that I was going to mess it all up somehow.

'You're looking good,' said Jill.

'Not as good as you.'

'I like your hair.'

'My hair? Oh. Right.' It was ten years since Jill had laid eyes on me. During that time, I'd started using hair dye. Keith had always been vicious about hair dye. Whether he thought it was a waste of money or he wanted me to feel bad about the way I looked, he'd given me such a hard time about my first dye job that I'd decided it wasn't worth the hassle.

A feeling like that can be hard to shake. But finally, after six long years of freedom, I'd picked up a packet of Clairol and turned back into a redhead.

'Thanks very much.' I didn't know how to respond. 'Emily thinks it looks cheap.'

'Well, I think it looks ballsy.' Jill hugged me again, then retreated a step and asked if I was going to be all right.

'Of course.'

'No problems?'

'None.' I glanced over at Nerine, who was sitting in my car. 'We have to do this. I mean, she's one of us, isn't she?'

'She is. She's one of us.' Jill squeezed my shoulder. 'Bye, Meg. Good luck. And thanks.'

'Same to you.'

'Drive carefully.'

That was easier said than done in a 1998 Commodore. But I slid behind the wheel and waited until Jill had manoeuvred her hulking great Toyota into a three-point turn. Once she was rolling down the drive, I started my own engine.

'Right!' I said. 'Everyone ready?'

'God, yes. Let's go.' Beside me, Nerine was gnawing at her fingernails. 'This place is so creepy. Why did we have to meet in a graveyard?'

It wasn't a graveyard, but I knew what she meant. In the glow of my headlights, the old church did look creepy.

I felt better when we'd left it behind.

No one talked much on the way home. Ana stared into the darkness. Colette fell asleep. I think Nerine may have dozed off too, though she was awake when we bounced across the cattle grid that spanned my front gate.

'Wait—is this it?' she said.

'Yup.'

'The Bolt Hole?' She had spotted the sign under my street number. 'It's seriously called the Bolt Hole?'

'That's right.'

'Jesus, Meg.' Her fingers were drumming nervously on the dashboard. 'Don't you think that's a dead giveaway?'

'No. It's fine.' Poor woman, she was anxious to the point of paranoia. 'I put that up years ago, when I first came here. Everyone knows about it. I felt like I was crawling into a burrow, you see?'

'Yeah. Jill mentioned that.' After a long pause, Nerine remarked, 'You met at some kind of support group in Sydney, right? Because you were both married to shits?'

I glanced up at the rear-view mirror. She caught me looking.

'It's okay,' she said. 'They didn't hear me, they're asleep. God, is all this yours? It's huge!'

'Not really.' The place was too rocky for cropping, too rough for sheep and too small for cattle. It was on top of a ridge, where the topsoil supported only native species that had evolved to survive high winds and variable temperatures. I didn't tell her that, though. It wasn't the time or the place.

'Jill said you'd been doing it tough,' Nerine continued, squinting out at the ghostly tree trunks that were flashing past. 'But this must have cost a fortune.'

'Nup. It was a weekender. No insulation. Tank water. The fencing isn't finished. And I bought it eleven years ago, when land was still cheap.' I'd also bought it with a small inheritance left to me by my father, but Nerine didn't need to know that.

Suddenly my high beams hit Zincalume. I heard the sound of barking.

'Here we are,' I said. 'That's Esme on the veranda. Don't worry about her—she loves kids.'

Nerine grunted. Pulling up at the garden gate I waited for her to make a move. When she didn't, I got out myself.

By the time I'd pushed the gate open, Esme had joined me, waving her plumy tail like a flag. From inside the car I heard an inarticulate cry of joy. Someone had obviously seen her.

'Not today, girl,' I said, ruffling her ears. Normally I would have let her hop into the front passenger seat while I parked. 'Hey, Nerine?' I called out. 'Can you hold Esme while you shut the gate behind me? I don't want to run her over.'

Nerine was staring at my house, which had all the street appeal of a demountable site office with its low roof and aluminium windows. I'd painted it olive green, added a veranda and a brick chimney and planted a lot of vines and bushes, but it still wasn't impressive. I knew that.

'Nerine?' I repeated.

She gave a start. 'Oh! Yeah,' she said. Then she slid out of the car and grabbed Esme's collar.

'Do you like the doggie?' I asked Colette as I climbed back into the driver's seat. She was wide awake and writhing with excitement. Even Analiese had perked up. 'She's called Esme and she loves children.'

Colette squealed something that might have been 'dog'. I released the handbrake, changed gears and crawled into the yard until I reached the front steps. Behind me, Nerine closed the gate. Then she released Esme, who bounded up to the car as fast as her rickety old legs would carry her.

Poor Esme wasn't getting any younger. I'd bought her soon after I bought the house, safe in the knowledge that Keith wouldn't be around to snipe at me about her hair and her drool and her wayward turds while he sneaked chilli into her food. I still couldn't believe I had a dog of my own. It was the dream of a lifetime.

'Yes, girl. I'm back, here I am.' I had to push her out of the way as I emerged from the car. 'Time for bed, kids. Do you want to pat the doggie before you say goodnight?'

But Analiese had already gone. The booster seat was empty, the door beside it was open and the front steps were creaking. By the time I'd lifted Colette out of the car, her elder sister was trying to push her way into my house.

'Hang on, sweetheart,' I said. 'Just let me get the key.'

Esme followed me onto the veranda, where I unlocked the front door. Nerine was still down by the car, unloading luggage, so I carried Colette through the living room, along the hallway, into the second bedroom. Here I'd made up the double bed and added two camp beds, just in case.

'This is where you'll be sleeping.' I put Colette down and she immediately flung herself at Esme, who stood patiently enduring her clumsy attentions. Analiese sidled into the room behind us, still clutching her pink rabbit. She looked around cautiously.

'Meg? Where are you?' Nerine called from the vestibule.

'In here!' I watched Analiese approach the nearest camp bed. She craned her neck to examine the rainbow doona cover.

'That can be yours, if you like,' I told her. She looked at me, unblinking.

Then Nerine appeared, lugging her suitcase. Her energy was so agitated—so anxious and alert—that she seemed to fill the room. 'Can you bring in the rest of that stuff?' she pleaded. 'I have to get these girls to bed...'

'Of course.' I spent the next few minutes emptying the boot and hiding the two safety seats in my shed. Meanwhile, Nerine changed nappies, washed faces and dug pyjamas out of sports bags. Soon the two camp beds had been stripped and refolded. 'Won't be needing those,' she explained. 'We always share a bed.'

I showed her the bathroom and the linen closet. I dragged Esme out of Colette's reach, dumped the Marcs bag in the kitchen and wheeled the camp beds into the laundry. I drew curtains and fetched tooth glasses. Then I said goodnight.

'Goodnight, Meg.' Leaning on her bedroom doorknob, Nerine looked pasty with fatigue. 'Thanks so much for this.'

'It's a pleasure. Really.'

'You're a brave woman.'

'No, no...'

'That dog.' She pointed at Esme. 'Is it a guard dog?'

'Well...' I glanced down at Esme's arthritic hips and trusting eyes. 'She's a golden retriever. They're not really *guard* dogs.'

'Would it bark if someone came near the house?'

I blinked. 'Of course, but—'

'Good. That's good.'

I gazed at her with some concern as her fingers worked away at the doorknob. 'Nerine,' I assured her, 'no one will come near this house. No one ever does.'

She dredged up an unconvincing smile.

'That's why I'm taking you in. Because it's safe here,' I

continued, feeling a profound sympathy for the poor girl. She couldn't have been much older than Emily, yet she looked as if every spark of hope, every glimmer of joy, had been drained out of her.

I knew that feeling. I'd lived with it for years.

'Honestly,' I said, 'if there was any risk at all, I wouldn't have agreed to do this. But there isn't. I swear. You're going to be all right.'

'Famous last words,' she mumbled.

Then she nodded at me and retreated back into her bedroom.

I used to tell Emily that she was going to be all right. I said it when she was bullied. I said it when she accidentally spilled milk all over her father's desk and broke his computer keyboard. I said it when she brought home a friend's guinea pig, and when she desperately wanted to go to riding camp.

But I was lying. It was never all right. The bullies kept bullying. Keith punished her for 'wrecking his business'. The guinea pig was sent straight back to the friend's place because there were never any pets in our family; they weren't tolerated. As for the riding camp, it coincided with one of Keith's black moods. He refused to pay for something so 'useless' and 'expensive' while he was 'haemorrhaging money'.

In the end my daughter stopped believing me, because it was pretty obvious that she wasn't all right. She was wary and defensive, and her self-esteem was terrible. She couldn't relax into anything for fear that her father would belittle, mock or thwart her. She didn't feel safe in her own home, any more than I did.

Nerine, however, was in an entirely different position. When I told her she was going to be all right, I really meant it.

If I hadn't, I wouldn't have taken her in.

SETTLING

'MEG! WAKE UP!'

I struggled out of a dream. Opened my eyes. It was still dark, though the hall light was on. A silhouette was framed in the doorway.

'Nerine?'

'I heard noises. Outside,' she said.

Sitting up, I peered at my bedside clock: 4:30 a.m. I'd been asleep for two hours.

'Do you have a gun?' she demanded. The word 'gun' hit me like a bolt of lightning.

'A *gun*?' Suddenly I was wide awake.

'In case it's Duncan.'

Jill hadn't told me the ex-husband's surname—only that he'd been abusive and that Nerine's warnings about him had been disregarded by the Family Court. When Nerine had refused to comply with the shared care arrangements, she had been hit with a recovery order. And that's when she'd run.

'Do you still have your old phone?' I asked her.

'Of course not. I was told to get rid of it.'

'Then it's not Duncan. How can it be? If he can't trace your phone, he won't know where you are.' All at once I realised she was holding Colette. Her other daughter was clinging to the hem of her pyjama top. 'Let's not talk about this right now, eh? Not in front of the kids.'

'They need to know the truth.' Nerine spoke in dull tones. 'If they don't, they can't protect themselves.'

'But—'

'I heard something, Meg. It was outside.'

Colette whimpered. Esme's tail thumped against the carpet.

'Okay. I'll take a look.' I swung my feet to the floor. 'It was probably a feral pig, or a goat. Or maybe a fox. That fence doesn't keep out foxes…'

'It sounded *big*.' Her voice was shaking.

I shuffled into my slippers and pulled on my dressing-gown, then padded out into the living room. Though my ears were pricked, I couldn't hear anything suspicious. Even the windchimes were silent. The only sound was Colette's whispery snuffling as she rubbed her face against her mother's shoulder.

'Where did you hear it? Out front?' I asked Nerine.

'Sort of. Yeah.'

I headed for the front door, but she hissed, 'Wait. Meg. Take something with you. Like a knife, or…or a fire iron.' She saw me wince and said fiercely, 'You don't know what he's like. No one does.'

'Nerine.' I didn't know how to calm her down. For the children's sake, I had to make her understand. 'If someone's out there, Esme would have barked.'

Nerine shook her head. 'He's clever. He might have sprayed himself with something.'

Sprayed himself? My expression must have said it all. She burst out, 'You don't believe me! No one ever believes me! They think I'm crazy, but *he's* the one who's crazy! He'd do anything!'

'I know. I understand.' I'd been married to a narcissist, and there's nothing a narcissist doesn't know about gaslighting. 'But you don't have to worry,' I assured her, trying not to look at Ana's frightened face. 'I'll have Esme with me. Why don't you put the kids to bed? There's nothing they can do...'

'Take a torch,' said Nerine.

So I went to the kitchen, dug out my torch, grabbed a broom from the cupboard in the vestibule and switched on the outside lights. Then I turned to Ana and said in a cheerful voice, 'I think there might be a naughty goat out there trying to eat my broad beans. But Esme will chase it back home.'

Ana just stared. She wasn't buying it.

Nerine muttered, 'Be careful.'

When I pushed open the front door, displaced air hit the nearest windchimes. I grabbed at them to stop the jangling. There were four sets of windchimes on the veranda—along with three wicker chairs, a lot of hanging baskets, a doormat, a dreamcatcher, Esme's second-best dog bed, a mosaic plaque, a boot-scraper and a wrought-iron umbrella stand. None of these things had been disturbed.

If there were possums about, they hadn't left any traces.

Esme slipped out of the door ahead of me. She trotted stiffly down the front steps as I listened, my torch beam sweeping across the yard. I heard her panting. I heard the distant boom of an owl. I heard the faint sigh of wind in the treetops. But nothing else.

I decided to check the fence, just in case. If a pig or a goat had pushed through it, I'd be able to see the damage. The gate was still shut. So was the shed. No strange car was visible. Slowly I circled the yard, comforted by Esme's cheery, bustling presence. It was very dark, and so quiet every rustle made me jump. I half-expected my wandering spotlight to freeze on something scary. A face. A corpse. A fleeing figure. But nothing sprang out of the darkness. The fence looked solid. The chickens stirred and grumbled in their little house. When my torch beam slid across its roof, I glimpsed a shadow skittering away. A very small shadow. Probably a bush rat.

Esme growled. She'd seen the rat too.

Slowly I moved past the tanks, the woodpile and the back gate. A scrabbling noise stopped me for a moment, making my nerves jump; I scanned the bush beyond the fence, but saw nothing unexpected. At last I found myself back at the veranda. The house seemed oddly silent, as if it was holding its breath.

I unhooked a couple of windchimes from the rafters and took them inside.

'Nothing,' I said. For some reason, the sight of Nerine's hovering figure came as a huge relief. Trudging up the front steps, I'd had the strangest, most illogical feeling that she wouldn't be there when I returned.

'Are you sure?' she demanded.

'All I saw was a bush rat.' I returned the broom to the closet, then laid my torch on the piano. 'Honestly, it's fine. Gate's shut. Esme's happy. But in case you're still worried, I'll hang a set of these on each door.' Jingling the windchimes, I showed her how noisy they were. 'They'll give Esme fair warning, even if they don't wake the rest of us.'

'Denga,' Colette muttered. Her eyes were on the chimes. Her pale little starfish hand reached for them.

'Tomorrow,' I said. Colette began to snivel, but I knew that if we wanted any sleep at all, she'd have to be kept away from clanging metal tubes.

By the time I returned from the kitchen, Nerine had vanished, along with her kids. Their door was shut. So I withdrew thankfully into my own room, taking Esme with me.

I was climbing into bed when I remembered something. The latch on my bedroom window was broken. I wondered if I should hang more chimes off the latch, or put something noisy underneath the window. Like a cutlery drawer, maybe? Even a scattering of screwed-up plastic chip packets might do the trick…

No. I shook myself, astonished at how badly I'd been affected by Nerine's irrational fear. It had probably stirred up old feelings and memories. I'd lived for years with a grinding, niggling dread, though Keith had never actually hit me; he'd been too smart for that. There had been slammed doors, weeks of silence, shouts, jibes, smashed glass, passive-aggressive puddles of urine around the toilet…but never a blow, because back then a blow was the only thing that could have landed him in jail. Anyway, just the threat of violence was enough. It used to hang over me like a thundercloud.

Nerine had obviously lived with more than a threat. I felt deeply sorry for her. And even sorrier for her kids.

My job, I decided, would be to calm them all down.

It took me a long time to get to sleep. I lay there worrying, the way you always do in the small hours. I thought back to Jill's first phone call, out of the blue after a two-year lull. I replayed it in my mind: the confession, the reasons, the request. It hadn't surprised me—not much, anyway. She had always been stronger than me, and fiercer. But she wasn't pushy. She had laid everything out and let me choose, insisting that I shouldn't feel pressured. I should only do it, she said, if I was really, really sure I wanted to.

By that time, however, she'd already mentioned the kids. Two little girls. How could I have said no? If two little girls needed my help I wasn't going to turn them away, no matter how scared I might be.

I'd failed Emily. I wasn't going to fail those girls.

When I woke again it was after nine. My guests were already up. I stumbled into the kitchen to find them surrounded by dirty plates and empty glasses. Colette was cuddling Esme. Analiese was sitting at the kitchen table, picking up crumbs with a moistened fingertip. Nerine was rinsing dishes and looking, I thought, surprisingly perky.

'We made toast,' she said. 'Hope you don't mind.'

Crestfallen, I threw open a cupboard, exposing three big boxes of cereal—one sugary and multicoloured, the other two healthy enough. 'Didn't they want these?' I asked.

'Sorry, missed those.' Nerine frowned. 'You didn't buy 'em at your usual place, did you?'

'No.' I shot an uneasy glance at Ana. Was she listening? It was hard to tell. 'No, I went to Bathurst. Bought in bulk like Jill said.'

'Okay. Good. Thanks.' Smiling at Ana, Nerine cheerfully remarked, 'Ana loves Froot Loops. Don't you, Big Bug?'

Ana nodded solemnly. She was still wearing yesterday's yellow fleece and white tutu. I'd have to get them off her at some point and give them a good wash, but I didn't want to deprive her of every familiar thing all at once.

Her plush rabbit, I noticed, was sitting on the table beside her. And that reminded me…

'I have to let the chooks out. Does anyone want to meet my chooks?'

'Oh, wow!' Nerine clapped her hands. I couldn't believe the change. The cowering fugitive from last night had turned into a bright and sparky young mum. She was even wearing makeup for some reason.

'Who wants to see the hens?' she chirruped. 'Hey,

Buggins—you wanna see the cluck-clucks?'

'Dok,' Colette replied.

'Come on.' Nerine scooped her up as I headed for the back door. Ana was watching me. I couldn't work out if she wanted to come or not; her face was impossible to read.

'Let's go, Big Bug!' Nerine exclaimed.

Colette began to whimper. 'Dok,' she repeated.

'Esme's coming with us,' I said. Esme, in fact, was already pushing past me. By the time Ana joined the rest of us outside, Esme was modestly doing her business behind one of the water tanks. I led everyone else across the yard to the coop, where the chickens were milling around looking annoyed. They were usually out of their pen by eight o'clock.

'Gna,' Colette crowed, on catching sight of them.

'Boy, that's a big chookhouse,' said Nerine.

'It has to be, for twelve chooks.' I released the gate-latch and the chickens came pouring out, making Colette laugh and squeal. Even Ana smiled.

'That's Nugget,' I said, pointing. 'And that's Chocolate, and that's Snowball, and I call that one Granny because she's the oldest...'

'The kids could easily hide in that.' Nerine's bright look had faded. Her expression was suddenly preoccupied. 'It would be a good place to hide if anyone comes.'

Ana's smile disappeared.

I took a deep breath. 'No one's going to come, Nerine. No one ever does.' Lowering my voice, I tried to make her understand. 'I don't even have proper neighbours. The ones to the north have dogs that'll rip you to shreds. The fence on the other side is electric. And there's a great big cliff at the back of my property, so no one's getting in *that* way.' Hoping to distract her, I added, 'Don't ask me why the Baumanns installed an electric fence. More money than sense, if you ask me. We'll have to make sure the kids don't go near it.'

'I'm worried about letting the kids out at all.' Nerine set Colette down to meet Esme, who was trotting towards us. 'I don't want anyone hearing them.'

'No one will hear them.' I glanced at Analiese, who stood mutely studying the chickens. She was still clutching her rabbit. Did she ever let it go? 'Hey, Ana—do you want to collect some eggs?'

She spun around, her eyes flaring. Then she nodded.

'See that bag over there?' I pointed at the canvas draw-string pouch hanging off a fence post. 'That's the egg bag. You can put all the eggs you find in that.'

I let her fetch the bag herself, even though she was a bit too small to lift it off the fence post. Giving kids a problem to solve isn't a bad thing, I've found. It keeps them occupied.

'Colette really loves Esme,' I observed. Poor Esme was stoically suffering the toddler's heavy-handed pats and slob-bery kisses. 'It must be hard if she throws herself at every strange dog in sight.'

'Collie loves dogs. We used to have one at home.' Nerine's face changed. 'Before Duncan killed it.'

I shot a quick look at Ana, but she was absorbed in the egg bag.

'He cut its throat,' Nerine continued. 'He said the neighbours did it because of the barking. That's what he told the police, anyway.'

'Oh my God.' I felt as if I'd been slapped.

'It was him, though. He was jealous because the kids loved the dog more than they loved him. And to warn me, of course. He was showing me what he would do if I didn't toe the line.'

'Ana? Sweetie? Let me just check inside the henhouse for you.' I was ashamed of myself, because I knew Nerine deserved a supportive ear, but I didn't want to hear any more. So I darted forward to peer into the coop. 'You see?' My voice cracked on a high note. 'Ruby and Belle are both sitting on their eggs, the lazy lumps. I'll just shoo them off, okay?'

Because I had to crawl into the henhouse, I didn't hear Ana's reply. I was too busy scooping my two broodiest chickens off their nests. Ruby was a great layer but a terrible mother. Belle was in a semi-permanent sulk. I was nudging them both into the yard when I caught the tail end of a muttered remark that seemed to be coming from Ana.

'What's that, pet?' I asked. My knees cracked as I hauled myself to my feet.

'Are they trying to look after their babies?' Ana repeated, in a worried voice.

'Oh, no! No, my eggs don't have babies in them.' Keen to divert her attention, I stepped back and waved at the entrance to the henhouse. 'Go on. You go and check all the boxes and bring back every egg you can find. And maybe later we'll eat some for lunch. Or dinner, if Mummy says it's okay.'

Obediently Ana dropped to her haunches. I went and joined Nerine, who said, 'I reckon we could all hide in that henhouse. It's big enough.'

'No.' I shook my head. 'It's filthy. You'd catch giardia or something.'

'I suppose so.' Nerine glanced around vaguely, ignoring Colette, who was pulling Esme's ear. 'But they need a hide-away. They always had one at home. It changed every time Duncan found it, but they always had a safe place to go.'

'Mmm.' I could see her point. 'Let me think. There's bound to be a spot somewhere...'

I thought about my house. It was small. It was cheap. It was cluttered. Where would I find a cosy corner big enough to fit two small girls and a plush rabbit?

'I counted five,' Ana called from inside the coop. 'Five eggs.'

'Wow! Five eggs! That's great!' said Nerine.

Suddenly an idea flashed into my head. It was a good one.

'Bring them all out, sweetie, and we'll put them in the fridge.' To Nerine I said, 'Don't worry. We'll set up a nice little cubbyhole for the kids, and they can play in there, and make it comfortable, and they won't have to roll around in chicken manure every time they want to feel safe.' Moving past her with Esme at my heels, I added, 'Why don't you take care of those eggs while I get dressed? Then I'll grab some breakfast and we'll have the hideaway sorted by lunchtime.'

'Dok,' Colette protested.

'In a minute, darling. Just give me a minute.' I'd forgotten how it was with kids. The urgency. The unfettered emotions. The way they filled up every corner of your life…

I decided to move my work-desk into my bedroom.

Emily wasn't an easy baby. She must have sensed something from the start. When she was two months old the clinic nurse said, 'She doesn't want to be here, does she?'

Emily was always crying, and I felt like a failure.

Keith agreed. He'd heard of the controlled crying method and insisted we use it, even though it didn't work until Emily was six months old. He often refused to sleep at home, storming out to spend the night with friends, lovers, workmates…I didn't really care. We were actually evicted from one flat; Keith blamed the baby, but I was pretty sure our neighbours had heard us screaming at each other night after night. In those days I was still fighting back. Later I realised it only made things worse.

I had plenty of milk, but sometimes Emily wouldn't take it. She had a lazy streak and if she didn't get a let-down when she first latched on—if the milk didn't instantly spurt into her mouth—than she would refuse to make an effort. I remember standing in the shower crying because the hot water had triggered a let-down just before a feed was due. I remember Keith glaring at me in disgust as I wailed that it wasn't fair, I tried so hard, she was failing to thrive, what would the clinic say?

'You're mad,' he said. 'What's wrong with you? If you're going to carry on like this you'd better find yourself a psychiatrist.' He couldn't believe one tiny baby was too much for me to handle. He thought I was overreacting, and he wasn't entirely wrong. Emily had filled up my world. Wherever I turned, there she was. Every small setback seemed like a massive disaster. Every mistake seemed life-threatening. The more miserable she seemed, the more useless I felt.

I calmed down as she grew up, but I still couldn't turn away. With Keith mostly out of the picture, I was always on the front line, feeding, clothing, bathing, comforting, teaching, playing, nursing. And every small setback was still a disaster, because that's the way it seems to a small child.

Years later, I came to miss that closeness. I mooned over it. I glorified it. I forgot that it can turn you into someone else.

With Nerine around, I was beginning to remember.

DAY OFF

MY VESTIBULE CUPBOARD didn't look like a very good hiding place. It was right opposite the front entrance, for one thing.

But appearances can be deceptive. Though fitted with a standard pair of sliding doors, the cupboard wasn't a standard size. The previous owner had obviously decided that he needed more storage but hadn't wanted to pay extra for bigger doors, so there was a lot of hard-to-reach space on either side of them. They were also slightly off-centre, and the whole cupboard had been constructed around the attic manhole. I'd often wondered why my predecessor had done that. Did he want to store his ladder near the manhole?

I certainly stored my ladder there, along with my broom, mop, vacuum cleaner, squeegees, picnic basket and screwdriver set. Needless to say, I relocated the screwdrivers before padding one dark corner with pillows and cushions. Then I added a set of coloured crayons, my torch, a blanket and a few plush toys that I'd bought at a Bathurst op shop.

'Look, girls.' When I summoned both children to the vestibule, Nerine came with them. 'This is your new cubbyhole. You can curl up in here and do anything you want. You can even draw on the walls.'

Analiese frowned. Nerine said, 'Really?'

'Why not? No one's going to see.' Lowering myself carefully to the floor beside Ana, I reached past a clutter of cleaning equipment to show her the crayons. 'Why don't you draw something nice in here? You could draw a window. Or trees. Or butterflies.'

Ana stared at the cosy retreat for a moment. Then she flicked a glance at her mother.

'The last time Ana drew on the walls, Duncan wrote "moron" all over her face with an indelible marker,' Nerine observed. 'She's scared to do it again.'

'Oh dear.' I felt winded. Why did Nerine have to keep ambushing me like this? 'Well...you must do what you want. You can play or draw or take a nap...anything.'

'I'll make a burrow,' Ana announced. 'For Mr Snuffles.'

'Is that your bunny? Good idea.' I scrambled to my feet again. 'And Mr Snuffles can be friends with the bears and the hippo. They're yours, now—yours and your sister's.'

Ana's expression didn't change. If she was pleased about her new toys, I couldn't see any evidence of it. But she did drop to her knees, and was crawling into the closet when my landline rang in the living room.

Ana froze. Nerine stiffened.

'It's okay,' I assured them.

But it wasn't. When I picked up the handset and said, 'Meg speaking,' no one answered. After a brief silence, there was a sharp *click*, followed by the dial tone.

I hung up quietly. Then I returned to the vestibule.

'Who was that?' Nerine demanded.

'No one.'

'What do you mean, *no one*?' The tension in Nerine's voice made Colette wail.

'Don't worry. It happens a lot.' I knew this wasn't going to satisfy Nerine, so I raised my voice over Colette's and said, 'Probably my ex-husband.'

Nerine blinked. Then she lowered Colette to the floor and gave her a little push. 'Ana, show Collie your new den. Go on.'

'What if I bring you some morning tea?' I was addressing the two girls, but before they could answer, Nerine grabbed my arm and pulled me away.

'What's the deal with your ex?' she asked softly, searching my face with narrowed eyes. She seemed genuinely interested—and suddenly much calmer. 'Is he harassing you?'

'I think so.' I took a deep breath. 'The calls seem to be coming from different payphones, but I'm pretty sure it's him.'

'Why? Jill said you split up with him fifteen years ago. Why's he still bothering you?'

'Because he's a shit,' I answered.

But that wasn't the real reason. Actually, it was because of his mum.

*

Keith was Carol's only child. I never blamed her for what he was like; I blamed his father. Carol divorced Harry Delgado when Keith was five years old, but by then the damage had already been done. Or perhaps it was something genetic. Whatever the reason, Harry's son became a chip off the old block: greedy, manipulative, narcissistic, underhanded and vengeful.

Carol's father had been a lawyer, and she inherited quite a lot of money when he died—enough to send her son to a top private school. Keith went on to study law at uni but soon flunked out because he had the world's shortest attention span. He never had any trouble getting jobs, but he had a lot of trouble keeping them. Over the years he worked as a personal assistant, an account manager, a salesman, a grant writer, a fundraiser, a 'microfinancier', a consultant, a human resources executive, an investment adviser, an entrepreneur and a restaurant owner. When I first met him, he was tooling around Sydney in pinstripe suits and a silver convertible. For Keith, it was all about image. That's probably why I appealed to him.

Believe it or not, I was a knockout back then. Lots of wavy auburn hair, chiselled cheekbones, big blue eyes. Short, of course, but slender enough to carry it. 'Good things come in small packages,' Keith used to say. I was finishing my music degree and planning to become a teacher, but Keith talked me into playing keyboards in a band. He was my manager for a while. Then he became my husband. I don't know why he took the plunge. Maybe he needed someone to look down on. Maybe he liked the way I did everything he said. I was four years younger than he was and fresh out of Taree.

Carol helped Keith a lot in those early years. She put up the money for his restaurant, his consultancy and two of the companies he founded to sell a special kind of exercise bike and a special kind of fuel additive (both doomed to fail). But as the years dragged on, he began to lose his lustre even in her eyes. Though she may have loved him, she didn't like him. And she certainly didn't trust him.

After Emily was born, she trusted him even less. I saw quite a lot of Carol while I was pregnant; Keith and I often made the trip to her big dark house on the North Shore. Carol was small, like me, but stiff and skinny and permed. She wore twinsets and cashmere. Her manner was cool and remote, but I soon discovered that underneath her brittle façade she was very, very shy. And shell-shocked. God knows what Harry Delgado did to her, but you can safely bet that he married her for her father's money. She'd been smart enough to keep a lot of it after her divorce, though. When I first met her she owned her own house and four rental properties, including a block of flats.

Two of those properties were sacrificed to fund Keith's ambitions but she baulked at selling the third, and that was what caused the rift. Keith blew his top instead of biding his time. For a while he tried to use Emily as a hostage, refusing to let his mother see her unless Carol coughed up the money he needed. 'We can't afford the petrol,' he would say, whenever Carol suggested we visit. And when she offered to visit us, he'd respond, 'We can't afford to entertain.'

In the end I had to meet her secretly, in parks and shopping centres. I was still under his thumb at that stage, because I didn't have a choice. New mothers don't. I was getting through each day by putting one foot in front of the other and trying not to think about where I was going.

I was also scared. When Emily was born, I suddenly realised I'd given Keith a weapon. I was afraid of what he might do to my baby if I didn't toe the line.

Not that he ever hit her. He didn't have to; his weapon was neglect. 'How was I to know...?' he would say. 'How was I to know she needed changing? How was I to know she wanted a feed?' He told me I was crazy anxious—that I had post-partum depression—that I should start taking Valium. Sometimes he would let Emily taste his beer. Sometimes he would leave her strapped in the car while he 'popped into' a friend's place. Sometimes he would tease her by pushing a spoonful of food into her open mouth, then withdrawing it quickly before she could close it. He did the same thing with her toys, making her struggle all the way across the room before snatching them away at the last second. 'I'm training her to crawl,' he'd say, but I knew it was a lie.

He just liked to torture people.

When I told Carol all this, it touched a nerve. Unbeknown to me, she changed her will. She was besotted with Emily, and must have known that if she left her money to Keith, his daughter wouldn't see a cent of it. So Carol made me her beneficiary—because Emily, at that point, was a child. Carol didn't mention the change to anyone but her lawyer. She certainly didn't tell Keith; perhaps she was afraid of what he might do. Even towards the end of her life, after she'd moved into a nursing home, she kept quiet about her decision. By that time she had sold the block of flats to fund her living expenses, and Keith had started visiting her again after years of neglect, probably with the aim of putting her in a cheaper facility. I don't think he was trying to make her change her will. He wasn't aware that it needed changing. He assumed he was the beneficiary, because he'd never been told otherwise.

When Carol died last year, he finally found out what she'd done.

You can imagine how he reacted. He went straight to court, claiming that a provision should be made for him under section 50 of the Succession Act. Luckily, the executor of the will was Carol's lawyer, David Blazek, so I didn't have to defend it myself. But I did have to go to a family provision mediation and sit in a room listening to Keith's lawyer drone on and on about Keith's 'significant financial needs' and how he'd 'fallen on hard times'. I wondered how someone who had fallen on hard times could be driving an Audi, but I wasn't allowed to ask about that. David did all the talking.

Later, David told me the Audi had been leased through Keith's employer. We were standing around in the corridor outside the mediation room, and David mentioned the car after observing that he still had a lot of questions about Keith's financial status. 'He's not been very forthcoming with his bank records,' David said.

'Well—Keith has a history of concealed bank accounts,' I

replied. 'I could never track down all his money when we got divorced.'

David's ears pricked up at that, and the mediation soon foundered. Subpoenas were issued. Letters were exchanged. David told me that all his own costs would be met by Carol's estate—and that if Keith was successful, *his* costs would be met by the estate too. I decided Keith was doing exactly what he'd done during our divorce. His technique then had been to hit me with so many lawyer's letters and court orders that I'd almost gone broke responding to them. I figured his latest plan was to deprive me of my inheritance either by challenging the will or by ensuring that every last cent of Carol's money was spent on lawyers.

The thing is, he didn't just want his fair share—he wanted all of it. That was why we went to trial. 'Legislation favours the lame duck,' David admitted to me early on in the process. 'If a biological child can prove he's in dire financial straits, then it really doesn't matter what his mother wanted.' All the same, he wasn't about to let Keith get away with my whole inheritance. 'His character and conduct have to be taken into account,' David said.

So we went to court and it was horrible. Courts always are. I felt as if I was divorcing Keith all over again—and by that time, of course, I was also dealing with the anonymous phone calls. They'd started a few weeks after Carol's death: heavy breathing that unnerved me so much, I actually approached Tearle Godwin for help. I didn't really know Tearle; he was a retired lawyer, and my divorce had put me off lawyers. We'd met while working together on the board of the Bulwell Arts Council, which neither of us had been able to stick for very long. He'd struck me as dry and a bit starchy but bright, so I wrote to him asking if we could meet. To my surprise, he said yes. 'I was delighted, in this day and age, to receive a properly worded letter,' he told me when we finally sat down together in the bar of the Palace Hotel.

He listened to my tale of woe and promised to look into the matter, testily refusing my offer of payment. Then, after showing me how to use Telstra's calling number display, he worked out that the calls were probably coming from a payphone, or several payphones. But, despite all his efforts, he couldn't prove that Keith was responsible—even though I knew in my gut who was ringing me at two in the morning.

'We can apply for an order, but I can't guarantee we'll get one without some kind of evidence,' Tearle warned me at our second meeting. 'Especially since Keith hasn't been near you.'

'But it's so obvious,' I said. 'He's pissed off. Because of the court case...'

'Yes. The court case,' Tearle said thoughtfully. 'This might be a tactic he's using to make you look paranoid, irrational and malicious. If I were you I'd think very carefully before taking out an order.' As I pondered his advice, my heart sinking, he added, 'It might be wise if you kept a diary. Just note down details of every call—date, time, duration—as a record for the police.'

So that was what I did. Date, time, duration. The calls usually happened late at night or early in the morning. They rarely occurred during business hours.

But they were becoming more frequent as I waited for the court to make its judgement.

I didn't want to explain all this to Nerine because it upset me too much. Instead I took her on a tour of the house, showing her how the washing machine worked, what to do with the rubbish and where I'd put the DVDs. My TV reception wasn't very good and the internet was too slow for streaming, but I had dozens of DVDs that I'd bought at a pawn shop in Bathurst.

The kids watched a Disney cartoon later that day, after we'd given Esme a bath. Then we played the piano and drew pictures. Colette had a nap after lunch, but Ana spent nap-time in the cubbyhole, whispering to her stuffed toys. She seemed more comfortable playing on her own; I noticed how mute and cautious she became whenever there were adults around. Even Colette was very quiet for a toddler. I wouldn't say they skulked, exactly, but I was relieved when Colette had a tantrum later that afternoon because Nerine took a piece of fencing wire away from her.

Nerine dealt with the tantrum by holding Colette very tightly and hissing in her ear. Watching them both, I realised what Ana had been doing in the cubbyhole. Nerine had a rest-less energy that suited small children. She seemed to get bored as quickly as her daughters did, hopping from one activity to the next: music, drawing, card game, TV, picking beans, plaiting hair, playing with the windchimes. She also asked a lot of questions. Most of them were about Emily, whose pictures covered my walls. Nerine wanted to know how old she was, what she did, where she lived, if she was married.

I explained that Emily was twenty-seven, that she was living with her boyfriend in England and that she worked as a restaurant manager. I didn't say that my daughter had once told me she would never, ever get married. Nor did I mention that Emily had left Australia to get as far away from her parents as possible. 'When you two are anywhere near each other, it's toxic,' she'd once announced. 'And since I'm the only connection between you, I'm better off elsewhere.'

She had always blamed Keith for making her feel like garbage and me for not stopping him. But I didn't want to discuss that with anyone else. So I told Nerine that Emily was a keen traveller with a passion for exotic food.

'Aren't we all?' said Nerine gloomily. I had to laugh. Much later, when we were dumping feed into the chook pen— because there was no other way of luring the chickens back in at night—she asked me if Emily ever visited.

'Not lately,' I said.

'Do you visit her?'

I shook my head. 'Too expensive.' Shooing Belle through the gate, I shut it behind her and fastened it with a wire loop.

'Why do you have to lock them in?' Ana wanted to know.

'Because otherwise a fox might eat them.' Her forehead crumpled and I added quickly, 'But the foxes can't reach them now, because it's safe in there. It's really, really safe.'

She didn't look convinced.

'We get a lot of foxes around here,' I said, 'and I've never lost a chook. Not since I built this coop. It's the safest place they can be.'

Then I took everyone back inside to choose a bedtime story.

Most of the books I showed to the girls came from an op shop, but some were Emily's. I'd kept her favourites just in case she ever had children of her own. Nerine lifted *Where the Wild Things Are* from its place on the stack and said, 'We don't read this one. You can take it away.'

'Oh.' I was surprised; the book had been Emily's favourite. 'Too scary?'

Nerine shrugged. 'Duncan gave it a new ending,' she explained. 'He said Max thought he'd left all the monsters behind, but they actually followed him into his bedroom and ate him for supper.' Seeing me wince, she smiled without a trace of amusement. 'I think he wanted the girls to understand that you can't trust anyone, no matter how friendly they are or how big a fuss they make of you.'

'Jesus, Nerine.' I didn't know what else to say.

'Luckily he never read to the kids much.'

Ana finally chose *One Fish, Two Fish* and a book about swimming. Later I heard her mother's muffled voice inside their bedroom, reading aloud in a peculiar kind of monotonous chant. Nerine was in the room for hours, finally emerging at about eight o'clock to ask for a beer. 'Getting Ana to sleep is a major achievement,' she admitted. 'She's probably got PTSD.'

I didn't ask how she knew. I didn't want to hear the details of what Ana had endured. 'Has she seen a psychiatrist?'

'Are you kidding?' Nerine threw herself onto the couch next to me and thrust her long legs out in front of her. Then she reached for the TV remote. 'Duncan hated spending money.'

I was so worried about those girls. As Nerine skipped distractedly between channels, I wondered if there was anything I could do to help. Bulwell Women's Health Collective had a doctor on staff named Sally Kristensen, who was well informed about local counselling services for children and adolescents. But I couldn't risk telling her about the girls; how could I? They weren't her patients, so she had no duty of confidentiality.

She might go straight to the police.

'I can't believe you don't have a gun,' Nerine suddenly remarked. 'You live in the middle of nowhere and you're a primary producer—you could easily get one.'

'I'm not a primary producer, Nerine.'

'Yes, you are. You've got hens.'

I laughed.

'You were talking about all the pigs and goats and foxes on this property,' Nerine continued. 'You're allowed to have a gun to shoot vermin.' After a pause, she muttered, 'It would be something to do, at least.'

'I don't want a gun. I don't need a gun.' Sensing that she was growing agitated again, I said, 'Neither do you. It's safe here. Honestly.'

'Nowhere's safe. Not in Australia.' For a while she stared at the television, but her eyes were blank. At last she mumbled, 'Is there anyone in your network who can get me a fake passport?'

I gaped at her.

'Or just get me out of the country,' she added. 'You don't need a passport for that.'

'Yes, you do.'

She turned to look at me. 'I used to know a biker who did business with deep-sea fishermen. They'd meet Asian boats and swap drugs for cash. A lot of fishermen are into drugs—I bet they wouldn't mind dropping me on an Asian fishing boat. Only I'd need a lot of money. And I don't have it.'

'Nerine...' I was appalled. 'You can't get involved with drug trafficking. What about your kids?'

'Got a better idea?' When I didn't answer, she said, 'I can't spend the rest of my life hiding out like this. My kids certainly can't.'

'Yes, but...' I racked my brain for words of comfort. 'If Duncan's as bad as you say he is, he'll probably end up in jail.'

'He's already been in jail. What good did it do me? Anyway, I'll still be arrested. And then the kids will go to foster care.' She fixed me with a fierce look, her pale eyes framed by smudged mascara. 'I grew up in foster care, Meg—there's no way I'm letting that happen to my kids. They'd be better off on an Asian fishing boat.'

Suddenly the landline rang. We both stared at the handset. Neither of us moved until at last the answering machine switched on. *You've reached Meg Lowry*, my recorded voice announced. *Please leave a message after the beep.*

There was a click, then a dial tone.

'Bastard,' said Nerine.

WORK

I USED TO wonder what I ever saw in Keith. The more you hate someone, the more you blame yourself for ever having been fool enough to love him—though I'm not sure if 'love' is really the right word. I adored Keith, but that's not the same. You adore gods, not people. I thought Keith was a superior being, and he certainly looked the part. I suppose what I saw in him was his bouncy hair, his long eyelashes, his lean body, his resonant voice.

Keith can put on a pretty good front for a while. At first he put on a pretty good front for me. And by the time I realised he wasn't a god, I was pinned to his life like a dead butterfly. He'd fought with my friends, alienated my parents, upset my career plans and dragged me from house to house until everyone had lost my phone number.

He'd also made me believe I was a flake. A loser. He had me convinced I wouldn't be able to look after myself if he wasn't around to do it for me.

Then Emily was born and I was shackled to him for another twelve years.

The most important thing I learned during my life with Keith was how petty, mean, vindictive and unrelenting he could be. Most people don't have the energy to waste on endless mind games, but Keith did. Manipulation galvanised him. So did revenge. Once, after he was fired, he went back to his office at night and spent hours pumping superglue into all the locks. Another time, after a client dumped him, he stopped anyone else from leaving a message on her phone by calling it repeatedly until there was no memory left on her answering machine.

So I knew he was the one making those anonymous calls to my number. I knew it in my gut. I just didn't know how I was ever going to prove it.

'We've had four hang-up calls this morning,' Nerine piped into the phone. '*Four*, Meg! Is that normal?'

Her voice was so penetrating I was afraid all the people in the waiting room would hear.

'I don't know if it's normal or not,' I said. 'I'm at work every Tuesday, remember?' My voice seemed very loud because the three women within earshot weren't making any noise. Gail Kerr was flicking through old issues of *House & Garden*. Mara Singh was on her iPhone. Becky Dussault seemed to be asleep. She was hugely pregnant and looked exhausted, poor pet.

'But does this sort of thing usually happen when you're at home? On your days off?' Nerine demanded.

I wanted to tell her my days off weren't really days off; I spent them marking exam papers for an online music academy. Instead I muttered, 'No.'

'Then what if it isn't your ex? What if it's mine?'

'That's impossible.'

'How can you be sure?'

'We've discussed this already.' Before Nerine could protest, the landline rang. 'I'll call you later, okay? We'll sort things out.' Then I broke the connection and picked up the other phone. 'Women's Health Collective,' I recited, trying to sound calm.

The Bulwell Women's Health Collective occupied a modest fibro cottage. What had once been the front bedroom now contained six easy chairs, a coffee table, a filing cabinet and a desk where I worked from nine to five every Tuesday and Thursday. The bedroom across the hall was Sally's surgery, and the bedroom behind that was occupied by a massage thera- pist named Mantra. The living room had become a venue for workshops, board meetings and talks, while the dining alcove had been transformed into a cubbyhole for Bridget, the office manager.

The bathroom and kitchen were for everyone—not just the staff. Sometimes new mothers had to warm up formula or use a breast pump in there. And when they did, you could hear the noise all over the house.

Normally it was a peaceful place, despite all the babies we saw. Thanks to the beat-up furniture, diffuser-scented air and friendly public-service messages plastered all over its walls, the centre had a very comforting atmosphere. During my seven years there I'd witnessed only a handful of traumatic episodes: a bathroom head injury, an early-stage miscarriage and a screaming breakdown involving a client with schizophrenia. Since men weren't allowed past the front desk, there had also been one or two tense exchanges with parents and partners. But our clients had come to expect a tranquil, nurturing experience—especially from the receptionist.

After talking to Nerine, I found it hard to keep my voice at the right pitch, though. I'd told her not to call unless there was an emergency. Since she had called, did that mean she was in a state of panic? I didn't like to think of her panicking in front of the children. What if she tried to leave? What if she did something crazy, like calling the police or boarding up the windows?

As I made an appointment for one of the McIntyre sisters, I decided that the time had come to stop Keith's nuisance phone calls. But I would need help.

Specifically, I would need Tearle Godwin's help.

'Gail?' Sally murmured, as she opened her surgery door. It was at least ten minutes since she'd said goodbye to her last patient; had she been gobbling down a sandwich? Sure enough, when I looked, the clock said twenty past twelve.

I called Bridget on the landline, because part of her job was to cover for me at lunch.

'Are you ready? I need to pop out.'

'It's not twelve-thirty yet.' Bridget was far more attached to the schedules than the rest of us were.

'All right. Ten minutes.' I dropped the receiver into its cradle, my mobile into my knitted bag, my hand cream into the desk drawer and my coffee cup into the bin. Then, at half past twelve precisely, I stood up and left, waving at Bridget as she entered the waiting room.

'Back in an hour,' I told her, and headed for Tearle's place.

Bulwell had spread out a bit over the years. But the old section of town, where Tearle Godwin lived, covered no more than a few blocks. As a collector of antiques, Tearle would never have considered living in a house built later than 1914. He'd moved to Bulwell because he needed something big, old and cheap; his North Shore mansion had been sold off during an expensive divorce, and he couldn't afford anything comparable in Sydney. Half of his collection had also been disposed of during the settlement, but he was committed to buying back what he'd lost—and determined that the pieces he still owned would be displayed in a sympathetic, spacious environment.

So he'd purchased the old Risdon place, which had six bedrooms, a tower, stained-glass windows and stone lions flanking the front steps. He'd hired an army of Sydney painters, carpenters and roofers to restore the mansion to its former glory, then filled it with a dazzling array of antique paintings, pillboxes, epergnes, napkin rings, cigarette cases and other rarefied objects. Most of Bulwell's residents thought he was a little touched, but I'd met enthusiasts before. I knew the type.

Tearle didn't socialise much. He had very little in common with his neighbours and preferred to spend his time on the internet, hunting down auction records. But for some reason he liked me. Maybe I reminded him of his antiques—tarnished and battered, but formerly quite choice. His ex-wife, a prominent art dealer, was certainly a collector's piece. She'd received a lot of press coverage over the years, and looked absolutely stunning in every photo I'd seen of her.

When I arrived at Tearle's house, I marched up the front path feeling sweaty and unkempt. Tearle's garden was immaculate, full of topiary and stone urns, and I felt hugely out of place in my Aldi cardigan and comfortable shoes. I'd never paid a call on Tearle for that very reason; I preferred neutral ground like the Palace Hotel or the Daily Grind café, where his sports jackets and brogues looked a lot weirder than my corduroys and Blundstones.

His bellpull was an antique, just like his doorknocker. I tried both. Then I waited, glancing at my watch and wondering if perhaps I should have called him instead of bearding him in his den. But Tearle wasn't great on the phone. Sometimes when I rang him I sensed that his attention was focused elsewhere. Perhaps his detached manner was misleading, but I'd decided that if I was going to get a result, I'd need to speak to him in person.

Opening the door, he said, 'Why, hello. This is an unexpected pleasure.'

'Can I talk to you for a moment?'

'Of course.' He stepped back to admit me, offering up one of his measured, closed-lip smiles. As usual, he was dressed in the kind of clothes you would expect to see on a golf course.

His silver hair was brushed back neatly from his narrow, beaky face.

'It's about Keith,' I said, as I crossed the threshold. Then I found myself gaping up at the staircase in front of me, which was lit by a stained-glass window. The walls were hung with Norman Lindsay etchings. The parquet floor gleamed like crystal. 'Well. This is nice.'

'Would you care for a drink? Or a sandwich, perhaps…?'

'Oh, no. No, thanks. I have to get back to work in a minute.' Tearing my gaze away from the museum-quality furnishings, I said, 'It's about those anonymous phone calls. They've been getting worse.'

'In what way?'

'Well—you know. More frequent.'

'Ah.'

'And I was thinking that maybe I should send Keith a letter. A lawyer's letter. Telling him to stop or I'll go to the police.' I had no intention of approaching the police—not while Nerine was in my house—but I was hoping that the threat might be enough. 'You'd get paid for it,' I added hastily, because I'd had a lot of dealings with lawyers and knew how they operated. 'I wouldn't expect you to do it for nothing.'

Tearle studied me for a moment, then asked, 'Have you established that Keith really is the one making those calls?'

'It has to be him. Who else would bother?'

'Meg, if you don't have evidence—'

'I know. But I'm sick of it. And if I don't do something, he's not going to stop.' I looked Tearle straight in the eye and said, 'Unless you've got a better idea?'

He pursed his lips. 'Let me give it some thought.'

'If the letter comes from a lawyer, he might take notice.'

'He might. On the other hand, it might aggravate him.' Tearle always spoke as if he were giving a lecture, carefully enunciating every word and never hurrying or stumbling. I found it hard to tolerate. 'You once told me that Keith is a narcissist. Narcissists enjoy litigation. At least a quarter of my clients were narcissists—going to court was a hobby, for them.'

My mobile chirped. I groped around frantically in my bag, but the phone had slipped under everything else and the call went straight to voicemail.

'If you change your number, Keith won't be able to ring you,' Tearle pointed out, not for the first time. Sally had said the same thing, and so had Jill. It was a suggestion that never failed to annoy me.

'I told you, I don't want to change my number. Why should I? I'm not going to let him run me ragged.' Suddenly my phone rang again. 'Excuse me,' I said, and squatted down to dump the contents of my bag on the floor.

Dirty tissues, shopping lists, throat lozenges, empty pill cards, keys, pens and bobby pins spilled out everywhere. It was embarrassing, but I didn't have a choice; I was afraid Nerine might be calling.

I plucked the phone from a nest of crumpled receipts and slapped it against my ear. 'Hello?'

'Meg?' It was Nerine, all right.

'Oh. Hello.'

As Tearle knelt down to help me shove all the rubbish back into my bag, I waved him off. I didn't want him picking up my old Bounty wrappers.

'What are you doing?' Nerine demanded. 'I thought you were gunna call me?'

'I will. But I'm talking to someone else right now.' Glancing up at Tearle, I added, 'A lawyer.'

'What?' She sounded alarmed.

'He'll know the best way to tackle Keith.'

'But what if it isn't Keith?' she wailed. 'What if it's Duncan?'

'Later, okay?'

'Meg—'

'Bye.'

I disconnected. 'Sorry. That was my daughter.'

'Really? She must be quite a night owl.'

I stared at him blankly as I struggled to my feet.

'Didn't you say she was in England?' He was watching me with a glint in his eye. 'It has to be after midnight over there.'

Then my phone rang again.

'Bye, Tearle,' I said, and scurried back outside.

When I arrived home that evening, all kinds of things had changed.

My clothes horse was standing in the middle of the living room, draped with damp laundry. More laundry was hanging over kitchen chairs, bedheads and towel rails. My side tables had been cleared of every sharp-edged item. There were puzzle pieces scattered across the coffee table and plush animals strewn across the floor. Esme was wearing hair clips.

On entering the kitchen, I found it awash in dirty cups and half-eaten biscuits. Something red and fragrant was bubbling in a pan on the stove. The table had been carelessly set, with paper and crayons swept aside and replaced by a handful of dumped cutlery. The bin was overflowing and there were fingermarks on the fridge.

'Oh, hi!' Nerine said, when I wandered in. 'Sorry about all the laundry, but I couldn't put it outside in case someone saw the kids' clothes.'

I stood rooted to the spot, staring at her. She'd dyed her hair brown and tied it back in a ponytail. She was sporting a heavy fringe that covered her eyebrows, and dark lipstick just like Emily's.

She could have been Emily's twin.

'I brought some different hair dyes, just in case,' she continued, on seeing me blink. 'And some lipsticks and sunglasses and stuff.' When I remained dumbstruck, she added, 'I'm a hairdresser. Did Jill not tell you?'

She was draining spaghetti into a colander with one hand as she cradled Colette with the other. To my relief, I saw that Colette's hair was still blonde. So was Ana's, as far as I could tell; most of it was hidden by a knitted cap with fluffy cat's ears.

'Do I look like your daughter?' Nerine asked me. After a day dotted with frantic phone calls, I'd been expecting to find her cowering in the bathroom behind a locked door, armed with a hammer or a set of old hedging shears. Instead she sounded quite calm and pleased with herself. 'I thought I should try a disguise, so you could say your daughter's visiting. Just in case anyone sees me.'

I didn't like that idea at all. 'Why would anyone see you?' I said, eying the axe that was now resting on top of the kitchen cupboards. 'You won't be going anywhere.'

'I mean if I'm out in the garden.' She seemed to notice where I was looking. 'The kids can't reach that high.'

'But an axe in the kitchen...' I protested feebly. 'Don't you think it would be safer back in the shed?'

'Not if Duncan shows up. Now—who's having sauce with their spaghetti and who's having cheese?'

Since she was about to serve me dinner, I decided not to fuss about the axe, the hair dye or the six times she'd called me that day. Instead I gathered up the pile of drawings from the kitchen table and moved them to a little shelf where I put foreign coins, spare doorknobs and other things I didn't know what else to do with. That's when I realised the topmost drawing showed a crying child covered in blood.

I nearly choked on my gasp of horror. 'Nerine...'

'What? Oh.' She spotted the picture and grimaced. 'Yeah, well...I guess it's all part of the process. Big Bug? Are you having sauce with this, or just cheese?'

'Cheese,' Ana mumbled. I searched her face for signs of distress, but saw none. 'We put the chooks to bed,' she told me.

I couldn't find my voice for a moment.

'Did you, sweetheart? Thank you.'

'So they'll be safe now.'

'They will. Very safe.'

'Meg?' Nerine interrupted. 'Could you get the plates, please?'

'Dok!' Colette had spotted Esme. I can't abide dogs under the table, so I hustled Esme out of the room and shut the door firmly behind her. Then I fetched four dinner plates and dealt them out like playing cards.

When I sat down next to Analiese, I saw that she was already wearing her pyjamas. Mr Snuffles occupied the chair to her left.

'What did you do today?' I asked her. 'Did you go for a walk?'

She shook her head, staring at me.

'How many eggs did the chooks lay?'

'Three,' she said.

'Did you eat them?'

Another headshake.

'Right!' Nerine dumped the colander onto the table and passed me the tongs.

I soon discovered that her sauce was fairly basic. Most food is when you have small kids. She ate her share of it while holding Colette on her lap, because we didn't have a high-chair; I'd been warned not to buy anything baby-related that couldn't easily be hidden.

Watching Nerine, I was unnerved. Emily might have been paler and shorter, with big brown eyes instead of small green ones, but Nerine had the same long neck and sloping shoulders. As for the hairstyle, it was identical—and profoundly disturbing.

'The bathroom's a bit of a mess,' Nerine admitted. 'Sorry about that. Colette wanted to give the dog another bath, and we used a lot of towels.'

'That's okay.'

'We also finished the last of the red food colouring. I figured you probably didn't need it.'

I felt a pang of annoyance before it occurred to me that I was behaving like someone who gets mad at babies on planes. I'd offered to house a woman and her two small children; what on earth had I expected?

'Were there any more calls?' I finally asked, raising my voice over Colette's squeal of delight as she threw a piece of spaghetti at Ana.

'No. *No.*' Nerine scowled at Colette, then shot me a speculative look. 'We haven't had any calls since five. What did the lawyer say?' She knew Tearle had called me.

'He said he'd have a quiet word with David. Hopefully David will have a quiet word with Keith's lawyer, and Keith's lawyer will have a slightly louder word with Keith.'

'Who's David?' Nerine wanted to know.

'Oh—just a lawyer friend.' Nerine didn't need to know the details of my court case. She had enough to worry about. 'Hopefully that'll do the trick. At least it'll be faster than a letter.'

Nerine didn't look convinced. She wrenched the saltcellar

out of Colette's hand, then shushed her fiercely when she began to cry. 'Did you talk to your contact?' she asked.

I was puzzled. 'My contact?'

'About passports.' Seeing my blank expression, she said patiently, 'You were going to talk to your contact about getting fake passports for me and the kids.'

I suddenly remembered making that promise earlier in the day, just to get her off the phone. My contact was Renee, a naturopath friend who raised alpacas just outside Taree. I'd thought of her at once when Jill had first called, because Renee's mud-brick house was an unofficial refuge for women escaping domestic violence; she had bought herself a large, intimidating dog for that very reason. She had promised to house my fugitives once her mother had finished chemotherapy, but that didn't mean she was a habitual lawbreaker. On the contrary, Renee was a gentle, retiring soul who had only agreed to help because of her experience with her own father. At school she had turned up every week with a new bruise or bandage.

I doubted she knew anything about fake passports.

'No, I didn't have time to call Renee. I don't even know if I should, from Bulwell. Last time I spoke to her, I was calling from Orange.'

'Well, when are you going to Orange next?' Nerine demanded.

'Um…'

'I'm worried, Meg. I'm really, really worried.'

'I know.'

'There's no future for us here. Even New Zealand would be

better. We need someone with a boat. We need new identities.'

'Dok,' said Colette, and began to grizzle.

Nerine ignored her. 'If we don't change our identities, Duncan's going to find us. He's really smart. And he scares people. We won't be safe until we're out of the country.'

I wanted to say that I'd signed up for house guests, not for identity theft or people smuggling. But I knew Nerine was desperate, and possibly suffering from PTSD. My only option was to be supportive.

'I'll call Renee from town on Thursday,' I promised. 'And Jill too.'

'I already did that before we came here.' Nerine sounded grumpy. 'She said she didn't know anyone who could help.'

'Well—let me think about it.'

'We don't have much time, Meg.'

'I'll see what I can do.'

'You can buy a gun. That's something you can do.'

'Nerine—'

'It's the only thing that'll stop him.'

'*Please* don't do this,' I entreated. 'Not in front of the kids.' Ana had stopped eating. She was staring down at her plate. I wanted to whisk her away and sing to her.

'You think they don't know?' Nerine said with a hollow laugh. 'You think they aren't sitting here waiting for him to turn up?' She clamped an arm around Colette, who was writhing and wriggling and trying to get down. 'He always turns up, Meg. That's what you don't understand.'

'But—'

'The longer we stay, the bigger the risk. That's why I'm telling you—get a gun.' She leaned across the table, gripped my wrist and fixed me with an intent look. 'It's for your sake as much as ours. Who do you think he'll blame for this? You need to start watching your back. I mean it.'

SAFETY

IT WAS THE barking that woke me. Esme had shuffled across my room and was yapping at the closed door. Then I heard Nerine's voice.

'Ana!' she was crying. *'Ana!'*

I scrambled out of bed. When I yanked the door open, Esme surged into the hall ahead of me.

All the lights were on.

'Nerine?' I croaked as I stumbled into the living room, but there was no sign of her. Esme barked again. She lolloped over to the front door and started scratching at it.

'Ana!' Nerine called from the laundry. A sudden, piercing wail told me she was with Colette. So I hurried to join them, nearly tripping over a doll in the process.

I found Nerine on her haunches, with her head in the laundry cupboard.

'What's the matter?' I blurted over Colette's screams.

'She's gone.'

'What?'

'Ana's not here.' Nerine sprang to her feet. She was wearing a baggy T-shirt covered in brown stains. Her hair was a mess. 'I woke up and she wasn't in bed. And now I can't find her.'

'Shhh. It's okay. She's probably—'

'Oh my God, Meg!' Nerine had brushed past me and was pointing at the back door. I saw at once that the safety chain was off.

'She's outside!' Nerine exclaimed. Then she shoved Colette into my arms and stretched up to grab the axe from the top of the cupboard.

'Wait! Nerine!' Colette struggled in my grasp, hot and sticky and frantic. Her shrieks were deafening. 'I'll go.'

But Nerine had already wrenched open the door. I was forced to step back as she raised the axe, her fingers clamped to its polished shaft.

Peering into the darkness, she spluttered, 'I can't see. Where's the light?'

I was reaching for the switch when Esme slipped past me. The screen door had a broken handle and swung open when she nudged it. Her barking reached a hysterical pitch that even silenced Colette.

I knew at once that something was wrong, even before the porch light flickered on. Its harsh glow illumined a yard speckled with blood and feathers.

'Oh my God…' The axe sagged in Nerine's grip.

'Get inside.' I thrust Colette at her. 'Nerine? Take your daughter inside.'

A volley of barks told me that Esme was over by the henhouse. I couldn't see her; there wasn't enough light.

'Nerine!' My sharp tone set Colette off again. It was the little girl's shrill voice that caused Nerine to snap out of her daze. She dropped the axe, which hit the floor with a ringing thud.

'Oh my God,' she whimpered.

'Take her. Now. She shouldn't be seeing this.'

'He's here.' Nerine's hands trembled as she reached blindly for Colette. 'It's Duncan...'

'It's a fox,' I snapped. I'd learnt the hard way how to recognise a fox's handiwork. My first hens had lasted just two weeks; after cleaning up their remains, I'd invested in the very best farmyard security money could buy.

'A fox?' Nerine echoed.

I pulled a torch from the nearest drawer. Esme was still barking.

'You stay here,' I said.

'But what about Ana?'

'I'll go and see.'

Cautiously I picked up the axe and crept down the back stairs. A surge of fury swamped my fear as my wandering torch beam swept over a clump of white feathers near the tanks.

Snowball was dead. And Granny too, by the look of it.

'Get him, girl. Get the bastard.' I was talking to Esme, who trotted stiffly around the coop's wire walls, spotlit by the torch. Suddenly I realised that the coop was wide open.

Someone had left its gate ajar.

'Oh, for...' I couldn't believe my eyes. The gate, of all

things! Nerine had put the chickens to bed and she'd left the bloody gate open.

I hurried towards it, counting corpses on the way. Poor Chocolate was in pieces. Freckle was lying in a pool of her own blood. Everywhere I looked there were gaping beaks, knots of grey intestine, jagged shards of bone.

So much damage in so little time. I wondered if there had been more than one fox...

A flurry of movement inside the pen made me gasp. But then I saw it was only Nugget. She looked shell-shocked—as did Perdita, Ruby and Barb.

My torch beam skimmed across shit and chaff and feathers. For a split second, as I peered into the henhouse, I thought I'd found another chook. Then I realised who was curled up in there.

'Ana? Sweetie?'

She didn't move. With a crackle of joints I hunkered down, terrified. But when I poked at her skinny flank, she stirred and mumbled something.

'Thank God,' I whispered. 'Thank you, God.' I raised my voice. 'Nerine! Ana's here!'

If Nerine heard me, she didn't say anything—or perhaps I just didn't hear her. Putting aside the axe and the torch, I crawled halfway into the henhouse and gathered up the sleeping child. When I dragged her out, she made a few sleepy efforts to push me away, muttering a protest. But as soon as I was on my feet again, cradling her in my arms, she laid her head on my shoulder and fell back into a heavy doze.

'Stay,' I told Esme. Then I staggered towards the house, feeling Ana's breath on my cheek. She smelled of soap and sour milk. The rash near her mouth looked worse. But she didn't seem to be injured.

'Oh my God.' Nerine pushed open the screen door to let me in, still clutching her younger daughter. 'Where was she?'

'In the henhouse.'

'Oh my *God*.'

'She's a champion sleeper.' I kept going, through the kitchen, down the hall, into the guest room. Here I dumped Ana onto the bed, which was already full of stuffed toys.

A muscle twinged in my back as I straightened. Rubbing it, I turned to Nerine, who had followed me in. 'She must have left the gate open,' I said. 'That's why the chooks got out.'

'Oh, Meg. I'm so sorry.'

'It's not your fault. It's not her fault, either.' Gazing down at the little girl in grubby pyjamas, I felt tears prick my eyes. 'It was my fault. I told her the coop was safe. I kept saying it. No wonder she went in there.' Before Nerine could apologise again, I added, 'You might want to wash her face and hands and maybe change those pyjamas. They're probably covered in chicken poo.'

'Poo!' Colette yelped.

'I'll be outside for a bit. I have to clean up.' Passing Nerine on my way to the kitchen, I added, 'We don't want the kids seeing any of this tomorrow morning.'

'Can I help?' Nerine looked pale and shaky.

'No—you stay here. Your kids come first.'

In the kitchen I paused for a moment to collect a roll of black garbage bags and a pair of rubber gloves. Then I went to shovel up my dead chooks.

I spent about an hour putting bits of chicken into three garbage bags. Once I'd covered up the bloodstains on the ground, I dumped all three bags into the boot of my car and went back to bed. By then it was nearly four-thirty.

But I didn't sleep again that night. I couldn't. I lay grieving for my poor hens and fretting about Ana. The depth of her fear was hard to grasp. The fact that she felt safer inside a stinking chicken coop than she did in a warm bed with her own mother…how could that have happened? How bad could her life have been?

And how much worse was it going to get?

I was haunted by a sense of culpability. She should have been seeing a psychologist. She should have been playing with other children and visiting the library and going to the beach. Instead she was being kept inside my poky little house in an atmosphere of unmitigated dread.

I knew that she would have lifelong problems unless something was done very soon. She would grow up to find herself battling with anxiety and depression. I'd seen what Keith had done to Emily when she was a child. He'd hacked away at her self-esteem bit by bit, and my attempts to repair the damage had failed because he'd been doing the same thing to me. I would never forget how Emily had emerged from her room one day dressed like a cheerleader for her dance class. Keith had roared with laughter. 'You look like a slut!' he'd crowed. 'A real little slut!'

She'd been eleven years old at the time.

Ana's father had probably done worse—and her mother (like me) had been trying to remedy the situation. But Nerine's fear was undermining all her efforts, creating an atmosphere that had driven Ana into a chicken coop. I didn't know how to help; my repeated assurances seemed to count for nothing. Instead of calming Nerine down, I was being infected by her unease.

I lay there scolding myself. What an idiot. Once again, I hadn't thought things through. I'd jumped at the chance of saving two little girls from domestic violence, but it hadn't occurred to me that the whole process of removing them from their abusive environment might expose them to other forms of stress. I'd had a picture in my head of children thriving and blossoming, far away from their father's malign presence. I hadn't imagined his presence would follow them from place to place.

But I should have. I should have known that, even in her father's absence, Ana would take refuge wherever she felt safe, her terror so great that the blood and filth hadn't been enough to scare her away. Unless she'd slept through the noise? Hard to believe the screech of dying chickens hadn't woken her, but she'd certainly been dead to the world when I carried her off to bed.

As dawn began to filter through the treetops I got up, dressed myself and went out to the car with Esme. After closing the gate behind me, I guided my old bomb onto the fire trail that bisected my land. The air was full of birdsong. Comfortably arranged on the front passenger seat, Esme barked once at a parakeet that flitted across the road. But for the most part she remained silent, rocking and bouncing as we crawled along.

I headed towards the Baumanns' fence line, through stands of banksia and wind-stunted mountain ash. At one point I crossed the shallow gully that became a creek during thunderstorms. Then I bumped over a compacted ants' nest and rattled across a patch of exposed bedrock. When we finally reached the electric fence, I followed it north for more than half a kilometre, past an ancient, rusty oil drum that had been disintegrating in the bush since I'd first arrived. Just beyond this relic was an area of half-cleared land where someone had once tried to open up a bit of grazing or maybe plant a potato field. It was an ugly scar full of weathered tree stumps and mouldering piles of rotten wood. After that came a dense thicket of tea-tree, which thinned as the track took a sharp right along the clifftop.

My property backed onto a wooded gorge slashed through a basalt hillside. Just beyond the track there was a sheer, naked cliff face that hit a slightly gentler slope about ten metres down. That was where the growth started: first came a fuzz of boronia and acacia bushes, then a thick curtain of trees that shrouded the side of the gorge all the way to the creek at its base. Up top, the cliff was so dangerous that there was an eight-metre gap between it and the fire trail, filled mostly with scrub. But at one point someone had cleared a track to the very edge of the gorge, where there was a huge, flat, jutting boulder to stand on. My own private lookout.

At first I'd been surprised that my house hadn't been built there, facing the magnificent view of the plateau opposite. Then I'd visited the place on a windy day, and a howling gale nearly swept me into the gorge. After that I decided I was perfectly happy living in the centre of my block, shielded from the wind by a wide belt of eucalypts.

The air was very still when I drove up to the cliff with my boot full of dead chickens. I'd thought about burying the corpses, but all that digging wouldn't have done my back any good, and I couldn't have done it before Ana and Colette woke up. I'd also thought about a cremation, but that might have sparked someone's interest. The Huggetts next door might have seen the smoke.

So I'd decided to do something that I didn't normally do: throw my rubbish off a cliff.

As I heaved the three garbage bags out of my car, I told myself it wasn't littering. Within a week, I knew, the bloody scraps would have been eaten by scavengers. Bushwalkers didn't come this way. There were no walking tracks along the gorge because the terrain was too steep—though not so steep that any stray body parts would plummet straight down to the creek bed. I hoped those bits would land in the forest and be gobbled up by birds, ants, lizards and the odd feral dog. Maybe the fox would finish what it had started.

Emptying the bags over the edge of the lookout wasn't easy. I'd never been good with heights, and the sight of my poor murdered hens made me feel nauseous. When I reached the lookout I dropped all three bags, removed the plastic ties and lowered myself awkwardly onto my hands and knees. Then I crawled to the very end of the stone platform, dragging one of the bags with me.

The view into the gorge was so hair-raising that I flung myself onto my stomach like a sunbaking lizard, and shook out the bag onto the olive-green canopy below. When the bag was empty I squirmed back from the cliff edge and went to repeat the process. By the time I'd finished, there were only three body parts visible on the wall of the gorge. One smudge of white feathers was sitting on top of a tree, where the next strong wind would bring it down. One mangled head had caught on a knob of rock about four metres beneath me. And there was a chunk of flesh wedged against a tuft of fern that had broken its fall.

Confident that a magpie or currawong would spy all these pieces and whisk them away, I returned to my car with the used garbage bags, which I tossed back in the boot. I'd been planning to take the kids on a nature walk later in the day but decided, as I slipped behind the steering wheel, that I wouldn't go anywhere near the lookout. It was too dangerous—and I didn't want anyone spotting the chook's head.

God knows, I didn't want to look at it myself.

'Move over,' I said, pushing Esme off the gear stick. Then I turned the key in the ignition and set off home, dreading my next encounter with Analiese. How was I going to make her understand that the dead chickens weren't her fault? How was I going to deal with her guilt and despair?

Maybe some new hens might distract her…

Back at the house, I found everyone in the kitchen. Nerine was hovering near the toaster while she dandled Colette on her hip. Analiese, dressed in a pink tracksuit, was methodically packing down spoonfuls of cereal. Like her mother, she looked a bit groggy—but I was pleased to see that her eyes weren't red and her cheeks weren't tear-stained.

'Hello,' I said, barring Esme at the threshold. 'No,' I told her. 'Not in here.'

'Dok!' Colette exclaimed.

'You're up early,' Nerine remarked. 'Do you want some toast?'

'No, thanks.' Shutting the door on Esme, I went to retrieve my coffee cup from an overhead cupboard.

Analiese said thickly, through a mouthful of stodge, 'Did you let the chickens out?'

I paused and glanced at her mother, whose grimace was hard to read. What was Nerine trying to tell me? That Ana hadn't mentioned her midnight stroll? That she didn't even remember it?

'Uh—no,' I replied. 'Not yet. But I will.'

'Can I help?' Analiese asked.

'Of course.' I took a deep breath. 'The thing is—there are only four chooks left now.'

The little girl stared at me. Her chewing stopped.

'All the others ran away last night,' I continued. 'And a fox ate them. I'm sorry, Ana.'

Tears welled in her eyes. Her bottom lip trembled. I shot a pleading look at Nerine, who said, 'The gate was left open. It was probably my fault.'

'We'll be more careful from now on,' I added quickly. 'We'll make sure the gate's always shut.' As Ana swallowed and put down her spoon, I made a desperate attempt to change the subject by adding, 'And I'll get some more hens. Brand new babies.'

Still Ana didn't speak. She sniffed and wiped her nose, blinking at the tabletop. Nerine said, 'It's very sad, Big Bug, but if you get too upset you're going to make me feel like it's my fault. And it wasn't my fault. It was an accident.'

I was startled by this comment, which didn't seem entirely fair to me. So I put an arm around Analiese and murmured, 'The one good thing is that the fox won't be hungry anymore. And perhaps his family won't be hungry, either.'

Ana sniffed. But she was listening.

'Some animals eat other animals,' I went on. 'It's what happens. It's what has to happen, or we wouldn't have creatures like lions or wolves or sharks.' I dug a used tissue from my pocket and handed it to her. 'The fox won't come back for a long time,' I promised. 'It must be very full, by now.'

'I'm full,' she said. 'I'm finished.' Then she slipped from my grasp and dropped to the floor, taking Mr Snuffles with her.

I waited until she'd disappeared down the hallway before addressing Nerine.

'Maybe you should go and see how she is.'

'All right. If you'll take the other one.' At that instant the toast popped up, and Nerine pushed Colette into my arms. 'I'll just butter these first.'

'Does Ana not remember last night?' I asked as I wrestled with Colette.

Nerine shrugged. 'I don't think so. She hasn't said anything.'

I found that hard to understand. 'Is she a sleepwalker?'

'Sometimes,' said Nerine.

'Does it happen when she's particularly worried?'

Nerine finished scraping butter across the first slice. She passed it to me and said, 'I guess so. Maybe.' Her tone was distracted. 'That piece is for Collie.'

'Well, then...' I had to pause for a moment as Colette lunged for the toast, crushing it in her small, doughy hand. She shoved it straight at her mouth; I had to catch one fragment that broke off and tumbled towards the floor.

'You'd better sit down,' Nerine suggested.

Obediently I parked myself where Colette could smear her greasy meal all over the table. Then I held her in my lap while I helped her break the toast into smaller, more manageable chunks. Her mother, meanwhile, was buttering the second slice.

'Nerine?' I said. 'Don't you think it's possible that...well, that Ana is so worried right now because you keep talking about Duncan and how he's bound to show up?'

The butter knife froze in Nerine's hand. She turned to

70

look at me and said flatly, 'He *is* bound to show up.'

'Yes, but—I mean, even if that were true—'

'It *is* true.'

'You don't have to keep saying it, though. Not in front of the girls.' I tried to make my tone as mild as possible. I didn't want her to think she was under attack. 'If you go on and on about it, Ana will just keep sleepwalking, or whatever it is she did last night. We have to give her a sense of security, or she'll get worse. What if she runs away in her sleep? What if she ends up bumping into the electric fence or falling off a cliff?'

Nerine studied me for a moment. 'You just don't get it, do you?' She sounded tired. Perplexed.

'Nerine—'

'Say Ana gets comfortable. Say she forgets what she's learnt. Say she hears a knock and answers the door and it's Duncan.' While I struggled to think of an appropriate response, Nerine took a bite out of the second slice of toast. 'You know what'll happen?' she continued, spraying crumbs everywhere. 'A disaster, that's what. As long as he can find us, she can't afford to forget about him. None of us can.'

'Bok,' Colette barked, trying to wedge a soggy piece of toast into my mouth. As I recoiled, Nerine headed for the door.

'There are worse things than sleepwalking. That's why we need to go,' she said. Then she went off to find Ana, leaving me weighed down with guilt because she wanted a passport—a gun—a way out—and I couldn't give them to her.

I wondered if a gun would really make her feel safe. Would

it calm her down? Stop her frightening the children? Even an unloaded gun might do the trick.

Sally's partner had a gun because the two of them lived on a farm. But I doubted they would lend it to someone like me.

GONE BUSH

KEITH DIDN'T LIKE the great outdoors. He liked football fields and beach views, but we didn't go for picnics or bushwalks or farm stays. The one time we went camping, it was because Keith wanted to impress a work colleague. When Steve Mazzoli asked us to join him on a trip to Jervis Bay, Keith accepted the invitation eagerly, then went out and spent hundreds of dollars on fancy new equipment: a tent, a gas stove, camp beds, sleeping bags, collapsible chairs, lanterns—even a portable storage unit.

But of course Keith didn't know what he was doing. He forgot to bring a gas bottle for the stove or a hammer for the tent pegs. And since I was in charge of packing the food, sheets, maps, towels, toiletries, cooking utensils, sunscreen, hats, clothes, washing-up bucket, detergent, medicines, insect repellent and alcohol, it made perfect sense to blame me for not checking that the hammer and gas bottle were in the boot as well. Not to mention Keith's sunglasses.

The trip to Jervis Bay was a nightmare. Emily threw up in the car, and Keith always hated it when she did that. He was furious, even though I had a change of clothes and plenty of sponges. He bawled at Emily for making the car smell bad, then accused *her* of smelling bad. He was angry at me for giving her breakfast because I wasn't supposed to feed her before we went on any long drives.

When we stopped for lunch, he refused to buy her anything. We had a big argument in the car until finally Emily screamed, 'I don't want lunch! I'm not hungry!' She was only eight years old, but I was already worried about eating disorders because Keith constantly monitored what she ate. He told me I fed her 'rubbish'. He said she had too much 'puppy fat'. He used health food as a kind of weapon: I was a lazy mother if I bought a packet of Tim Tams.

When we finally reached Jervis Bay, we were barely speaking. I suppose we weren't used to spending so much time together. Keith was always so busy with his schemes and his networking that Emily and I rarely saw him except when he needed laundry done or an investor entertained. I was relieved when we were at last able to spread out across the campsite—especially since the Mazzoli family were already there. When other people were around, Keith would generally keep a lid on his temper. He was careful not to look bad in front of the men he worked with.

As it turned out, Steve and his wife Greta were lovely. They had three kids, two boys and a girl. Greta was a great cook and Steve loved children and they had brought all kinds of extra equipment: bats and balls, flippers and snorkels, boogie boards, fishing rods, a kite, a blow-up raft, a set of binoculars. The campsite was fantastic—wooded, well serviced and right on the bay. There were fish in the surf. There were wallabies and possums; we even saw an echidna. Emily was frightened of the waves, but the Mazzoli kids were very kind to her. The oldest boy, who was thirteen, taught her to use a boogie board.

We would have had a wonderful time if Keith hadn't been there. As it was, he ruined everything. To begin with, he made a hash of the tent. We both did, but I copped the blame while he shook his head indulgently. If we'd been alone he would have shouted and kicked things. With Steve there, he was restricted to making jovial comments like, 'When she gets all flustered, she can't understand the simplest instructions' and 'Musicians, eh? No practical skills.'

I let it go. I'd learnt that fighting back led to streams of abuse or, if we were in public, to more subtle forms of revenge. At the camp, for instance, he needled me for bringing generic-brand snack foods ('She gets a high from the chemicals'), for undercooking the meat ('Artists are such flakes') and for insisting that Emily wear something on her feet while showering. ('Meg is a very anxious mother. I was hoping we might all get to relax on this trip, but apparently I was wrong …')

To his credit, I don't think Steve appreciated Keith's bitching. Greta certainly didn't. She spent more and more time away from my husband, and made a very conscious effort to take me on beach walks and shopping trips without him. His attempts to ingratiate himself—by comparing our own daughter unfavourably to hers—went down like a lead balloon. When he asked Greta how she'd raised such resilient, outgoing kids, she replied bluntly, 'Well, I don't criticise everything they do. That helps.'

She had obviously noticed the way Keith kept taking away his daughter's books and forcing her into the water with the other kids. He also dumped a lot of scorn on Emily for not distinguishing herself at charades or fictionary. Competition brought out the worst in Keith, no matter how friendly it might be. By the third night, there were no more campfire games. The Mazzolis seemed reluctant to take part. And the next day they announced they would be leaving before lunch, instead of in the afternoon.

This was my fault, naturally. Keith said I knew just how to press his buttons, and now Steve was running away from the toxic atmosphere I'd created. No doubt I'd been whining to Greta, telling her all kinds of pathetic lies about our marriage. 'Well, I hope you're satisfied,' he spat at me. 'I hope you realise you've probably torpedoed my chances. Is that what you wanted? Less money? Less respect? I'm guessing you're *scared* to move up because you're so fucking embarrassed about your loser background and lack of education.'

I didn't argue: it was better to let him blow off steam. I just went and said goodbye to the Mazzolis, then started to pack.

Not long afterwards, Keith drove away. I'd already stuffed a lot of food and equipment into the boot while Keith was chatting with some of the other campers. But then, as Emily and I were pulling up the tent pegs, he climbed into the car and roared off without a word of explanation. At first I thought he was headed for a pub somewhere, and I worried about drink driving. When he wasn't back by lunchtime, I thought he'd decided to eat somewhere nice while Emily and I were left with trail mix. Then, when he hadn't returned by our official check-out time, I began to think that he really had gone back to Sydney. Standing there next to our gas stove and folded tent, I tried not to panic. I told myself that it was only half an hour's drive to the nearest town, that there was bound to be a motel, that I could always ring Carol and ask her to pick us up…

In the end, I did panic. I went around the camp begging for a lift to town, making an awful fuss. In my defence, I was worried about being charged for another day. I was also worried because the family who'd booked our campsite had arrived, and I didn't know where to put our stuff. I remember sitting on someone's camp stool, surrounded by a cluster of concerned holidaymakers who were busily discussing my options. Someone offered me a ride into town. Someone else suggested phoning the police. It was five-thirty in the afternoon, with only a few hours of daylight left; I was just about to stand up and load our tent into the back of a complete stranger's four-wheel drive when I spotted Keith's car bumping down the trail towards us.

Needless to say, he managed to make me look like a fool. He kept insisting that he'd told me he was going off to meet with a business prospect down the coast and that he'd promised to be back before dinner. 'I must have reminded her half-a-dozen times,' he insisted. 'She can be very vague. She's a musician.'

It wasn't long before people started to think I'd been over-reacting. They were all in vacation mode anyway, so they didn't want to entertain the possibility that anything serious had occurred. It was easier to believe I was neurotic and possibly on some kind of medication. God knows, I didn't blame them. *I* wouldn't have wanted to tangle with Keith.

After he'd loaded the tent and the gas stove into our car, we took off, heading straight home without stopping for dinner. We hardly spoke for the entire trip. I felt wrung-out—defeated—and because Keith was obviously quite pleased with himself, he didn't need to vent. Instead he smugly let me stew, occasionally ordering Emily not to kick the back of his seat.

And that was the only time our family ever explored the bush together. I used to take Emily to the park all the time, but not with Keith. Parks were too boring for Keith. I was too boring for Keith. He said that knowing the names of native birds was 'autistic', I guess because he saw nature through a money lens. Views were valuable, especially water views. Timber was valuable. National parks weren't doing enough to monetise their assets.

After our camping weekend, I sat Emily down and told her that her daddy was very stressed and that she wasn't really gutless or dim. She looked at me for a moment, her face heavy, and replied, 'But he says the same things about you, Mummy. So how would you know?'

It was a good question.

'Stay on the track, Big Bug,' said Nerine. 'You mustn't go in the long grass—there might be snakes.'

'Not really. Not at this time of year,' I assured her. We were heading for the Baumanns' electric fence, making very slow progress because Colette had insisted on walking. When toddlers walk, there's always a lot of stopping and sitting down, so to keep Analiese from getting bored I'd been feeding her snippets of information. I told her about the time I heard a lyrebird imitating a nail gun. I showed her a blue flax lily and explained how you could eat the fruit and make the leaves into woven bags. I took her on a slight detour so she could look at the old bowerbird bower I'd found. Under a screen of tea-tree, two modest tufts of carefully arranged sticks were surrounded by a wide, well-trodden dance floor. The floor was scattered with blue parrot feathers, blue plastic bottle caps and scraps of blue tarp.

The bower enchanted Analiese. Even her mother was impressed. 'They should do *Renovation Rescue* with bowerbirds,' Nerine joked. But then she hurried everyone away because there was an ants' nest nearby. 'Bull ants can bite you,' she warned her girls. 'They really, really hurt when they bite.'

She went on to relate how a march-fly bite had once landed her in hospital. She seemed to see nothing but threats in the natural environment. Her focus was on cliffs, thorns, wasps, spiders, ticks, leeches, snakes and falling tree limbs. She asked me if there were any old mine shafts in the area. She described how you could catch psittacosis from bird droppings and lyssavirus from bat saliva.

I could see that my scrubby, undernourished land bored her because her gaze never lingered on anything. It made me wonder if she was fussing and fretting just to invest the bush-walk with drama.

By the time we reached the Baumanns' fence, I was getting quite irritated. My intention had been to make the kids realise how dangerous electricity could be, but after Nerine had warned them off nearly everything in sight, I was concerned that they wouldn't see the fence as a serious threat—despite all the hazard signs scattered along it. Nevertheless, I did what I could. I explained how one little touch could be very painful even for an adult, and how small children might get burned.

'Don't the people next door like you?' Analiese asked, her forehead creasing.

'Sorry, sweetheart?' I didn't understand.

'Do they want to keep you out?'

The penny dropped. 'Oh, no—no, they just want to keep their cows in.' Not that I'd ever seen the Baumanns' modest herd of Angus cattle anywhere near my boundary. The country was too rough, and too far from the Baumanns' lowland grazing, to offer any kind of attraction. 'Cows are so big that they can knock fences over, you see,' I continued. 'But not if the fence gives them an electric shock.' Seeing Ana's face fall, I added quickly, 'The cows never come up here, though. And even if they did, it would only take one little shock to stop them from coming back.'

'Like when you burned yourself on your dad's cigarette lighter,' Nerine interposed, her eyes on Analiese. 'You never picked that up again, did you?'

Ana winced. I clenched my teeth. Colette was squirming fretfully in Nerine's arms, because I'd insisted that the toddler be picked up before we went anywhere near the electric fence. 'Colette's getting bored,' I said. 'Perhaps we should head home.'

'Before someone spots us,' Nerine agreed. 'We probably shouldn't be out this far anyway.'

'Oh, we're fine here,' I assured her. 'The Baumanns live right down in the valley, when they're around at all. It's the Huggetts we have to watch.'

'The Huggetts?'

'On the other side. The son's always out doing road work but the father's retired. Mostly he stays inside with his dogs, but sometimes he goes for a stroll.' As we set off for the house, retracing our steps, I found myself adding, 'I think he came onto my property once and stole my eggs.'

'Really?' Nerine perked up. 'What makes you say that?'

'Well...I noticed strange footprints around the henhouse when I got home from work. And the nests were empty.' Before Nerine could question me further, I admitted, 'It only happened that one time, though, when I first got the hens. Before Esme arrived.' Glancing at Esme, who was bringing up the rear, I said, 'She must have scared him off, somehow.'

'Ugh. Imagine having a creepy old guy wandering around your backyard.' Nerine shivered, then paused to put Colette down again because we weren't near the fence anymore. 'I can't believe you don't have a gun.'

'Meg?' It was Ana's voice. She was using my name for the very first time, and I felt a little flush of pleasure. 'What's over there?'

'Over where, sweetie?' I saw her wave at the track to our left. 'Oh, that leads to a cliff. We don't want to go there.'

'Why don't we?'

'Because you might fall off.'

'Remember what I said, Big Bug?' Nerine was steering Colette away from a pothole. 'You must never go outside unless Mummy's with you. It's too dangerous.'

'Not around the yard, it isn't,' I said quickly, because I didn't want Nerine's anxiety to keep them permanently house-bound. 'You need to be a little bit careful out in the bush, or you might get scratched by spiky plants. But you'll be fine as long as you stay on the paths.'

'And well away from all the rusty metal.' Nerine pointed at a knot of discarded wire. 'If you cut yourself on *that*, you'll have to get a needle in your arm.'

Ana shrank away from the wire. When she took my hand, I felt another stab of joy. But then guilt swamped the happiness, and I reminded myself that she wouldn't be staying for very long. If we grew too fond of each other, the pain of parting would only add to her stress.

'Look down there, Ana. See that? That's wallaby poo.' I stopped beside a dusty clump of turds. 'Sometimes wallabies come here, but never near the house. They're too scared of Esme.'

'Poo!' Colette cried. She was stumbling towards me, her face alight. Nerine immediately swept her back up into the air.

'Not the poo. You're not touching the poo,' Nerine scolded. 'You'll get sick.'

'How do you know it's not dog poo?' Ana asked me.

'Because of my little book. My book has pictures of all the different kinds of poo you can find, and tells you what animals they're from.'

Ana stared up at me, wide-eyed. 'There's a book about *poo*?' she demanded.

Nerine gave a honk of laughter. 'You're really something, Meg.'

'Where is it?' Ana was tugging at my hand. 'Is it at your house?'

'Yes,' I replied.

'Can I have a look?'

'Of course.'

'Does your book have dog poo in it?'

'Yes.'

'And chicken poo?'

'Hmmm…not really.' I was conscious of Nerine snorting away in the background, but tried to concentrate on what Ana was saying. 'You don't see chickens in the bush, and this book is about bush animals.'

'Like kangaroos?'

'Yes.'

'And rabbits?'

'Yes, there's a picture of rabbit poo. Except it's not called poo. It's called scats.'

'Cats?'

'No, *scats.*'

'Why?'

'I don't know.' After a moment's thought, I said, 'Maybe it sounds more scientific.'

Nerine snickered.

'Does the book have people poo in it?' Ana inquired.

'No.'

'Why not?'

'I don't know.'

'What about fox poo?'

'Yes, it has a picture of fox scats.'

'What about bat poo?'

'I'm not sure. We'll have to look…'

Ana and I talked about turds all the way home. We talked about them over lunch, as well. After lunch, we went out to look for animal traces in the bush around the house, and found some possum poo. Ana insisted on putting it in a labelled jar. She confided that she was going to start a 'poo museum' and spent the whole day poring over my pamphlet. She read it while she was cleaning her teeth, then took it to bed with her. I'd never seen her so animated. She even tried to copy the pictures into her own little exercise book.

'I guess we've been in the shit for so long, she feels comfortable with it,' Nerine drawled, after both her kids had finally fallen asleep.

'She's a very clever little girl.' We were both slumped in the living room, drinking wine. I don't usually drink wine, but sometimes you need it after a day with small children.

'Oh, she's smart,' said Nerine. 'She takes after her dad. Duncan's smart. Too smart.'

'Maybe you could talk to her about museums tomorrow. While I'm at work.' It worried me that Ana wasn't going to pre-school. 'If she's interested in biology, you can build on that.'

Nerine grunted. She looked so much like Emily that I found myself wheedling and placating, even though she had her feet on my coffee table. 'Is there anything you want me to get you from Bulwell tomorrow?' I asked.

'Oh, yeah. That's right. You're going to work.' She fixed me with a speculative look, her mascara smudged and her shirt smeared with chocolatey fingermarks. 'You should call that friend about getting fake passports.'

'Right. Yes. I'll do that.' My heart sank at the thought. 'You shouldn't get your hopes up, though.'

'I know. For one thing, I'd need lots of money. And I don't have a cent.' She sagged in her chair like someone much, much older. 'It's just…I worry so much about the kids.'

I worried about the kids too. But I didn't think trying to smuggle them out of Australia would do them any good.

A lot of people thought I should have left Keith long before I did. Emily was one of them. She blamed me for hanging around 'like a dog on a lead'. She accused me of being gutless. Masochistic. Stupid.

All I could do in my own defence was try to explain. I'd stayed with Keith because I knew what would happen if I didn't. And I was right; when I finally did leave, he fought me tooth and nail for full custody. When he didn't get that, he insisted on equal parenting arrangements. I had to let Emily stay with him almost every weekend, even though she didn't want to. If I hadn't, I might have lost her entirely.

Though she rarely talked about it, I understood how bad things were at Keith's place. After every visit she would withdraw into herself, or act out, or stop making an effort. Sometimes Keith would be living the high life with an older professional woman—who was able to pay the bills—or with a beautiful girl barely out of her teens. Sometimes he was scraping by in a dingy rental flat with one bedroom and a sofa bed. I preferred it when he had a partner, because it meant there was someone around to look after Emily when he took off on one of his 'business' jaunts, which tended to involve golf or strip clubs or harbour cruises. The older women were usually the more reliable child-minders, though the younger ones were often decent enough. Emily would occasionally mention that she'd spent Saturday evening on the couch with Sammi or Parker or Danielle, eating pizza and watching TV.

I got quite fond of Danielle. In fact I helped her out when she broke up with Keith. That was another thing Emily had to put up with: lots of domestic quarrels. I'm sure I didn't hear about half of them, but I do know clothes were tossed out of windows, holes were punched in walls and cars roared off at two o'clock in the morning. One woman was zonked on Valium half the time.

But even someone on Valium was better than no one at all. Because when Keith was forced to look after Emily by himself, things got really bad. Normally it only happened when he was unable to afford a babysitter—and normally *that* only happened when Carol refused to cough up more money for him. So of course he would be in a filthy mood, punishing Carol by refusing to let her mind Emily and taking out his anger on the closest available target. When he was living in a one-bedroom rental, the closest available target was his daughter.

He would 'help' her to do homework by prodding and harassing and confusing her. 'You think that's right? Really? Well, it's not. It's wrong,' he would say. 'How the hell did you get that answer? What was your brain doing? Show me. What does that mean? Huh? I don't get it. You're not making any sense.' If she'd been told to read something, he would make her do it aloud and correct her pronunciation. If she'd been told to write something, he would criticise her handwriting. She was never quick enough for him—never neat or clever or articulate enough.

When he wasn't looming over her, he was yelling at the TV, or at someone on the phone, making it impossible for her to concentrate. And he wouldn't buy her cardboard or glue or pens for her assignments, so I would buy them and send them with her to Keith's, where something bad would always happen: he would put his wet glass on the cardboard, or throw the glue away because she'd smeared some of it on his kitchen table. She would cry about it afterwards, and I'd have to say, 'It'll be all right.' But it never was. She often lost marks for sloppy work.

Even when Keith was being nice, it was for a reason. I once heard how he'd got all dressed up and taken Emily to a yacht club, where a 'nice lady' with a little girl had stopped to say hello. By the following week, Keith and Emily were visiting the lady's palatial home, where Emily played with the little girl's astonishing collection of toys while Keith sucked up to whatever rich divorcee he'd managed to manipulate by playing the deserted father.

He used Emily as bait, and it tormented me. More than once he had her call an ex-girlfriend to say, 'We miss you.' It was outrageous, but it was nothing I could take to court. We just had to put up with it, Emily and I, until she turned sixteen and flat-out refused to visit him anymore.

'I won't,' she growled. 'You can't make me.' And I couldn't—not legally. So I didn't.

I had always known how bad it would be for her when I finally made the break. That was why I'd waited. By the time Emily was twelve, I'd decided that she was probably old enough to cope. And of course there was the Clive Denny incident. When that happened, I knew we had to get out.

Keith had partnered up with a dubious man to sell some kind of product that had probably fallen off the back of a truck. The man's brother, visiting from overseas, had needed a place to stay—so Keith had offered him our couch. We were living in a two-bedroom flat at the time, and Clive treated it like a squat, leaving clothes on the floor and food on the couch and dirty frying pans in the sink. He was about thirty years old and behaved like a teenager, endlessly playing Keith's computer games and using up all the shampoo. Every time I turned around, there was Clive, balding, unshaven and hunched on the couch with a console.

But none of this would have driven me away if he hadn't seemed so interested in Emily. It didn't take me a day to decide that something was off. She was the only person he bothered talking to. I even found him in her room once; he told me he was looking for a pair of scissors.

I went straight to Keith and told him what I suspected, but he shrugged it off. Thinking back, it's possible that Clive's brother had something on him. Or perhaps Keith simply cared more about his deal than he did about his daughter.

'Either Clive leaves or I do,' I announced. But Keith ignored me. So I started making plans, which took about three weeks and involved a lot of photocopying and visits to the bank. Finally, one day while Keith was out with Clive, I hired a car, packed up as much as I could and went to stay with my brother in Albury. It even crossed my mind that if I moved quickly I could get out of the country before Keith had a chance to alert the police.

I have to admit it was never a serious consideration. I realised that there was no easy way out—that I would have to struggle through as best I could.

But I understood why Nerine was so keen on the alternative. After all, it wasn't as if Keith had ever cut our dog's throat.

VISITOR

AT WORK THE next morning I told Sally what had happened to my hens. She was very sympathetic. 'Oh, Meg. How awful,' she said in the deep, melodious voice that didn't quite match the rest of her. Sally was as short as me, thin and small-boned, with blonde hair and freckles. But her voice made her sound dark and rangy, like a six-foot Amazon.

'It was my fault.' I couldn't say Nerine had left the gate open. 'Eight of them dead because of me. It was a massacre.'

'Are you going to replace them? Because Dinah and I are thinking of selling some pullets.'

'Really?'

'It's getting a bit cramped at our place. There's been a baby boom.' Sally's smile was gentle and a little sad. She and Dinah, a former vet, had been trying to have a baby for years and had recently decided to adopt. 'Why don't you come over for lunch on Sunday and have a look?'

'Well…'

I didn't like to leave Nerine and the kids, but I did need more chickens.

'Dinah was just saying it's been too long since we caught up with you.' Sally leaned across the reception desk as I settled myself behind it. 'Nothing fancy. Just a casserole, or something. Twelve o'clock?'

'Okay. Thanks. That would be great.' I felt a lift of the spirits when I thought about getting away from Nerine's constant anxiety—though I also felt sad that I couldn't show Analiese the animals on Sally's farm.

'You'll have to admire our new hive. Di's been showing it off to everyone.' Sally's smile faded as the front door opened to reveal her first patient of the day. 'Hello, Ciara,' she said. 'I'll be with you in a minute.' She disappeared into her office.

I was a little twitchy because of Nerine. I'd warned her not to ring me unless the roof collapsed, but I was fully expecting to be bombarded by agitated reminders that I should call Renee about the passports. Then there was the ever-present threat of hang-up calls, though I hadn't received any the previous day. Nerine was such a bundle of nerves that she was bound to start pestering me if Keith started pestering her.

When the landline rang I actually jumped in my seat. I hadn't slept well; Colette had been up during the night, and her sobbing and wailing had unsettled Esme, who had prowled around the house for a while before climbing onto my bed for comfort.

I wondered if I was ever going to get a full night's sleep while Nerine and her kids were in residence.

'Bulwell Women's Health Collective,' I said calmly into the handset.

At that instant my mobile rang. I ignored it until it finally stopped. But the next time it trilled, a few minutes later, I picked it up with a sigh.

'Yes?'

'Meg!' Nerine was whispering. I could hardly hear her.

'What?' I said.

'There's someone in the backyard.'

'There can't be.'

'There is. An older guy. Bald. Big gut.'

I couldn't believe Fred Huggett would dare sneak onto my property, though the description certainly sounded like him.

'He's poking around the chicken coop. I'm watching him through the window.'

'Where's Esme?' I could hear her barking in the background.

'Right here.'

'I told you to leave her outside. That's what I normally do.'

'She was scratching and whining to come in. I thought it might look suspicious if someone showed up.'

She was right. I could see that. But without Esme guarding my fence line, Fred Huggett had obviously felt safe enough to trespass.

'What's he doing now?' I was trying to keep my voice low as Sally ushered Ciara Campbell into the surgery.

'He's just checking things out,' Nerine replied. 'What am I gunna do, Meg? What if he steals something? What if he tries to get in?'

'He won't.' I was more worried that he'd hear Colette. 'Where are the kids?'

'In the hideaway.'

'That's good.' It was practically soundproof. 'Leave 'em there till he goes.'

'But—'

'I can't talk. I'm at work.' Another patient had just sidled through the front door, looking lost. 'Ring me if he does anything.'

'Maybe I should I speak to him. Say I'm your daughter.'

'No.' I hung up and smiled at the new patient, who was hovering halfway between the door and my desk. She was in her late teens, droopy and pale, with lank hair and lots of piercings. Her nails were bitten down to the quick, poor pet.

'Bryony?' I said, to encourage her.

She nodded.

'You haven't been here before, have you?' I asked.

She shook her head.

'In that case you'll need to give us a few contact details.' Offering her the usual clipboard, with its leashed biro and registration form, I added, 'Would you like to fill it in yourself, or shall I?' We always gave the patient a choice, in case she was illiterate.

Bryony mumbled something and took the clipboard. Then she shuffled over to a seat and lowered herself into it so carefully that I wondered if she had a urinary tract infection.

'There's tea and coffee in the kitchen if you'd like some,'

I said. 'Dr Kristensen is with another patient at the moment, but she won't be long.'

Bryony grunted. I sensed that no amount of friendly chit-chat was going to make her comfortable, so I politely turned my attention to the latest delivery of test results.

But I found it hard to concentrate, because I was tensely awaiting Nerine's next call.

It was a busy morning. At one point we had three babies in the waiting room, all screaming their heads off. Then the electric kettle shorted, tripping a fuse, and some medical equipment arrived at the front desk in several enormous boxes. Nerine also rang me twice before lunch: the first time to tell me that the intruder was sniffing around my shed, the second time to announce that he'd gone. Both times she suggested I come home. 'Pretend you're sick,' she said.

By twelve-thirty I was badly in need of a break.

'Just getting something to eat,' I told Bridget on my way out the door. The sunshine and fresh air calmed me down a bit, though I was still keyed up at the prospect of calling Renee. It seemed like a bad idea; I wasn't far from home and Jill had told me to call my contacts only when I was outside my normal stomping ground. I also knew that Renee wouldn't have any advice about fake passports or people smuggling or anything else that smacked of organised crime. Even the marijuana she smoked came from a lovely man who lived near Dorrigo and grew organic bush food.

But I'd promised Nerine. So I headed straight for the only

public phone in Bulwell—a grubby glass box outside Peter Fry's post office-cum-gift store, just opposite the Daily Grind. I'd never used this particular phone box before; though it smelled bad, I had to close the door behind me because people were passing and I didn't want anyone to overhear.

'Hello? Renee?' I said, when my call was finally answered. 'It's Meg.'

'Oh. Hi.' She sounded wary. Normally she would have sounded thrilled. I felt sad that Nerine's arrival had cast a pall over our comfortable, uncomplicated friendship.

'How's it going?' I asked.

'Fine. How are you?'

'Good. I'm good.' I squared my shoulders and took the plunge. 'Look, I'm sorry to bother you, and I realise this is a bizarre question, but do you know anything about smuggling people out of the country?'

There was a brief silence. 'What?'

'I'm calling for Nerine.'

A face appeared in front of me, beyond the glass. Tearle. He gave me a crooked smile and a brief wave, then headed across the road. 'Bugger,' I blurted out.

'What?' said Renee.

'Nothing. Sorry. It's just that I promised I'd check with you because Nerine's been talking about fake passports and fishing boats and I've no idea what to tell her. The poor thing's a nervous wreck. It's not her fault.'

'Fishing boats?' Renee's tone was bewildered. 'Meg, I live in Taree.'

'Of course. I'm sorry.'

'I had a girl stay here once who changed her name and went to Western Australia to get away from an ex-boyfriend,' Renee said, 'but I don't know anyone who's left the country. Except on holiday.'

'No. I understand.'

'It wouldn't be a good idea. Not with kids.'

'I've told her that. She's just…' I tried to think of the right word. 'Very anxious,' I finished lamely.

'You sound pretty anxious yourself.'

'I'm all right.'

'It's difficult, isn't it?' Renee's calm, gentle delivery was hard won. She'd spent years doing yoga and meditation and various kinds of therapy just to get over her childhood. 'When you're dealing with someone who's scared, the energy they project can be very infectious.'

'It's harming the children.' I glanced around, scanning the street. The only people in sight were old Mrs Bass, who was posting a letter, and two roadworkers eating pies in their truck. 'What should I do, Renee? Those poor kids are so stressed and their mum's making it worse. The younger one has night terrors…'

'Does she meditate? The mother?'

'Uh—I don't know. I don't think so.'

'Show her those breathing exercises I taught you. And St John's wort can be helpful.' Renee paused for a moment, thinking. 'What about Esme?' she said at last. 'Do the kids like her?'

'Oh, they love her.'

'Well, maybe she can sleep near them. Companion animals are really therapeutic.'

'That's a good idea.' I hadn't thought of moving Esme's bed into the guestroom. 'Nerine would feel safer with the dog there, too.'

'And what about you, Meg? How are you holding up?'

'Fine. I'm fine.'

'You don't sound fine.'

I didn't want Renee to wonder if housing Nerine and her kids might be too much for me. It would be a disaster if she changed her mind about taking them. 'It's Keith,' I said. 'He's still making anonymous calls to my landline.'

Renee clicked her tongue. 'Mindfulness, Meg. Set aside a few mindful minutes for yourself each day.'

I tried to imagine doing that with Colette around. 'I'll try,' I said doubtfully. 'How's your mother?'

'Fighting. One more chemo cycle to get through.'

'Poor thing.' After enduring Renee's dad for thirty-odd years, Renee's mum deserved an easier life, but she hadn't got it. I liked Renee's mum. And I didn't blame her for not protecting her daughter from her husband; after all, I hadn't protected Emily from Keith. 'Well—I'd better get back to work. Sorry to spring this on you.'

'That's all right. I'll call you in a few weeks, shall I? When I'm free to help. In the meantime, take it easy. And remember to put yourself first, sometimes.'

'Okay. Thanks. Give my love to your mum.'

'I will.'

After hanging up, I sprayed hand sanitiser on everything I could reach, including the keypad and my face. I was just pushing my way out of the phone box when Tearle's voice made me jump.

'Hello, Meg.'

'God!' I rounded on him. He was all decked out in a blue blazer and shiny brogues, though as far as I could tell he was simply grabbing a takeaway coffee from the Daily Grind. 'You scared the life out of me!'

'Sorry.' His nose wrinkled as he caught a whiff from the phone box. 'Are you all right?'

'Of course I am!'

'You look a bit...' He hesitated, carefully choosing his words. 'Frazzled,' he said at last.

'That's because it stinks in there.'

'Is your mobile not working?'

'No.' To distract him from the subject of phones, I asked, 'Did you talk to David?'

'I did. He promised to have a word with your husband's lawyer.'

I was struck by a sudden thought. 'When? I mean—when did you speak to him?'

'Yesterday.'

'That's interesting.'

'Why?'

'Because I didn't get any hang-up calls yesterday.' As we exchanged a speculative glance, I added, 'Maybe it worked.'

'Maybe.' Tearle inclined his head. 'I think it's a little early to be sure.'

I was about to argue when my mobile rang. We both peered at my bag.

Tearle raised an eyebrow.

'Well. That's weird,' I mumbled, as the blood rushed to my cheeks.

'Aren't you going to answer it?'

'Not right now. I've got things to do.' Then I said goodbye and went off to buy lunch, conscious of Tearle's quizzical look. By the time I'd banged into the Daily Grind, the ringing had stopped.

I was beginning to wonder if I should just turn my phone off and pretend it had died. Otherwise, I felt sure, Nerine was going to ruin my day.

That evening I came home to fairyland.

The house was all shut up like Fort Knox. But when I pushed open the front door, it brushed against a dangling star made of cardboard and aluminium foil. Then Esme rushed at me—and I saw that she was wearing paper wings. So were the stuffed toys scattered around the living room, where more silver stars hung from the ceiling fan. I recognised the angel from my Christmas tree; it was sitting on the mantelpiece.

'Look, Meg!' Analiese suddenly appeared in the kitchen doorway. 'We're fairies!'

'You certainly are,' I said, my heart melting. She was dressed in her white net tutu, a tinsel crown and wings made of fuse wire. Nerine must have found my Christmas decorations.

'Esme's a fairy too,' Ana said.

'I know. She looks lovely.' I dumped my bag on a chair and found Nerine in the kitchen with Colette on her hip. They were both draped in tinsel. Colette was chowing down on something pink and green. Fairy cakes were piled on the nearest benchtop.

'Wow.' I was impressed. 'You've been busy.'

Nerine gave a tired nod. Her fingernails sparkled and her skin was dusted with some sort of glitter, but she looked drained. Her daughters, I noticed, were wearing the same silver nail polish.

'Macaroni cheese tonight,' she said, gesturing at a pot on the stove. 'I couldn't manage anything else.'

'That sounds great. I haven't had macaroni cheese for years.' Pushing Esme out of the room, I asked brightly, 'What if I make a salad to go with it?'

'Dok!' Colette protested.

'Not in the kitchen, sweetheart,' I told her. 'Esme can go and play with the fairy bears and the fairy bunnies.' To Ana I said, 'Is Mr Snuffles the king of the fairies? I see he has a crown on.'

'No. He's a fairy princess,' she replied. Then she seized my hand and urged me to come and see the fairy cave. So I went and inspected the vestibule cupboard, where paper doilies, white sheets and Christmas decorations had been used to create a very convincing winter wonderland.

'How long did it take you to do all that?' I asked Nerine

much later, when the kids and their stuffed toys had been put to bed. I'd decided to take down the silver stars in case we had unexpected visitors. But I hadn't messed with the fairy cave.

'Oh—you know. Hours and hours.' Nerine was lolling in her usual chair, holding a glass of wine. 'We couldn't go out because of that guy, so I had to do something special.'

'You did it very well.' I'd resigned myself to the fact that my aluminium foil was all gone and the bathroom vanity was covered in smears of glittery nail polish. 'Maybe tomorrow we can make a fairy dell outside. With flowers.'

'We can't go outside, Meg.' Nerine looked at me as if I'd suggested flying to Portugal. 'What if we run into that guy?'

'Fred Huggett? Oh, he won't come anywhere near us. Not while my car's here.'

'How do you know?'

'Because he never has before.'

Suddenly Esme lurched to her feet and gave a short, sharp yap. As she lumbered towards the front door, I shushed her.

'What's wrong?' Nerine demanded.

'Nothing. Just a possum. Or a wallaby…'

But Esme barked again—and something about her pricked ears made my stomach clench.

Then I heard the windchimes. They weren't jangling in a stiff breeze, along with my other sets of windchimes. They were playing alone—and they were playing a tune.

Twinkle twinkle little star.

'Jesus,' Nerine croaked, her eyes widening.

I jumped up and made for the door. Nerine grabbed my wrist as I passed.

'Wait!' she whispered. 'Take the poker!'

I dashed over to the fireplace while Esme gave another yap and Nerine flung herself at the front window, which was shrouded in layers of white gauze.

'Why the hell don't you have a gun?' Nerine mewled.

I didn't answer. The poker in my hand felt heavy and solid; it reassured me as much as Esme did. And the thought that Fred Huggett was probably out there, trying to scare us, filled me with more fury than fear.

I slapped on the veranda light and yanked open the front door. 'Who is it?' I snapped. 'Is that you, Fred?'

No one answered. I couldn't see much beyond the front steps: just the glint of my car in the distance. Then Esme surged past me and I followed her into the night, taking one step, two steps, three…

'Hello?' I said loudly, before remembering the children. I didn't want to wake them.

The veranda was deserted. Esme was sniffing around the wicker chairs. My torch was in the kitchen, so I retreated back into the living room, calling to her as I did so.

The screen door crashed shut behind her wagging tail.

'What did you see?' Nerine's face was a mask of terror.

'Nothing. No one.' I plunged into the kitchen, scooped up the torch, snapped on the outside light and slammed through the back door with Esme at my heels. Then I flashed my torch about. It still wasn't easy to see; there was no moon and the torchlight cast long, dense shadows as it raked across the tanks.

The silence was so deep I felt as if I had wax plugs in my ears.

'We're calling the police!' I yelled into the darkness. Esme was already weaving across the yard, head down, tail up. I called to her and began to make a circuit of the house, still clutching my poker. By this time I was fairly sure the intruder had gone, or Esme would have been barking. But I kept a cautious eye on those big, bulky tanks as I approached the first corner, conscious that a whole gang of people could easily be hiding behind them.

Esme padded past me. I couldn't grab her collar because my hands were full, so I charged straight after her, around the side of the house, skidding to a halt when my torch beam hit the guestroom window.

The flyscreen had moved. Instead of being clamped to the frame, it was leaning against the wall.

FEAR

'IT'S HIM.' NERINE paced the living room, gnawing on her thumbnail. 'It's Duncan.'

'Wait. Let's think about this.' My heart was still racing, but I knew better than to panic. Shakily I lowered myself into my rocking chair. 'Fred Huggett must be seventy-odd. For all we know, he has dementia. Who's to say he doesn't wander about at night, playing with people's windchimes?'

'For God's sake!' Nerine rounded on me. 'Why would your next-door neighbour take the screen off my window?'

'That screen's fallen off before. It's very old—it was here when I moved in.'

Nerine rolled her eyes.

'Anyway, how would Duncan know it's your room?' I asked. 'You're not thinking straight. I don't blame you, but—'

'He's been watching us, Meg! Don't you get it? He's out there! In the bush!' Nerine turned on her heel and marched down the hallway. 'I'm leaving. And I'm taking the kids.'

'Nerine. *Nerine*.' I jumped to my feet and ran after her, catching up just before she reached her bedroom door. Behind it her daughters were asleep; I didn't want to wake them. 'Don't. Please,' I begged, lowering my voice. 'Where will you go? You can't check into a motel. And I'm guessing the police know all your friends.'

'We'll sleep in the car.'

'And then what?' I tugged her back into the living room. 'We have Esme, remember? If anyone comes near the place, she'll let us know. She's very protective.' My tone was the soothing one I used at work with agitated patients. 'We're safe in here, I promise. We've locked the doors. We've locked the windows.' Not my bedroom window; its lock was broken, but I wasn't going to mention that. 'I'll leave the outside lights on and I'll sit up tonight, if you want me to. And tomorrow I'll go over to the Huggetts' and find out what the hell's going on.'

Nerine suddenly snatched up the phone and slapped it to her ear. 'At least the line's not cut,' she murmured.

'Nerine. Look at Esme.' I pointed at the dog, who was grinning up at us, panting and wagging her tail. 'She's fine. She's happy. She wouldn't be if someone was outside.'

Nerine stared at Esme for a moment, then returned the handset to its cradle. 'We can't stay here,' she said.

'We have to. We don't have a choice.'

Tears shone in her eyes. 'You have to think of something, Meg.'

'I will.'

'Or get a gun. At least get a gun.'

A gun. She was fixated on it. 'Will you really feel safe if I get a gun, Nerine?'

'A gun's the only thing that'll stop him.'

'You don't think an axe might do the trick?'

Nerine thumped the wall with her clenched fist, making me jump the way I used to when Keith banged things. He was always slamming drawers.

'You don't know Duncan,' Nerine snapped. 'He's crazy.'

'Look—'

'He'll kill us all!'

'No, he won't. Because he doesn't know where you are.' Her paranoia was beginning to irritate me—perhaps because I was so unnerved. The thought of being stalked by someone was terrifying, even if that person happened to be old Fred Huggett. 'How could Duncan have found you when you don't have your phone?'

'I'm not sure, but he's smart. He could do it.'

'Then why hasn't he already killed you?' I argued the point gingerly, conscious of the children asleep in their beds. I even hustled her into the kitchen and closed the door so they wouldn't hear us. 'Why muck about with windchimes? Why didn't he just bash me over the head when I went out to look for him?'

Nerine blinked. Then her gaze turned inwards. 'Maybe he wants us to leave,' she finally said. 'Maybe he's done something to the car. Maybe he wants to catch us outside...'

'Then let's stay inside.' I watched the wheels slowly turn

in her head. 'I can't call the police. You know that. And there's nowhere else I can take you—not right now. It's the middle of the night.'

All at once Nerine collapsed onto a kitchen chair and buried her face in her hands. Her movements were always abrupt, like a rubber band snapping. You could feel the displaced energy.

'God,' she whimpered. 'God, God, God.'

'It's okay.' I patted her arm. 'We'll sort it out.'

She mumbled something that I couldn't quite hear.

'What was that?'

'We need a gun.' She raised her head, exposing red eyes and quivering lips. The traces of glitter in her eyebrows made her look pathetic. 'Either we get a gun or we go.'

'Nerine—'

'It's a matter of life and death. You don't understand. If you can't send us somewhere else, we'll need a gun.'

'What if Esme sleeps in your room?'

'*We need a gun.*'

There was an edge to her voice that alarmed me. So I raised my hands and said, 'All right. Okay. I'll get a gun.'

'Really?' Her eyes narrowed. 'You can do that?'

'Maybe. There's someone I can talk to.'

'When?'

'Soon.' I doubted Sunday would be soon enough for Nerine, but I wasn't about to call Sally and ask if I could borrow Dinah's rifle. The only way of making such a peculiar request, I decided, was to raise the subject during lunch on

Sunday, while discussing the fox and the chickens.

'What about finding us another place to stay?' Nerine was studying me with sombre eyes. 'Wouldn't that be easier?'

'Well...no.'

'There's nobody else?'

I shook my head. Sally's farm was certainly big enough. And she'd be sympathetic; she was on the board of a domestic violence refuge in Bathurst. But she wouldn't break the law. Not Sally.

Renee would, because she knew what it was like to be desperate. She knew that, occasionally, you have to do what has to be done.

'It wouldn't have to be for long,' Nerine pointed out. 'Just until your other friend can take us...'

'Yes, but how will that change things? If Duncan can find you here, why wouldn't he be able to find you elsewhere? Have you thought of that?'

Nerine's face fell. There was a long silence. At last she said, 'Just see what you can do, Meg. Please?'

'I'll try.' The prospect made my shoulders sag. 'But I really think it was Fred Huggett who did this. And I think he must have dementia, because the whole thing was so loopy. Why would your ex be creeping around playing tunes on windchimes?'

Nerine fixed me with a weary, impatient look. 'You should know,' she said. 'Why does *your* ex keep ringing you up?' Before I could answer, she shot to her feet and reached for the axe, which was still sitting on top of the kitchen cupboards.

'I'm taking this to bed with me,' she declared.

I was aghast. 'Oh, but Nerine—the kids—'

'I won't let 'em near it. I'll take the dog too.' She nodded at my knife block. 'You should grab one of those. And maybe hide the rest around the house, just in case.'

I was gaping at her, speechless, when the phone rang in the living room. Its shrill piping made me flinch.

Nerine stared at me in surprise as I flung open the door, marched over to the side table and snatched up the handset.

'Fuck off!' I screeched. Then I slammed the phone back down again.

It didn't make sense. I understood why Nerine was scared of Duncan. But why did she think he was clever enough to hunt her down?

'Is he a private investigator?' I asked.

She snorted. 'No.'

'Is he good with computers? Does he work for a phone company?'

'God, no.'

'What was he in jail for?'

'Dealing drugs.'

'Oh.'

'He's a lowlife. A piece of shit.'

'But he must have a job. What does he do?'

'Plumber.'

'Is he part of a criminal syndicate? Is that what you're afraid of?'

'I don't wanna talk about it.'

'Is there something you haven't told me?'

'I don't wanna talk about it.'

She never wanted to talk about it. She never discussed Duncan, or her home, or her work, or her family; it was as if her whole life was a fresh wound, too tender to touch. Though I picked up a few details here and there, they didn't add up to a full picture. She'd met Duncan through her half-brother, Leon. She'd done a hairdressing course at TAFE. One of her foster-mothers had accused her of stealing food. Duncan had punched her in the stomach while she was pregnant with Analiese.

But whenever she mentioned the past at all, there was an underlying current of fear, constant, pervasive and jarring. She glanced out the window repeatedly. Jumped whenever my landline rang.

She talked about Duncan as if he were inescapable, like a werewolf or an epidemic. I couldn't for the life of me work out what gave him such power over her. If he'd been a Mafia hitman or even a cop I might have understood. But a plumber?

It wasn't as if she'd disappeared down a pipe.

That night I hardly slept a wink. Every little noise roused me. I kept sitting up in bed, taut with nerves, listening to possums squabble and chooks mutter. The sound of windchimes made my skin crawl; I wondered if I should just pack them all away.

At daybreak I rose and dressed. Esme heard me from inside the guestroom. She scratched at the door until I opened it for her, then followed me into the kitchen. I have to admit, I was nervous about leaving the house. Though Esme seemed perfectly serene—though the fresh morning sunshine made everything look quite harmless—I pushed open the back door cautiously, clutching a heavy saucepan in my right hand. Hinges squeaked. A startled currawong flapped up onto the roof.

Nothing else stirred except Esme. She headed straight for the chook pen. When I caught up with her, she was nosing around its gate, saying hello to Belle.

She would never have done that if a stranger had been nearby.

I let the chickens out and watched them for a few minutes, reassured by their fussy, preoccupied demeanour. If they had PTSD, it wasn't obvious—though I knew they hadn't been laying the last couple of days. Ana had told me so. She gave me constant updates on the chickens.

If I bought some of Sally's pullets I would name one of them Analiese.

By this time Esme was relieving herself near the tanks. I set off in the same direction because I wanted to have a look at the guestroom window and check the flyscreen for broken clips. All the clips were made of plastic and I'd had trouble with them before—especially on the western and northern sides of the house. I'd once found my bedroom screen lying on the dirt near the back steps, so it was possible that the guestroom screen had slid down, bounced once or twice and landed against the wall.

I trudged past the tanks, trying to remember whether I'd put the spare clips in the shed or the vestibule cupboard. I'd just decided they were in the cupboard when my gaze fell on the dirt under the guestroom window.

My plants had never done well on the western side. The azaleas had been a mistake; I'd been forced to move them. The hebe had died, for some reason. Even the grass was scarred with big patches of dirt that turned to mud in the rain.

When these patches were dry, however, the soil was fine and pale and perfect for capturing footprints. That was why I saw them right away—the footprints in the dirt. Two of them. Bigger than mine and much clearer.

I froze. It took me a few seconds to process what I was looking at: a swirl of scuff-marks, some of them mine, some of them Ana's, some of them probably Nerine's. And clearer than all the rest were two corrugated prints made by someone far heavier than I was.

Someone like Fred Huggett.

Rage engulfed me like a hot flush. Without even checking the flyscreen clips, I rushed back into the kitchen, dumped the saucepan, grabbed my keys, scribbled a note on the back of a shopping list—*Gone to neighbours*—and charged outside again. Esme bustled along beside me as I made for the car; I decided to take her along so that the Huggetts would think twice about setting their dogs on me. They had two: a German shepherd and a nasty little staffie cross, neither of which barked much, thank God, because Fred hardly ever went out. But I always knew when the Huggetts had visitors. It was like listening to a tornado hit an animal shelter.

Driving from my house to the one next door took longer than expected, thanks to the number of gates and potholes I had to negotiate between my front yard and the Huggetts'. The whole trip was a drama; it stoked my simmering resentment. Their driveway was like a dry creekbed in some spots, all jagged rocks and deep gullies. You practically needed a four-wheel drive. What if the fire service had to get in there? Or an ambulance? Or some poor bloody plumber? It wasn't just antisocial—it was downright dangerous.

When I finally arrived, the Huggetts' dogs were baying and slavering at the garden gate. Instead of fighting my way past them to ring the doorbell, I had to sit in the car and sound the horn. It didn't seem like a neighbourly thing to do at six o'clock on a Friday morning, but the barking would already have woken both men inside.

Sure enough, Neville soon came stomping out of the front door with shaving cream on his chin. He was small, dark and sturdy, just like his house, and looked sunburnt even in winter. His face had settled into dull, belligerent folds that told you exactly how he was going to react to any kind of request.

I paid particular attention to his boots as he stormed over to the gate. They were chunky work boots but I couldn't see the soles. Not from where I was sitting.

'Geddout! Gorn!' he yelled at the dogs.

They ignored him—and their barking reached a crescendo when I climbed out of the car.

'What is it?' He peered at me suspiciously, then aimed a

kick at the German shepherd. 'Shuddup.'

'Is your dad here?' I asked, getting straight to the point. My anger was draining away, as it always did when I was addressing a disgruntled man, but I'd come too far to retreat.

'My dad?' he said. 'Why do you want my dad?'

I raised my voice over all the snarling and yelping. 'Someone was sneaking around my house last night. I wondered if it was your dad. Or you.'

Neville scowled. '*Me?*'

'I found footprints.'

'For fuck's sake.' He sounded genuinely appalled. 'Why would I wanna go sneaking around your house?'

'For my eggs?' I suggested, but he wasn't listening. He was bellowing at the dogs.

'Get inside. *Get. In. Side.*' As he gave the nearest dog a shove with his foot, I caught a glimpse of his boot sole. Its pattern wasn't corrugated—more like a ring of studs. 'Get! Gorn! Out!' he roared, pointing at the front door, which was flanked by mounds of junk: firewood, car parts, rusty wire, broken furniture, lengths of guttering. Junk had also spilled out into the yard; there was an old fridge by the garage and a bath by the kennel.

The shepherd began to slink away. The other dog didn't budge.

'Is your dad the full quid, Neville?' I asked.

'What?'

'Has your dad got dementia?'

'Dementia? No!' he spluttered.

'I was just wondering—'

'Why the hell would you even say that?'

I couldn't tell him that Nerine had spied Fred on my property the previous morning. Both the Huggetts probably knew that I worked in town on Thursdays. 'Whoever was there last night mucked around with my windchimes,' I said. 'It was a weird thing to do.'

'Well, it wasn't Dad.'

'Are you sure?'

''Course I'm sure.'

'Because the person didn't have a car.'

'I guess they parked on the road, then.'

'Why?'

'How the fuck should I know?' Neville's voice rose as his temper flared, and the staffie cross started barking again. 'Shuddup, Deesie,' he spat, then turned back to me. 'Haven't you got some bastard ex-husband, or something? Maybe it was him.'

I was shocked. I couldn't recall ever mentioning Keith to the Huggetts. 'How do you know about my husband?'

'For Chrissake, everybody knows about him.' Neville wasn't even looking at me; he was glowering at the dogs, as if daring them to utter a sound. 'What do you expect when you call your place the Bolt Hole? It's a small town. People talk.'

I stared at him. It had never crossed my mind that Keith might be responsible for messing with my screens and windchimes. I'd been fixated on Fred because of Nerine's sighting.

But when I thought about it, sneaking around was exactly the kind of thing Keith would do. He'd been making anonymous calls to my phone. What if he'd gone further?

'Look, just call the fucking cops, okay?' Neville must have sensed my sudden doubt, because when he spoke again, his voice was more of a grumble than a yelp. 'Talk to your ex. Figure it out. This has nothing to do with us. We haven't been near your place.'

'Your father has, though. In the past.' I summoned up my last ounce of courage to issue a veiled warning. 'I think he might have taken my eggs.'

'Bullshit.'

'I'm just saying. Someone was there without a car.' Before Neville could argue, I turned and went back to my own car, where Esme was waiting for me on the front passenger seat. Her tail began to thump as I climbed behind the steering wheel.

'My dad wouldn't set foot on your place,' Neville declared loudly. 'Reckons it would give him AIDS or something.' Then he swung around and marched back inside, leaving the dogs to hurl themselves at the gate unchecked.

'AIDS?' I muttered to Esme. 'What does he mean, AIDS?'

I was halfway down the pitted, furrowed driveway when it struck me that Fred Huggett must have decided I was a lesbian.

*

When Keith and I were getting divorced, I had to put up with a lot of very nasty stuff. It wasn't just that he told his lawyer to gut me. It wasn't just that the two of them claimed I had serious mental-health issues—that I was flaky and spaced out and unfit to look after a child. Keith also took my punishment into his own hands, with lots of sneaky stuff that was impossible to pin on him.

He put dog shit in my letterbox, and in several others nearby so it wouldn't look as if I'd been targeted. He switched off a couple of my fuses one day while I was out, defrosting all the meat in my freezer. I'm pretty sure he replaced all the washers in my outside taps with faulty ones, running up my water bill and forcing me to hire a plumber when I could barely afford food.

After that, I learned how to replace my own washers.

He also kept doing things to my car, an old Corolla that wasn't hard to get into. One time he put diesel in the tank and everyone thought I must have had a senior moment at the petrol pump. Another time he left a dead snake tucked in next to the spare tyre; I never quite got rid of the stink and no one would believe that the snake hadn't crawled into the car and died there. I even began to have doubts myself. But then something else would happen—a nail in my tyre, a dead rat in the compost bin, a sock missing from the clothesline—and I would know that someone was engineering my uncanny run of bad luck.

It sounds paranoid. I realise that. But you had to know Keith, and I knew Keith. I certainly knew he hated windchimes.

He once said I liked windchimes so much because they sounded just like me: pointless, tuneless and noisy. He said I had windchimes in my head instead of brains.

In fact, now I thought about it, if anyone was sending me a message with windchimes it had to be Keith Delgado.

GOOD NEWS

WHEN I ARRIVED home, everyone was up and eating breakfast. Colette was grizzling, but gave a squeal of joy when she spotted Esme. Nerine looked exhausted.

Analiese gazed at me with wide, troubled eyes. Her mouth was full of cereal.

'Dok,' Colette crowed.

'Esme—out.' I nudged her back through the kitchen door. 'Later, sweetie,' I said to Colette. 'You can feed her later.'

'What happened?' asked Nerine. She didn't seem to care that the kids were around.

I did, though.

'It was fine,' I muttered.

'What did they say?'

I picked up a slice of bread and made for the toaster. 'They denied it.'

'Dokibah,' Colette snivelled.

'I told you.' Nerine plucked her from the floor and parked

the little girl on her hip. 'I told you it was Duncan. It's just the sort of thing he'd do.'

I saw Ana stiffen and suddenly felt annoyed. 'No—it's just the sort of thing *my* ex would do,' I said, dropping my bread into the slot. 'And he knows where I live.'

Nerine frowned. 'You mean—'

'Keith's done this kind of thing before.' I punched the lever, then bent down to pull a plate from the cupboard.

'But that's still bad, Meg. I mean, if he's hanging around...'

'I know. He might have seen you.' The jam jar and butter dish were near Analiese, so I sat opposite her to wait for my bread to toast. Normally I ate wholemeal, but I'd bought a packet of white sliced for the kids. 'Even if he's seen you, though, that's trespassing. He wouldn't risk going public. And if he's around, I'll find out soon enough. Bulwell's a very small place.'

'I still think we should leave.' Nerine was jangling a set of measuring spoons in front of Colette. Analiese had stopped eating; she was staring down at her half-empty bowl. The sight of her obvious distress prompted me to change the subject.

'We'll talk about this later,' I told Nerine firmly. To her elder daughter I said, 'When you finish your breakfast, we can play the piano. Would you like that?'

Ana raised her eyes.

'Or you could sing a song with Esme,' I went on. Seeing a spark of interest in her peaky little face, I leaned across the table and confided, 'I have a special musical instrument that makes Esme sing whenever I play it.'

'What inssument?' Ana wanted to know.

'I'll show you in a minute.' Turning back to Nerine, I smiled and said briskly, 'There's some marking I have to do, but that can wait. If you want to take a shower or a nap or anything, I'll watch the kids.'

For some reason, Nerine took offence at this. 'Fine,' she retorted. Then she dumped Colette in my lap and flounced out of the room, leaving me with a whimpering toddler, an anxious preschooler, one slice of rapidly cooling toast and Esme, who'd sidled back into the kitchen because Nerine hadn't closed the door.

I managed to keep Colette amused by feeding the dog. Then, after Ana had eaten her cereal, I dug out my old accordion—the instrument that made Esme wail like bagpipes. Her yowls and yodels entranced the children for at least an hour. Both girls also had a lot of fun trying to play the accordion. We even sang a few songs together, though Esme's attempts to join in made Ana break off and laugh, again and again. I'd never heard her laugh before. She sounded just like Emily.

But Colette finally grew bored, and Ana lost patience with her. There were a couple of sharp, almost vicious exchanges. When Ana slapped Colette, I had to suggest that Ana go and sit in her fairy cave with Mr Snuffles if she felt really angry.

'Your sister's only little,' I said. 'She can't help being annoying.'

'A fairy would make her go away,' Ana grumbled.

'To fairyland?'

'No.' She spoke flatly. '*I'm* going to fairyland.'

'All by yourself?'

'Yes.'

Then Colette began to cry, and Ana rolled her eyes with such exaggerated frustration that I had to suppress a grin. Though I tried to comfort the younger girl, I couldn't work out what was wrong. In the end I had to admit defeat and appeal to her mother, who had emerged from a long scented bath and settled herself at my dressing table, where she was applying makeup with grim determination.

'Oh, she's in a mood,' said Nerine. She gave Colette one of her lipsticks and let the toddler draw on every mirror in the house.

I finally ate my breakfast at about ten o'clock. Afterwards, I shut myself in my room and marked exams. Whatever Nerine and her girls did in the meantime, they did it very quietly. In fact they did it so quietly that I assumed they must have gone outside, until the landline rang.

When I went to answer it, I found Ana and Nerine lying motionless on the living-room floor. Ana was cradling Mr Snuffles. Colette was crawling all over her mother. Esme was snoozing on the couch.

'We're playing dead,' Nerine explained as I grabbed the phone.

'Hello?' I said sharply.

'Meg?'

'Oh.' I exhaled. 'Hi, David.'

'Are you sitting down?'

'What?'

'I've got some news.'

My heart sank. I dropped into the nearest chair. 'What?'

'It's good news.'

'Really?'

'The judgement came down and you'll be getting seventy per cent.'

David began to rattle off all kinds of information about orders and funds and directions hearings but I couldn't take it in. I must have looked fuddled—ashen—because Nerine suddenly picked up Colette and rose, staring at me, while Esme lurched to her feet and lumbered over.

'...I doubt he'll appeal. An appeal has to be based on an issue of law and he doesn't have the grounds,' David was saying.

'Wait—um—hang on.' I was trying to process what I'd just heard. 'So how much will it be, do you think? After costs?'

'Your provision?'

'Yes.'

'I would say...about two hundred and thirty thousand dollars,' he told me, and my jaw dropped. For a moment I couldn't breathe.

Nerine started to make frantic gestures. She mouthed, *What is it?*

'But if Keith tries to appeal, that may be further reduced,' David added.

'He will,' I croaked.

'Mmmm. Maybe. I'm sanguine, though. As I said, he doesn't have grounds.' David paused for a moment before adding, 'This will all take time, of course. What I'm saying is, don't hold your breath.'

'No—I'm—I won't.'

'But it's a good result.'

'Oh, yes! It's...God, it's wonderful.' Or was it? I could only imagine how Keith would react. What if he was skulking on a nearby fire trail? What if his lawyer was telling him the news at this very instant?

Or what if Keith had already been told? What if *that* was the reason behind the windchimes business?

'Okay, so do you have any questions?' David asked, and I realised I'd been sitting in silence, staring blankly at Analiese—who was curled up near the coffee table, watching me with haunted eyes.

'No.' Then I corrected myself. 'I mean, yes. When did you find out?'

'This morning. I called you right away.'

'Oh.' In that case, it was unlikely that Keith's lawyer had been told the previous night. 'Well—thank you. Thank you for everything.'

'My pleasure,' David said blandly. He sounded very pleased with himself. He always did. 'And don't worry about Keith. He'll threaten to go to the Supreme Court, but I'm not concerned.'

'What if he does something else instead?' I spoke before thinking, and David's voice sharpened slightly in response.

'What do you mean?'

'It's just...well...' I was worried that if I mentioned the

windchimes, David would start making noises about the police. So I said vaguely, 'He's that sort of person. He's harassed me before.'

'If he makes one move against you, call the cops.' When I didn't answer, David asked, 'Do you want to take out an AVO? Do you have any specific concerns?'

'No. It's all right.' I gave a very unconvincing little laugh— just as Colette, who had been playing with Nerine's earring, squealed like concert feedback.

Nerine immediately whisked her out of the room.

'I had a word with Bryce Malouf. Keith's lawyer,' David went on. 'That friend of yours—Tearle. He rang me.'

'Yes.'

'He said you'd been getting hang-up calls.'

Again I didn't answer. I didn't know what to say.

'I honestly wouldn't worry about Keith. If he's going to get stuck into anyone, it'll be his lawyer. I know the type.' David's breezy attitude was something I'd encountered over and over again during my divorce. No one really understood the depths of my ex-husband's malevolence—certainly not the professionals I'd consulted. They never actually said so, but I was pretty sure they thought I had some kind of anxiety disorder.

I felt a sudden pang of sympathy for Nerine. Perhaps I was being equally obtuse about Duncan.

'So how does it feel, Meg?' David's jocular tone contained just a hint of disappointment. 'You seem a bit underwhelmed.'

'Oh, no. It's amazing. I'm…it's the shock.'

'Don't let Keith put a dampener on things. Go and celebrate. You fought long and hard—you deserve to crack open a bottle of bubbly.' He chuckled. 'God knows you can afford one now.'

'I will. Thanks, David.'

'And I'll give you a call when I have more news. I need to go through all this more thoroughly. Write you a letter. Contact Bryce.'

'Okay.'

'So you have a good weekend and I'll talk to you later.'

'I will. You too. Bye, David.'

I was putting the phone down when Nerine burst back into the room. She was still clutching Colette, whose face was smeared with chocolate.

'Well?' said Nerine. 'What's going on?'

I hesitated. There was so much to tell.

'What is it, Meg?'

'I've been fighting my ex-husband in court. Over his mother's will.' I began to stroke Esme's ears as she laid her head in my lap. 'That was my lawyer on the phone. I mean, the estate's lawyer.'

Nerine waited. She was staring at me. Everyone was staring at me: Nerine, Ana, Esme, even Colette.

I took a deep breath and mumbled, 'Keith was contesting the will because his mother left me everything. He wanted it all himself. But he didn't get it.' Seeing the question in Nerine's eyes, I dodged it by saying, 'He might still appeal. That could affect the final payout, though David says he doesn't have grounds...'

After a pause, Nerine said, 'How much?'

I honestly couldn't speak for a moment. The money felt to me like fairy gold—like something that would vanish if I actually gave voice to it. I found myself touching the nearest piece of wood before I said hoarsely, 'Two hundred and thirty thousand dollars.'

Nerine wanted to celebrate. When I told her I didn't have any champagne, she suggested we bake a cake instead. I reminded her that some of yesterday's fairy cakes were still in the cupboard. 'That's okay,' she said. 'Those are kids' cakes. I'm going to make you an adult cake.' Then she raided my supply of cooking alcohol and cobbled together a rum-and-raisin torte using milk chocolate instead of dark and sultanas instead of raisins.

The torte didn't look very adult by the time Ana and Colette had decorated it with jelly snakes and rainbow sprinkles, but I was touched anyway. Nerine seemed genuinely delighted; she babbled and grinned and even hugged me before dancing around the kitchen singing, 'Ce-e-e-elebrate good times, come on!' Her mood was so infectious that the two girls joined in—until Collette's dancing had us laughing so hard we had to take a break.

'So,' Nerine finally asked me, 'what are you going to do with it?'

'With what?'

'The money, you nong!'

'Bunna!' Colette exclaimed.

'That's a lot of money, Meg. You must have some idea.'

'Well…' It had crossed my mind, more than once, that Carol had left me her estate because she knew I would use it to help Emily. I had a feeling that Emily herself wasn't the direct beneficiary in case she ended up with a manipulative partner. After all, it had happened to Carol, and to me. Why not to the next generation?

'Emily's renting,' I said. 'With Carol's money, she'd have enough for a deposit on her own flat.' I felt a flutter of hope at the thought of ringing Emily with news like this. Most of the time she didn't pick up when I called, forcing me to leave a message that rarely prompted a reply. But this time I knew she would answer. This time we really did have things to discuss.

'You'll keep some for yourself, though, won't you?' Nerine offered me an encouraging smile. 'You deserve it, Meg.'

'I don't know. Maybe.'

'Money's there to take your worries away, and you've got a lot of worries. Plus Emily's going to get all this in the end, right?'

'Mmmm.'

'You should do something that makes you feel good. Like—I dunno. A trip? A new car? A charity?'

'It's too soon to worry about that.' I didn't want to discuss my plans. Not with Nerine. I wanted to mull them over in private. 'It'll be ages before I get the money. David said so.'

'Did he say how long?'

I was about to answer when the landline rang. So I darted into the living room and answered it.

Tearle was calling.

'I just spoke to David Blazek,' he said after I'd greeted him. 'I was trying to find out if he'd spoken to Keith's lawyer and he told me your news.'

'Oh.'

'I'm not sure he should have. It wouldn't have been my choice, had I been representing you. But then I'm from an era when privacy meant something.'

'I'm not exactly David's client, Tearle.' Not wanting him to hear Colette's squeaks and crows, I headed into the front yard, where four lonely hens were scratching around. 'He's acting for Carol's estate, remember?'

Tearle grunted. He and David had been in muted competition since the very first time they'd met, always completing each other's sentences and subtly critiquing each other's advice. I didn't know if it was because they were lawyers or because they were men.

'That's true,' Tearle had to concede. 'Even so, I'm assuming you don't want to go public with this? *I* certainly wouldn't. There's always going to be someone who'll try to tap you for cash.'

'They can try all they like. I don't have it yet and I probably won't for a very long time.'

'You must be pleased, though. Aren't you?' He had obviously detected a hint of doubt in my voice.

I was about to agree, but instead found myself admitting that I was worried about my ex-husband. 'He'll be furious. He might do something.'

'Like what?'

'I don't know.' Scanning the bush beyond my fence, I wondered if Keith was out there at this very moment, watching me. 'He's pretty creative when it comes to revenge.'

Tearle said nothing. He had always been clever with his silences, using them to coax information out of people, and it worked on me every time. I was incapable of letting a silence drag on.

'Since you live in the middle of town,' I said at last, 'and you know what Keith looks like, could you keep an eye out for him? If he's around, he'll be using a motel or a B&B—he's not a camping person.'

'Is something wrong?' Tearle's voice was as calm and dry as ever.

'Oh, no. I'm just worried. I always worry about Keith.' My little laugh was a very sad effort. 'I reckon it's good to be prepared, that's all.'

'You think he'll lash out?'

'I know he will.'

'In what way?'

'Kill my chickens? Burn down my house?'

This time the silence felt like an accusation. But when Tearle spoke again, his tone was gentle. 'Those are criminal acts, Meg. You think he'd commit a crime?'

'Absolutely.'

'Based on past conduct?'

'That's right.'

'Yet you've never taken out an order against him?'

'Well—no.' I hadn't needed the aggravation.

'I'll look into it now, if you want.' Before I could reply, Tearle added, 'I understand your concern. This judgement could be viewed as a possible trigger, given the man's history. Rest assured, if I do see him in Bulwell, I'll go straight to the police. In fact we could always have a quiet word with some of the hotel managers—'

'No! No.' The last thing I wanted was attention. I realised suddenly that I was digging a hole for myself. What if word went around and people started calling me about suspicious strangers—or worse still, showing up at my house? 'Forget it. I'm being stupid. I always overreact when Keith's involved.' Again I attempted a laugh, which sounded more like a strangled cough. 'Maybe one of these days I'll get over him.'

'And in the meantime he's ruining your moment of glory,' Tearle said. I wondered if he was being snide or sympathetic—it was hard to tell sometimes—until he continued, 'Actually, I thought we might celebrate. Would you care to have dinner with me tonight?'

For a moment I thought I'd misheard. Dinner? With *Tearle*? When I opened my mouth to answer, nothing came out.

'I'm an excellent cook, in case you were wondering.' He sounded as if he was presenting a summation in court. 'All I need to know is whether you have any allergies or aversions.'

Aversions. How very Tearle.

'Hello? Meg?'

I realised I was being rude. 'Yeah, I'm here. I was just...'

Just what? 'Checking my calendar.'

'I could show you my collection,' Tearle offered, and suddenly I understood. This wasn't some pathetic, sleazy come-on. He was genuinely looking for someone to admire his antiques.

Admiring them by himself must have been getting a bit lonely.

'All right.' I felt I owed him. He'd gone all the way to Sydney with me for my court hearings; the least I could do was pretend to be impressed by his Edwardian cigarette-holders. 'What time?'

'Six?'

'I'll see you then.'

'Any allergies, Meg? Or aversions?'

'Nope. If you cook it, I'll eat it.'

His raspy chuckle reached my ears. 'Good,' he said and hung up.

I walked back into the house.

'More news?' asked Nerine, who was still at the kitchen table; she and the girls were licking chocolate icing out of a bowl.

'No.' Unsure of how she would take it, I reluctantly confessed, 'Someone's invited me out for dinner tonight.'

She raised her eyebrows. 'On a date?'

'God, no.' But I flushed, and she smirked.

'Meg's got a da-ate,' she chanted.

'It really isn't.'

'How much better can this day get?' Nerine's tone was

indulgent, but also slightly sharp around the edges. 'Wealth… romance…'

'It's not romance.'

'We'll be fine. Won't we, kids? We can eat scrambled eggs and watch *Pocahontas* while Meg is being wined and dined.' Nerine obviously wasn't expecting an answer from either of the girls, though I noticed that Ana raised her head, like an animal sniffing the wind. But her mother didn't sound anxious, or annoyed, or even glum; she grinned at me and said, with a glint in her eye, 'So what are you going to wear to this unromantic dinner?'

I stared at her blankly.

'Because *I* think we should check out your wardrobe. *I* think we should have a little fashion parade. Don't you, Big Bug?'

Ana nodded.

I said, with mounting dismay, 'Oh, no.'

'Oh, yes. It'll be fun. We're going to style you for your big night out. Shoes. Bag. Makeup. And then…' Nerine surveyed me critically from head to toe. 'Then I'm going to cut your hair.'

Grooming was never my strong point. I blame my father for that—in fact I blame him for a lot of things. He was an old-style country copper, hard as nails, and he had certain opinions about women. You were either a nice girl or a whore, and if you were a whore you drank in pubs, hung out with men, wore short skirts and lots of makeup, went to rock concerts, had babies out of wedlock and walked around the streets after dark. He wanted his only daughter to dress like a nice girl, so I did, in Alice bands and flat shoes and clothes that weren't supposed to draw attention. Even jewellery annoyed him. He could cope with a gold cross or a wedding ring; anything else was regarded as a lure.

When Dad showed any interest in me at all, it was to chide me for studying music, which he said was a bludger's game. If I really wanted to spend three years wasting my time with a bunch of perverts and drug addicts in Sydney, I'd have to find the money myself, he said. He didn't hit me—he never hit women. But he showed his contempt in all kinds of other ways.

Dad died a couple of years after I married Keith. They didn't get along, and Dad stayed away from our wedding, but I'm pretty sure I got involved with Keith because of Dad. They were both controlling men who withheld their approval—or so my counsellor in Sydney once said. She said I'd fallen for Keith because I was still trying to win over my father.

But Keith wasn't a bit like my father at first. That was the whole point. He paraded me about like a luxury car, lavished me with praise, told me I was gorgeous, admired my singing, foretold great things for my musical career...

I honestly think he meant it at the time. He always meant it, whether he was talking about women or work or cars or colleagues. It was just that his enthusiasm never lasted very long.

His enmity, though—that could last forever.

DINNER

'GOOD EVENING,' SAID Tearle. He looked alarmingly formal in his silk bow tie, but I reminded myself that he always looked formal—even at the supermarket.

As he stepped back and held open his front door, I thrust a bottle of wine at him. 'I don't know much about wine, but Gary at the bottle-o told me this is a decent one,' I blurted out.

Nerine had insisted I buy wine on my way to Tearle's. She had also insisted I wear the dress I'd bought for Bridget's wedding—a bright, gauzy thing with a hippy twist to it. But I'd refused to wear the matching shoes, the hoop earrings or Nerine's coppery eye shadow. I'd also refused to let her cut my hair.

'Everyone knows I get my hair cut by Luka Durst's cousin when she's in Bulwell, and she hasn't been in Bulwell,' I'd said. 'We don't want people asking questions.' I hadn't let Nerine pin my hair up, either. Most of my friends knew that a pony-tail was about the limit of my capabilities.

'Thank you,' Tearle said, examining the bottle. 'This looks like an excellent drop.'

'I didn't know whether to go for red or white, but I thought—well, it's not summer, so I'll get red.'

I was babbling. Why? It might have had something to do with the room Tearle ushered me into, which had a marble fireplace, a glittering chandelier and an ornate plaster ceiling. The walls were lined with glazed wooden cabinets. The couches all looked very old; I sat down on a bulky leather chesterfield opposite a crimson plush thing with clawed feet and two backs.

Tearle went to open my bottle of wine. There was a drinks tray on the sideboard next to him, stocked with a crystal decanter and a silver ice bucket and everything else you would possibly need for a cocktail party. The painting on the wall above his head showed a very pale nymph (or goddess or maiden) being attacked by some very dingy satyrs (or huntsmen or savages).

'So I'm guessing that's your collection,' I said, with a glance at the nearest cabinet.

'That's part of it, yes.' Tearle filled a glass and offered it to me.

'What are those?' I asked, squinting at an array of shiny things mounted on velvet stands.

'Buttonhooks.'

'*Buttonhooks?*'

'You'd be amazed at the attention that was lavished on buttonhooks once upon a time.'

'And those?'

'Cigar cutters.'

I had to laugh.

Tearle inclined his head. 'In many ways I'm not a serious collector because my interests are too broad,' he admitted, as I went to have a closer look. 'There's width to the collection but not much depth.'

'Are those your smoking caps?' I peered into one cabinet that was full of silk and satin and velvet. 'I've heard about them.'

'Really?' His inquiring look shut me up for a moment, as I remembered that his smoking caps had been mentioned to me as an example of how obsessive and peculiar he was.

'I don't wear them,' he drawled, his mouth twitching into a half-smile, 'because I don't smoke.'

After looking at the smoking caps and buttonhooks we moved on to cigar cutters and pillboxes, then went into the dining room to examine his epergnes. There were so many of these elaborate dish-stands that all four walls of the room were lined with display cabinets. Some of the epergnes were studded with sculptured palm trees, some with carved emu eggs or cricket matches. But it's hard to know what to say after your seventh epergne, except the obvious question: why would so many people have spent so much money on something so useless?

After circling the dining room, refreshing our glasses and grabbing a handful of pecans, we inspected a library full of books and prints and paper knives. Tearle explained at great length that paper knives were blunter than letter-openers, which were sharp enough to damage uncut pages.

I liked his paper knives. Some of them were very pretty. I wasn't such a fan of his prints, though. You wonder about the private life of a man with a taste for Norman Lindsay nudes.

'Hang on.' I picked up a framed photo from the desk. 'Who's this?'

'That's me with my mother.'

'Jesus, Tearle, you look like Montgomery Clift!'

'You sound surprised,' he said drily.

'Well, I used to be a bit of a pin-up myself, believe it or not, but never like this.'

'Nonsense. I'm sure you were quite the bobby-dazzler.'

Tearle couldn't have been much older than me, but sometimes he sounded like an octogenarian. Feeling slightly awkward, I put down the photo and sauntered over to a solid-looking door fitted with a keypad on a dead latch.

'What's in there?' I asked.

'That's the old breakfast room. It's where I keep my guns.'

I'd been reaching for the doorhandle, but jerked back as if zapped by an electric shock. 'Your *guns*?'

'They're antique.' He joined me on the threshold and tapped a passcode into the keypad. I heard the click of tumblers unlocking. Then he pushed open the door and led me into a small, octagonal room with security screens on the windows. Every inch of wall-space was taken up by more display cabinets, but these ones had reinforced glass, multiple locks and no visible hinges.

Inside the cases were about twenty antique pistols, sporting lots of engraved brass and mother-of-pearl inlay.

'That's my oldest piece.' He pointed. 'Manufactured by Thomas Mortimer between 1780 and 1809. He was the King's gunsmith.'

'For God's sake—do these things actually work?'

'They're percussion flintlocks, Meg. You'd need musket balls and black powder to fire them.' He began to unlock one of the cabinets with a jingling bunch of keys. 'Unless you want to use this one here,' he added, pulling out a strange little gun with four barrels. 'This is a pepperbox caplock revolver. They made special percussion caps for these.'

When he offered it to me, I stepped back.

'No, thank you.'

Tearle smiled and returned the gun to its velvet-lined nest. 'It's perfectly harmless. The only piece I own that fires actual bullets is in this box here. It's what they call a suicide special, manufactured between 1870 and 1890. I've decided to sell it because it doesn't really belong in this collection; it was an impulse buy.' He unlocked a steel strongbox sitting on a low shelf and pulled out a very ornate revolver. 'I've a weakness for the decorative and this one has wonderful engraving, as you can see. Nickel finish, pearl grip, five-shot Hopkins and Allan rimfire...'

'Put it away.' For a fleeting instant I remembered Nerine, and thought about asking to borrow the thing—but then I realised how hard it would be to convince Tearle that I needed it for killing foxes. 'Guns are nasty. I'd rather look at something else.'

'They're historical artefacts, Meg. That's all.' Suddenly Tearle's phone buzzed. 'Ah!' he exclaimed. 'The lasagne's ready. Would you mind if we suspended our tour? I thought we should eat in the kitchen, since I don't want to leave you all by yourself in the dining room.'

I was relieved to get out of Tearle's armoury, which had changed my view of him. Previously I'd viewed him as a bit of a relic: uptight, slightly eccentric, essentially harmless. Now I wondered if there was something sinister about him after all. Count Dracula had liked living in old houses...

Tearle's kitchen looked like something out of a magazine, old-fashioned but brand new. It had marble splashbacks, ceramic sinks, a six-burner stove and a big refectory table lined with bentwood chairs. Everything was so perfect that I was surprised to see placemats on the table instead of a cloth. But the tossed salad was in a beautiful crystal bowl, while all the cutlery, according to Tearle, was made of solid silver. 'William Chawner II, 1833,' he said. 'I can't stand silver plate.'

I had to smother a snort. Then I went to fetch the wine from the living room as Tearle whipped his lasagne out of the oven. Soon we were sitting across the table from each other— and it didn't feel as odd as I'd expected. We'd shared a meal once before, at the Paradise Hotel, and Tearle was just the same on his home turf as he was in public: stiff and starchy and careful about every mouthful of wine.

His lasagne was impressive.

'This is great,' I told him. 'When did you learn to cook?'

'Since the divorce.'

'Keith couldn't cook to save his life.' As I drained another glass, I realised that I would have to stop drinking if I wanted to make it home unscathed. 'Mind you, that wasn't why I divorced him. I divorced him because I was his emotional punching bag. But don't get me started.' Realising I'd stumbled onto a topic that I didn't really want to talk about, I said quickly, 'Why did you divorce your wife?'

'She divorced me.'

'Oh. That's right.' I'd forgotten. 'Was it your collecting? I bet it was.'

The words were hardly out of my mouth before I regretted them. It occurred to me that I'd already drunk too much.

Tearle fixed me with an unreadable look. 'Why would you say that?'

'Well—collecting's like posh hoarding, isn't it? And some people don't like having lots of stuff. Minimalist people who paint their rooms white and buy modern art…' I trailed off.

Tearle raised an eyebrow. 'Have you been googling my ex-wife, Meg?'

'Um—yes. As a matter of fact.' Seeing his mouth twitch, I defended myself. 'You've never said a word about her, even though I've told you all about Keith.'

'What do you want to know?' he asked.

I shrugged and swallowed a mouthful. Silence fell, broken only by the ticking of multiple clocks. At last Tearle said, 'You're not entirely wrong, as it happens. My collection *was* a problem for Bettina.'

I stopped chewing and looked up.

'There was one aspect of it in particular that she couldn't tolerate.' Tearle gazed for a moment into his wine glass, then added, 'She didn't like the corsets.'

I nearly choked on my lasagne. 'The what?'

'I've sold them all. It was too painful to keep them.'

'You collected *corsets*?'

'A lot of people do.' He frowned as I struggled to control my expression. 'Corsetry is a dying art,' he pointed out. 'Some corsets are engineering masterpieces. Sarah Jenyns, for example—she revolutionised corsetry when she designed fan lacing, right here in Australia...'

It was no good. No matter how much he talked about lumbar support and exquisite detailing, I couldn't take him seriously. A man with Lindsay nudes and a corset collection obviously had a taste for vintage naughtiness—and it was a weakness that made him more endearing, somehow.

'It's all right, Tearle. Your secret's safe with me.'

He looked pained. 'It's not a secret, it's an investment. A good Edwardian corset can go for hundreds of dollars.'

'Hey, whatever floats your financial boat.' I was about to say I could use a corset myself, but decided against it. Talking about my 'full figure' would only get us into trouble. 'Personally, I don't see why Bettina was so freaked out by the corsets. I'm more freaked out by the guns.'

Tearle laid down his knife and cleared his throat. 'I'm sorry to hear that,' he said. 'I didn't want to make you uncomfortable.'

'I'm not.' We needed to change the subject. 'You know, if I

ever get Carol's money, I might give it to Emily. To buy a flat. That would be okay, wouldn't it? Even if the flat's in England?'

I'd been worried about taxes and duties and all the other government red tape that tends to crop up whenever you want to do anything with money. It had occurred to me that Tearle might know how to move large sums across borders.

He scooped up the last of his lasagne and chewed for a while. Finally he said, 'You're not thinking of using it yourself?'

'Well…no. I mean, what would I spend it on?'

'A house closer to Sydney?' He sipped his wine and waited for a response. When none came, he continued, 'You mentioned once that you came here for the same reason I did—because real estate was cheap. If you sold your house and used your inheritance, you could probably afford something further in.'

'Oh, no.' I waved the suggestion away. 'I don't feel like that anymore. That was years ago, before Emily left for England. There's nothing to keep me in Sydney now.'

'Ah.' He set down his glass.

'Besides, I like it here. I've got a job. A home. Friends.'

'You certainly have friends.'

'Why would I want to leave? I'm fine here.'

Tearle smiled one of his costive little smiles. 'Good.'

Then he went to fetch dessert.

Antique objects are very calming, I've found. When I go into a museum and see a set of leg-irons or a piece of hideous-looking Victorian surgical equipment, it's always rusty or dusty. Unused. Unneeded. The people who created it are dead;

its very purpose is sometimes a mystery. I look at these obscure objects under glass and it really puts my life in perspective, leeching the drama out of stuff I thought was terribly important. Because how important are your issues and obsessions really? In the context of human history, they're not important at all.

So I admired Tearle's buttonhooks and epergnes and napkin rings and tried to picture the tight little world from which they'd emerged—a world of stringent daintiness and elaborate refinement. A world of restrictions. Then I thought about Nerine and her little world, all dread and despair. And I saw it for what it was: a mental projection. A self-imposed trap.

I thought to myself, *Somehow I've got to get her out of that loop*.

'Hey, Tearle,' I said, as I helped him wash up, 'did you ever have any dealings with stalkers, when you were still working?'

'Stalkers?' he echoed. 'Oh, yes. But a cease and desist letter usually does the trick.'

'Really?' I found that hard to believe.

'Or an AVO.' Tearle placed his precious dishes in the drying rack very carefully. 'Most stalkers know they don't need to do much. Once they've instilled anxiety, it percolates. The threat is as effective as the act.'

I had to agree with him. There were occasions after I'd left Keith when I could have sworn he'd killed one of my pot plants, simply because he'd also been stealing my laundry and putting shit in my letterbox.

Was it possible I'd been blaming Keith for something

that had really been Fred Huggett's handiwork? Was I letting Nerine's paranoia undermine my common sense?

'If you're still worried about your ex-husband—' Tearle began.

'No.' I cut him off. 'Not at all.'

'Good. Because I'd hate to think you were fretting.'

The warmth in the glance he threw me was almost enough to make me forget the corsets.

I left for home at a quarter to nine, after inspecting Tearle's miniatures. By that time I was pretty worn out, despite the coffee I'd drunk with my tiramisu. After a string of disturbed nights, I didn't have enough energy for a late evening—and two glasses of wine had just about sent me to sleep.

'Are you sure you'll be all right getting home?' Tearle asked, as we exchanged a chaste peck at his front door. I wondered for a moment if he was going to offer me one of his bedrooms for the night, but then he said, 'I can always give you a lift.'

'God, no.' I almost winced at the thought. 'I'm not that tired. I can manage.'

In fact I was managing well enough to remember that I should keep an eye out for Keith's Audi on my way home, even though I was probably being overanxious. For that reason I slowed down as I passed the Heritage Motel, which was so small that I was able to take it all in from a single vantage point. Though I couldn't see anything that remotely resembled a luxury vehicle, I did wonder about the GoGet rental out the front. Would Keith have rented a car just to cover his tracks? It seemed unlikely; he'd always loved to flaunt his fancy European coupes. On the other hand, a boring old Japanese sedan would have been the perfect disguise…

I wondered suddenly what kind of car Nerine's ex drove. It occurred to me that I knew very little about him: just that he was a cruel, violent plumber who sold drugs. I didn't know how old he was or what he looked like. I didn't even know his surname. But just in case he was around, I sat for a minute by the motel's entrance, studying the array of non-rentals parked under the glowing carriage lights that flanked every door. There were only five cars that hadn't been hired. Two had Victorian plates, so I ignored those. Nerine hadn't come to me from Victoria. One had a Christian vanity plate— GOD2GO—which didn't seem right for Duncan, somehow. The other two were a dark blue Kia sedan and a silver Toyota hatchback. I paid particular attention to the sedan because I could see the silhouette of a kid's booster seat through the rear window.

If Duncan had come for his kids, he might have brought car seats with him.

No one emerged from any of the motel rooms while I was idling nearby, so I finally changed gears and headed off again. There were two pubs in Bulwell and I passed both of them at a crawl, eyeing the rows of bumpers lining the kerb. Most of them belonged to familiar vans and utes. I also recognised Ravi Singh's Jeep and Steve McIntyre's Morris Minor with its heritage plates. There was only one strange car parked outside the Palace—a dark grey Mazda—and as I rolled by, its tail-lights suddenly flared. I'd almost reached the highway when I realised the Mazda was leaving Bulwell too.

At first I didn't pay much attention. It was Friday night, so there was quite a bit of traffic about—and most people, like me, were taking the highway out of town instead of the back way. The Mazda turned left behind me, and that wasn't unusual either, even though right turns were more common. But when it followed me onto Cox's Ridge Road, I sat up and took notice.

It wasn't that no one ever used this route, which led straight to a colliery and a long, meandering line of hobby farms. I often zipped past coal trucks and horse floats on my way home. But I rarely saw other motorists on the road at night, and when I did they were usually heading in the other direction, away from the colliery.

The car behind me didn't belong to either of the Bernardi boys, or to Val Weller, who worked at the mine. Apart from the Huggetts, I didn't know the rest of my neighbours on Cox's Ridge Road—but I'd often glimpsed their properties, many of which were scattered with rusty old car bodies and abandoned water tanks and tumbledown sheds and half-finished fences. The Mazda, I thought, was too glossy a car for people like that. It was the kind of car a colliery manager might drive. But wasn't it a little late to be heading to work?

When I reached the bottom of Spinney Creek hill I expected the Mazda to pass me in the overtaking lane. Most vehicles roared past with an almost audible sigh of relief if they got stuck behind me on that hill. To my astonishment, however, the Mazda kept chugging along behind me as my speedometer needle dropped and dropped, until I began to feel not only suspicious, but slightly alarmed.

'It can't be him,' I said, because Keith didn't drive a grey Mazda. Duncan might have, for all I knew, but there was no way in the world that he could have identified my car. *You're being neurotic*, I told myself. *There's probably a simple explanation*. Maybe the grey Mazda had an engine problem. Maybe it was being driven by a very nervous old man who didn't like overtaking at night. Maybe the driver was drunk and being very, very careful.

I peered in the mirror again but saw only headlights. As I finally crested the hill, my wheezing old Commodore got its second wind and began to speed up.

The Mazda speeded up too. In fact it accelerated so much that it was practically nudging my bumper bar.

'Shit! You moron...'

Surging forward at a bend in the road, I found myself drifting over the centre line. It looked as if the driver behind me *was* drunk. Maybe he'd left the pub feeling angry and had decided to taunt the harmless old cow in the car ahead of him.

Shooting past a road sign, I identified exactly where I was. There was a fire trail up ahead, so I decided to pull over when I reached it. This meant slowing down—and as I did, the car behind me blasted its horn. I veered slightly, shocked by the noise.

'Dickhead!'

The next dip in the road marked the fire trail. Signalling,

I swerved onto loose gravel and bumped over a shallow pothole before crunching to a halt. The Mazda zoomed by, still sounding its horn. By the time I'd parked, it was up the other side of the dip and vanishing into the night, tail-lights dimming.

I sat for a moment, clutching the wheel and breathing deeply. My hands were shaking. I was on the verge of tears.

Men, I thought. What woman would have done a thing like that? If I hadn't been so shattered, I would have been furious.

I wasn't quite ready to drive, but home was only five minutes away and I couldn't sit in the dark forever. Besides, I didn't feel safe where I was, so I checked the road, flicked on my blinker and eased the car forward, gathering speed as I mounted the next rise. I had a picture of Esme in my head; once I reached her, I knew I'd be safe.

I couldn't ring any of my friends. Sally, Dinah, Bridget— even Tearle would probably fly to my rescue if I called. But they had to be kept away from my house while Nerine was there. And contacting the police was out of the question.

Anyway, I didn't have the Mazda's rego.

Rounding a bend in the road, I was slowing in preparation for a left-hand turn when I spotted two red lights up ahead. It took me a second to realise that they weren't moving; they were sitting on the verge some distance past my driveway.

I braked automatically. It was stupid, with the blind corner behind me, but I wasn't thinking straight. Like a frightened rabbit I sat staring at the car in the distance, my pulse racing.

The one thing I knew was that I couldn't keep heading home. Not while the Mazda was there. Whoever the driver was, I didn't want him to see where I lived.

His number plate was too far away to read.

Suddenly his rear blinker began to flash. I watched, astonished, as his car pulled out onto the road and roared off, tyres screeching dramatically. A horn blared, again and again. The third honk lasted so long that it started fading into the distance.

I waited until the Mazda's tail-lights had disappeared. Then I waited some more. Then I realised that I was sitting in the middle of the road, perfectly positioned to get rammed up the rear, so I took my foot off the brake and rolled forward.

When I reached my own driveway, the gate was open. I bounced over the cattle grid and trundled through the trees, continually checking my rear-view mirror. It had crossed my mind that the Mazda might be parked further along the road, waiting to terrorise me all over again. When I didn't appear, it might turn around and come looking for me. Or its driver might give up and set off home, satisfied with a job well done.

I'd told Nerine not to worry about leaving all the lights on, since I would have done it anyway before going out, to discourage burglars. So when I halted in front of the garden gate, I was greeted by a warm glow from the living-room window and the noise of Esme barking inside.

My hands were still shaking so much that I had a hard time releasing the gate-latch. As I climbed back into the car, drove it up to the front steps and returned to close the gate again, my ears were pricked and my eyes were peeled. I was listening for the sound of an engine. I was watching for the flash of headlights bobbing down the driveway.

Esme was in the vestibule, waiting for me, when I finally stumbled inside. I was careful to shut the front door and throw the deadbolt before dropping to my knees and hugging her.

'How was it?' asked Nerine, from the living room.

I didn't answer. I just buried my face in Esme's neck.

'I wasn't expecting you so early,' Nerine went on. 'To tell the truth, I thought you might not come back tonight. Did he make a move? I want all the details...'

Her arch voice grew louder as she entered the vestibule. But then I raised my head and she saw my expression. Her avid look changed to one of alarm.

'What is it?' she said. 'What happened?'

'I don't know.' Road rage? Drunk teens? A targeted attack by Keith or Duncan? 'Honestly, I just don't know...'

OUT OF TOWN

I HAD ANOTHER terrible night, and not just because of the alcohol. Nerine and I sat up until one in the morning trying to work out what was going on. I couldn't decide if Keith was harassing me or if I'd been chased by some random hoon. Nerine, for her part, insisted it was Duncan. She was very, very frightened.

'He's closing in,' she said. 'I can feel him. Oh, Christ...'

'Does he drive a dark grey Mazda SUV with roof racks?' I asked.

'How should I know? He could be driving anything.'

'But when you were together—'

'He had a red ute. Which he wrapped around a bollard just before I left.' Nerine jumped up and began to pace the kitchen, wringing her hands. 'I need to get out of here. I'm putting you in danger.'

'Nerine—'

'Listen.' She stopped in front of me. 'I realise you don't know anyone who'd take me in right now, but if I had some money—if I could get to the coast and find a way out—then we'd all be safe.' Seeing me blink, she gabbled, 'I wouldn't need much, just a few thousand dollars, and I know I shouldn't be asking but he nearly killed you out there and I don't want it to happen again.'

'A few thousand dollars?' I could barely get my head around what I'd just heard. 'I don't have that much to spare.'

'You will, though.'

'Yeah, but...' I was starting to feel uncomfortable. 'David told me not to hold my breath. Besides, we still don't know if this is Duncan.'

'It has to be!'

'How?' Without waiting for an answer, I said, 'If it really is him, why hasn't he told the police where you are?'

'Because he wants revenge! I told you!'

'And I think you're jumping to conclusions.' I flinched as she flung herself across the room and bounced off a wall like a crazed bluebottle. 'Keith had a thing about windchimes. And he knows where I live. So before you rush off and do anything dangerous, I want to make sure exactly who we're dealing with.'

'For God's sake, Meg—'

'I'm getting the gun on Sunday.'

She froze in her tracks. As I'd hoped, this news seemed to calm her a little—or at least give her pause.

'Seriously?' she said.

I nodded. 'A friend's invited me to lunch and I'll ask if I can borrow her rifle.'

Nerine stared at me for a moment, chewing on her bottom lip. Her eyes were bloodshot. Her hair was hanging in her face. She no longer looked like Emily, who'd learnt to hide her feelings while living with Keith. By the time she left for England, Emily had the most inexpressive face I'd ever seen.

'And in the meantime?' Nerine demanded. 'What about tonight? What about tomorrow?'

'Tonight we'll let Esme look after us.' I caressed the dog's ears; she hadn't left my side since I'd walked through the front door. 'Tomorrow I'm going to do some digging. See if I can work out where Keith is.'

'But—'

'You should go to bed, Nerine. *I'm* going to bed. We'll need our sleep because it's important we stay calm—for the kids' sake.' Seeing that my argument didn't seem to impress her, I coaxed her along by adding, 'We'll make mistakes if we panic. Just keep cool. Stay focused. Don't let it get to you.'

This was easier said than done. I lay in bed for hours afterwards, worrying and planning. Any pleasure I'd felt from David's legal victory had completely evaporated. I wondered gloomily if I would ever get paid, and what Keith would do to stop the payment. Then I thought about Nerine's request for cash. It had shocked me at first, but once I'd had time to reflect, I'd come to the conclusion that it wasn't much of a surprise really. Nerine was desperate. She had kids. She knew I was expecting a windfall. Of course she'd asked for money.

I wasn't about to empty my bank account, though. I didn't want Nerine dumping its contents into the hands of some people smuggler. There had to be a better way.

I was trying to figure it out when I finally dozed off.

My sleep was restless, full of disjointed dreams and confused awakenings. At one point I was roused by Colette's high-pitched yowl. A little later, in a state of semi-consciousness, I realised that Esme had returned to my room. And in the morning I woke with a gasp, propelled out of a nightmare in which I'd opened the vestibule cupboard to find something big and dark lurking in the children's hideaway.

The dream did give me an idea, though.

'Morning all!' I stumbled into the kitchen to find everyone awake, as usual. But it was drizzling outside and Nerine was fractious; the tense, unhappy atmosphere made me wonder what was going on. Analiese was sitting at the table, clutching Mr Snuffles and staring at an empty cereal bowl. Colette was whimpering on the floor, her face smeared with jam and tears.

'What's the matter?' I asked.

'Oh, nothing,' Nerine snapped. 'Everything's just great.'

Ana seemed to shrink into herself. I realised that her mother was in a mood—and it was the kind of mood that filled the whole house like a black fog.

'Well, listen. Something just occurred to me.' I decided not to wait, since Nerine's spirits couldn't have sunk any lower. 'Have you used your credit card, lately?'

'Of course not,' she said.

'And you left your phone behind?'

'Yes.' She gave an impatient sigh. 'I told you that.'

'Then maybe you should go and check everything you *did*

bring. Make sure there isn't some kind of bug or tracker hidden away in your stuff.' As Nerine stared at me, open-mouthed, I said apologetically, 'I know it sounds far-fetched, but there are things you can buy on the internet—'

'No! You're right! You're absolutely right!'

I was standing just inside the kitchen door, and she plunged towards me with one of her abrupt, unbridled movements that sent me scuttling out of the way. Crossing the threshold, she cried, 'Will you look after the girls?' Then she disappeared down the hall, making for her room.

It took me a few seconds to recover. Even Esme looked startled. Colette had begun to sob in earnest, so I scooped her up and said, 'Esme! Out!'

Her ears drooped. She wagged her tail.

'Go on. You know you're not allowed in here.'

She loped off reluctantly, with many a mournful backward glance. I shut the door behind her as Colette yelled, 'Dok! Dokka!' and struggled to escape my grip.

'Has anyone let the chickens out?' I asked her sister.

Ana frowned. 'It's raining.'

'Then let's get the umbrellas.' I picked up a tea towel and began to wipe Colette's face. 'Do you know where they are?'

'Yes. I know.' Ana slipped from her chair and darted out of the kitchen.

Colette was trying to suck the tea towel, so I let her get on with it. Peering through the window at the damp, gloomy backyard, I wondered if I should buy gumboots for the kids while I was shopping in Bathurst that afternoon. It wasn't as if anyone would see me doing it. And I had a feeling that we were in for a fair bit of rain.

At least that'll discourage Keith, I thought. He'd always regarded bad weather as a personal affront. His revenge scenarios were like cricket: slow, drawn-out, strategic and subject to rain delays.

When Keith first heard about nanny cams we were living in one of Carol's properties. He'd gone bankrupt—his fancy bistro had failed—so he'd appealed to his mother for help, even though he'd managed to find some kind of job that kept him out of the house for days on end. He said he was delivering luxury cars to interstate customers. I didn't know if this was true and I didn't really care. I was just pleased that he was away most of the time, because Emily was two years old and getting into everything. Whenever she spilled food on the floor or drooled on the couch or smeared paint on the curtains, it was easier if Keith wasn't there. He didn't want to live surrounded by chewed biscuits, he said. How could he bring friends back to a place where everything was sticky?

So I kept the mess to a minimum, even though Carol didn't mind. She adored Emily, she understood what toddlers were like, and in any case the flat was a rental, with lots of high gloss paint and dark grey carpets and stone benchtops that didn't mark. It was a lovely flat in Waverton, not far from Balls Head Reserve, and one of the nicest homes we ever had. I preferred it to the gigantic house Keith once rented in Cherrybrook, which was miles from anywhere and much too hot upstairs because there wasn't enough insulation in the roof.

One day Keith came home to the Waverton flat unexpect-edly and found his wife and daughter asleep in the middle of the afternoon. I always tried to nap when Emily did—though not, of course, if I had to clean or cook or make calls or do anything else that you can't manage with a toddler clamped to your knee. Keith immediately got it into his head that I spent most of my days lolling around. He suggested I apply for a waitressing job, and when I asked who would look after Emily he suggested the unemployed teenager downstairs. I pointed out that we knew absolutely nothing about the unem-ployed teenager downstairs. Did he really want to entrust his daughter to her?

'That's okay,' he said. 'We'll get a nanny cam.' He went on to describe, with enormous relish, how people in America used concealed cameras all the time to find out whether their domestic staff were stealing or slacking off. 'You can buy teddy cams, doll cams, robot cams, stroller cams, pen cams…There's a security shop in Dulwich Hill that sells 'em. We could wire the whole place up.' His enthusiasm about spy technology seemed so pointed that I felt a chill run down my spine. Was it my imagination or was he eyeing me with a sly, speculative look?

The next day I pulled the place apart. I'd spent half the night remembering how often, in recent weeks, he had accused me of wasting food and spending too much time with the woman next door. I'd assumed he must have been chatting to the neighbours or counting the number of bags in the garbage bin. Now I wondered if he'd installed a secret camera. So I checked every lamp, every shelf, every picture on the wall. I dismantled the stereo system. I even tore open Emily's stuffed toys, intending to sew them back together when I had a moment. It wasn't as if Emily cared—she enjoyed playing snow with the stuffing.

Keith said I was mad. 'You're insane,' he growled, when he saw the disembowelled teddies. 'You're a paranoid hysteric.' On realising that I'd somehow loosened one of his speaker wires, he blasted me with a two-hour harangue that condemned my stupidity, sloth, clumsiness, gullibility and lack of organisation. By the end of it, he'd convinced me he was right. I'd been imagining things. I was losing it. I needed help. And I had to stop watching domestic thrillers on the TV.

It was only years later that I realised he'd probably set me up, deliberately planting the idea of surveillance just to mess with my head. I certainly never found any evidence that he'd installed cameras or listening devices. When I think about it, he probably wasn't up to the challenge; his computer skills were fairly basic. He was good at manipulating people, not technology. Even if he bought a spy camera, I'm not sure he would have been able to use it. Especially if it involved any kind of software.

All the same, I knew that such devices were available. I also knew that, if Duncan was as smart as Nerine said he was, he might easily have inserted a tracker into one of his kids' toys.

Nerine must have thought the same thing, because when

I finally emerged from my bedroom, decked out for the day, she was sifting through her face powder and checking her lipstick caps.

'It's not in the makeup,' she said. I'd spent no more than five minutes getting dressed, but in that time she had recruited Analiese to feel along the seams of Colette's pyjamas for lumps or wires. The three of them were parked on their bed, in a tangle of clothes and toiletries, like flotsam washed up on a beach.

I didn't really approve of getting the kids involved, but I knew my objections would fall on deaf ears. Nerine's sullen air had turned feverish; she was obviously determined to inspect every single item they'd brought with them.

'There's nothing hidden in the suitcase, either,' she said, then frowned as she caught sight of my handbag. 'Are you off now?'

'It's quite a drive.' I hesitated, watching Ana swipe the hem of a T-shirt through her stick-like fingers. 'Do we have everything you need on the list? Last chance to add a packet of biscuits…'

'No, we're fine.'

She didn't look fine to me. She looked jumpy. Manic. And Colette was a snivelling mass of snot and tears. 'I could always go tomorrow.'

'You've got that lunch tomorrow,' Nerine pointed out.

'I could cancel.'

'No!' She glanced up from her mascara wand. 'The gun's more important than the groceries.'

'Nerine!'

'What?' Her shoulder twitched as if she was shrugging off a fly. 'The kids are gunna know about it soon enough.'

Sometimes I felt as if Nerine and I were on different continents, staring at each other across a wide, dark ocean. But there was nothing I could do about it. I couldn't chide her for talking about guns in front of the girls without talking about guns myself.

'Take care of Esme, will you, sweetheart?' I said to Analiese. 'And maybe I'll bring you a special present from the shops.'

Ana raised her eyes from her sister's pyjamas. 'What present?' she asked.

'You'll see.' I wanted to give her something to look forward to because I sensed she wasn't going to have much of a day. Not that I was overly worried; leaving her with her mother wasn't like leaving Emily with Keith. For one thing, Nerine knew how to bathe, feed and entertain a child.

But as I walked out the door I had a niggling sensation that reminded me just a little of the overwhelming dread I'd always felt when dropping off my daughter at Keith's place. It could have been Ana's dull expression—the look of a child burdened by a job she didn't want to do. Or the anxious, preoccupied way her mother was tackling the search for a tracker, so fixated on her own concerns that she reminded me of Keith.

Or perhaps it was the fear in the air. Keith had always been good at generating fear—fear of blame, fear of failure, fear of retribution. The fear now was different, but still pervasive. It made me reluctant to leave the children.

Whenever I sensed fear, my instinct was to whisk up the nearest child and run.

I had to pass Bulwell to reach Bathurst—and for the first time in a long time, I was nervous on the road. Pulling out of my front gate, I peered in both directions, almost expecting to see the grey Mazda lying in wait for me. But the coast was clear.

I set off for the highway, repeatedly glancing in the rear-view mirror, my fingers tight on the wheel and my heart racing. It was still wet; I had to drive slowly, especially on Spinney Creek hill, and there were some bends closer to Bulwell that slowed me down even more. Luckily, I didn't see a soul on the road except for a couple of trucks heading in the opposite direction. No one sat on my bumper as I crawled around the bends. No one tried to pass me on the flat stretch between Greenpoint Farm and the highway, where sprays of fading plastic flowers stuck to a road sign commemorated a young man who did try to overtake.

When I reached the Bulwell turn-off, I was sorely tempted. Why not do a quick recce of Mayne Street to see if the grey Mazda or Keith's Audi was parked anywhere? But I resisted the urge and kept going, through a cloudburst and a state forest, past roadworks and a nursery and the Yetholme Motor Inn, until the weather started to clear a little. By the time I reached Raglan, it had stopped raining and the clouds were a lighter shade of grey. Then the shops and pubs and service stations of Kelso closed in, covering the paddocks, and I found myself relaxing a little. In Bathurst, at least, I would be safe. No one knew I was here except for Nerine.

My first stop was Bathurst railway station, which was elegant and elderly, with a slate roof and bay windows. The circular car park in front was practically full. I knew my presence wouldn't excite any interest as I locked the car and bustled over to the station's front veranda, where a pay phone sat next to a ticket machine.

The phone took coins, thank God. I didn't want to use my credit card.

'Jill?' I said, when she picked up. 'It's me.'

'Oh!' She was on her mobile and I could hear voices in the background. 'Hang on a minute, would you?'

I waited for a few seconds, listening to scrapes, rustles and bangs. Finally she spoke again. 'Sorry—people here. How are you, Meg?'

'Well…a bit mixed, to be honest.' After the events of the previous few nights, I'd decided that I needed more information. I needed to find out where Duncan was, if only to reassure Nerine. 'We've had a couple of incidents and Nerine's in a terrible state—'

'Incidents?' Jill interrupted. 'What incidents?'

'Harassment. Hang-up calls. A car. I think it's Keith—I won the court case, and—'

'Oh, Meg! That's fantastic!'

'Not if it gets Keith all worked up.' I took a deep breath, glancing around to make sure no one was listening. A mini-bus had just pulled into a space near the memorial steam train, but the only person who got out was the driver—and he was miles away. 'Nerine thinks all this is her ex. Nothing I say makes any difference. So I was wondering if you could do a bit of digging for me.'

'Digging?'

'It would be great if I could tell Nerine that Duncan's still at home or at work or whatever. That he isn't hanging around my place.'

Silence fell at the other end of the line. I thought for a moment that the signal had dropped out. Then Jill said, 'Nerine got rid of her phone, Meg. How could he have found her?'

'I know. I told her that.' Wanting to stress how crazy things were getting, I added, 'She's been checking her clothes for trackers.'

'Trackies?'

'*Trackers*. GPS things.'

'Oh, dear.'

'Do you think you could speak to your contact? I just want to know where Duncan is.'

Again there was a pause. At last Jill said, 'All right. I guess I can do that.'

'Could you do it soon? Only I'm in Bathurst, and I'll be heading home in a couple of hours—'

'Give me an hour. Then call me back.'

'Okay.'

'How are you going otherwise?'

'Nerine's a challenge,' I had to admit. 'If only she'd calm down...'

'I'll see what I can do.'

'Thanks, Jill.'

'You hang in there.'

'I will.'

'Talk to you soon.'

I felt much better as I returned to the car. Jill had always made me feel better, ever since our first shared lunch, when we'd discussed our support group and Jill had said, 'What a bunch of survivors we are. Not victims—survivors.' She was able to identify a narrative of hope in the messy, broken details of other people's lives and use it to fill those people with a new sense of purpose. I'd never thought I was particularly brave or intuitive until Jill told me I was. Then I realised that I wasn't, perhaps, a complete failure—that my expert handling of Keith's moods had probably prevented a lot of physical violence, over the years, and that there was no telling what might have happened to Emily if I'd left Keith any earlier. 'You did your best,' Jill had insisted, again and again. 'You did your best and it was pretty damn good. Maybe one day Emily will realise that.'

Driving back to Bathurst's main shopping street, I let some of my anxiety drain away, focusing instead on what I was going to buy for Ana and Colette. Special cereal, of course, and little pots of custard, and bananas, and nappies, and perhaps some yoghurt bars. But I wanted to get something extra as well—something a bit special. A chocolate treat for both of them. Maybe a sticker book for Ana and a bath toy for Colette…

After I'd parked and plunged into the mall, I went to inspect the range of sticker books on offer at the Reject Shop, finally choosing one about animals. I also picked up a board book for Colette that had furry, sparkly, sticky, bumpy and fluffy patches in it. I couldn't find any children's gumboots, and the cute kids' umbrellas were too expensive. So I left the shop with a single plastic bag, which I slung into a trolley alongside my reusable ones before patrolling the aisles at Woolworths.

I had a very long grocery list, because Nerine and her kids had eaten their way through my entire pantry cupboard in less than a week. It wasn't only staples like bread, milk, meat and margarine I needed, but also a weird assortment of other things: flour, prunes, baking cups, tinned spaghetti. I bought the blandest cheese I could find and white rice instead of brown. I chose a jumbo packet of Coco Pops and twenty-four toilet-paper rolls.

Then I turned a corner and heard someone cry, 'Meg! Hello!'

It was Dinah Hodges.

BAD NEWS

DINAH WAS A tall, raw-boned woman whose confidence and efficiency made me feel like a wimp. Though she spent most of her time working with cows and tractors, she always looked stylish in her jodhpurs and khakis and down vests—probably because she had long legs and a tan.

'How are you?' she said. 'I'm just buying stuff to feed you with tomorrow. Can't get decent spices in Bulwell.' She glanced into my cart. 'I didn't know you shopped here.'

I'd broken into a cold sweat; adrenaline was making my heart pound and my hands tremble. I hadn't reached the nappies yet, but I was afraid that my party-pack of Freddo frogs would arouse Dinah's suspicions.

'Oh, I'm just catching up with a friend.' This wasn't a complete lie; I had, after all, phoned Jill. 'Thought I'd pick up some stuff while I'm here.'

Dinah nodded. She was usually more talkative than Sally—perhaps because Sally spent most of her time chatting to patients, while Dinah worked with large, dumb animals. 'We've got three pullets lined up for you: one Australorp and two ISA Browns. I'm sorry about what happened to your girls. Bloody foxes. Those bastards are almost impossible to keep out.'

I suddenly saw a way of distracting her from my juice boxes and cheese slices. 'It was awful,' I agreed. 'And I think the damn thing's still around, you know? I've smelled it.'

'Mmmm.'

'If this happens again, I swear, I don't know what I'll do. That's why I've ordered a fox trap. Online.' Before Dinah could comment, I took a deep breath, stiffened my spine and said, 'But once it's trapped, I don't want to hit it on the head with a rock. So I was wondering if I could borrow your rifle.'

Dinah blinked. 'My *rifle?*'

'To shoot it with.' I casually sidled in front of my trolley as Dinah absorbed this.

'Well…the thing is, that's not something I'm strictly allowed to do,' she said quietly. 'Not unless you've got a fire-arms licence. Have you?'

'No.'

'Have you ever fired a gun before?'

'No.' I felt suddenly as if I was ten years old. 'Forget it. Don't worry. I shouldn't have asked.'

'No, no. It's perfectly reasonable. I'd shoot any fox that came near my hens.' She pondered for a moment, fiddling with her fleecy grey hair. 'Let me talk to Sally. We can discuss it tomorrow, okay?'

'Sure. Yes. Whatever you think.'

'You wouldn't have any trouble actually getting a licence. And for storage I could always give you the lock box I use in the truck...' She stood for a moment, lost in thought, then gave her head a little shake. 'I'll think about it,' she promised. 'Let me see what I can do.'

'Thanks, Dinah.'

'Not a problem.' She was turning away when something made her change her mind; all at once she swivelled around again, her face brightening, and said, 'I hear you had dinner with Tearle last night?'

The look on my face made her laugh. She patted my shoulder. 'It's a small town, Meg.'

'How the hell...?'

'He bought a tiramisu at the IGA and Amy was on the register. Then Amy had an appointment with Sally, and then Sally left work late last night and saw your car parked outside his house.' Dinah leaned against the nearest pole, like someone settling in for a good long gossip. 'We didn't know you two were getting on so well. But I always thought there was more to him than met the eye.'

'Not really,' I said with a sinking heart. The news was probably all around Bulwell by this time. 'We were just celebrating, that's all.'

'Celebrating?'

'I've won my court case.'

Dinah was thrilled. I'd never seen her so excited. I tried to hose her down by pointing out that Keith would probably appeal, but she shrugged off my fears. 'You have to be really good to serve on the Supreme Court and no one that good is going to put up with Keith's bullshit,' she said.

She didn't ask how much money I was expecting, but she did want to know how I would spend it. When I muttered something about Emily, her face softened.

'Of course,' she agreed. 'That's exactly what I would do.'

By this time it was nearly midday and I needed to call Jill. So I told Dinah I was expected for lunch, without saying where.

Dinah smiled and nodded. 'We'll see you tomorrow. About twelve?'

'Twelve. Right.'

'It'll be a celebration. Do you like margaritas?'

'Not when I'm driving.'

'Hah!' She gave me a smacking kiss and a crushing hug. 'It's great news, Meg. I'm so pleased. You deserve it.'

Then she strode away without a backward glance, steering her trolley one-handed, her hair bouncing, her embroidered bag swinging, her sturdy boots squeaking on the linoleum.

I headed in the opposite direction, taut with nerves. On my way to the checkout I grabbed three enormous packets of disposable nappies, which I shoved through the register in a panic. Only when they were safely concealed in my grocery bags did I finally relax a little. But I kept my eyes peeled for Dinah, rehearsing what I would say if she spotted the Huggies logo tucked between my tissues and toilet paper. My Bathurst friend, I would explain, had two kids and no time. I was shopping for her. She lived over near the university, though she was moving to Queensland very soon…

Sally and Dinah wouldn't approve of disposable nappies, I thought as I hurried back to the car. If they ever managed to adopt, they'd probably shell out for a cloth nappy service— providing they could find one that would drive all the way to their farm. Or Dinah would wash the nappies herself.

Loading up the boot, I reflected gloomily that Dinah was the sort of person who'd be happy scraping shit off terry towelling. Compared to mucking out stables or cleaning up a cow's afterbirth, washing nappies would be a piece of cake.

I headed back to the station, where a train was due any minute. People were being dropped off with their luggage. Other people were sitting in their vehicles, reading newspapers or screens. I had to park quite a distance away and walk past a couple of noisy families, all hugging and kissing and bickering. But no one was using the station phone, thank God.

Jill answered on the first ring. 'Hello?'

'Jill?'

'Hi, Meg.'

'Any news?'

'Yeah…'

Something about her tone alarmed me. 'What?' I said. 'What is it?'

'I talked to my contact.' A pause. 'The thing is, Duncan's disappeared.'

I swallowed.

'Left town, apparently. No one knows where he is.' There was another long silence. 'Meg? Are you there?'

'I'm here.'

'This doesn't mean he's down your way.'

'Mmmmm.'

'My contact doesn't have a lot of details, unfortunately. She doesn't know if he told anyone his plans. He could be off shooting pigs or looking for work or pub-crawling on the Gold Coast—there are lots of rumours.' After a brief hesitation, she added reluctantly, 'One of them is that he's gone after Nerine.'

'Christ.'

'Which he hasn't. I mean, he might be looking but he can't have found her. We made sure of that.'

I glanced around, taking note of the passing faces. The parked cars. The distant traffic.

'I know this won't make things any easier with Nerine,' said Jill.

'No.'

'You were wanting reassurance and I can't give it to you. I'm sorry.' She heaved a gusty sigh, then remarked, 'You could lie, I suppose.'

I grunted. Lying wasn't something I did very well. In any case, I didn't think it would help anyone. And if Nerine found out, she'd lose whatever trust she had in me.

'I've told my contact to call once she hears anything,' Jill said. 'When that happens, I'll let you know, okay?'

'Thanks.'

'And don't worry. There's no way Duncan could have

tracked you down—he's probably gone off to harass Nerine's relatives.'

'Jesus, Jill! I hope not!'

'Sorry. That was stupid. Are you all right?'

'Yes.'

'You're doing so well, Meg. It's already been a week—just three more and you'll be out the other side. Hang in there. I know you can do it.'

She went on for a while, giving me a pep talk, until I finally decided it was time to go. There was milk in my car; I didn't want it spoiling on the drive back.

'Jill,' I said, interrupting her extended goodbyes, 'could you find out from your contact what Duncan was driving when he left?'

'Why?' I could almost feel her muscles tighten. 'What's going on?'

'I just want to know if he's in a dark grey Mazda SUV. With roof racks.' A rise in the noise level and a sudden burst of activity suggested that the long-awaited train must be pulling into the station, though I couldn't see it from where I was standing. 'Call me if he's been spotted in something like that, will you?'

Then I hung up and hurried back to my car, anxious to be gone before I was caught in a flurry of passengers.

Esme's barking greeted me when I pulled up outside the house, about an hour later. The sky had cleared, though the ground was still damp and the trees were heavy with silvery droplets.

No one opened the front door as I went to close the gate. No one helped me heave all the shopping bags out of the boot and dump them on the veranda.

Only Esme was waiting in the vestibule. 'Nerine?' I called, but no one replied. I checked the cupboard. Empty.

'Hello?' I said. No answer.

So I lugged the bags into the kitchen, wondering if the kids were having a nap. Esme followed me from door to table, table to fridge. I put the meat, milk and cheese away, then headed for Nerine's room.

Deserted. She wasn't in the house and neither were her kids.

'Where have they gone?' I asked Esme. She stared up at me, panting.

There were no obvious signs of a disturbance, though the place was such a mess I don't think I would have noticed anything short of cyclone damage. Nerine hadn't repacked since checking her possessions for bugs; clothes, toys and makeup were spread across every surface in her room. Stray socks and plastic wrappers littered the hallway. The bathroom was dusted with face and baby powder, the kitchen with sugar and biscuit crumbs.

I grabbed a banana, then pushed open the back door and walked down the steps. Ruby was the only hen in sight. She looked quite content and didn't even glance at Esme, who was trailing after me. I was about to call Nerine's name when I decided against it. What if Fred Huggett heard?

'They must have gone for a walk,' I said to the dog, though

I was puzzled. Nerine had always seemed so frightened of going outside; why would she do it now? Then something occurred to me. I scurried back around the front of the house and checked the driveway for tyre marks. The earth was still so soft from the rain that I could see my own marks very clearly.

No other tracks were visible.

I decided to try the path to the Baumanns' fence. If Nerine had gone for a walk, she'd probably have taken a familiar route. There were puddles in the potholes and one or two muddy patches, but most of the ground was too stony for footprints—until I came to a stretch of sand. Then I spotted a couple of marks that looked pretty fresh to me, and were small enough to have been left by Colette.

'Nerine?' I said in a ringing voice. 'Ana?'

A breeze rustled the treetops. A currawong cawed nearby.

I trudged on, telling myself not to panic. If Nerine had gone for a walk it was a good thing—unless she'd been running away, of course. But running away from what? There hadn't been any strange vehicles in my yard; I would have seen traces.

Ahead of me, Esme kept stopping to sniff at rocks and roots. The electric fence was in plain sight when she suddenly became very interested in a thick clump of grevillea. I thought at first that she must have found a trace of fox musk or possum scat, until I spotted a fleck of white in the dusty green. Stopping, I nudged Esme aside and bent down to part the stiff branches.

Wedged near the base of the plant was one of Colette's shoes.

I can't pretend I didn't feel a twinge of fear. *She probably dropped it*, I thought. *Nerine's probably carrying her.* The shoe was a cheap, rubbery little thing without laces; I could easily imagine it falling off while Colette struggled on her mother's hip.

'Nerine?' I said loudly. 'I have Colette's shoe!'

The only sound was Esme's panting. I picked up the shoe and set off again, trying not to knead it like a stress ball. When I reached the fence, I glanced down the fire trail that ran along it, but saw no one. Would Nerine have headed for the gorge after I'd warned her not to?

She might have, I realised, if she was looking for one of her kids. What if Colette had wandered off, for some reason? It would explain the missing shoe...

'Find 'em, girl. Find 'em,' I told Esme. She wasn't a bloodhound and didn't understand the words, but it made me feel better to break the enveloping silence as I followed her towards the cliff at the back of my property, watching her for signs of distress or excitement. She displayed neither; instead she sauntered along, her hips wagging, her nose in the dirt.

All the same, I felt a growing dread on my approach to the lookout, which was deserted when I reached it.

'Stay!' I said sharply, glaring at the dog. Then I edged forward, glancing back once or twice because I was afraid that someone would rush out and push me into the gorge.

But there was no one.

No one was lurking in the bushes. No one was lying at the foot of the cliff—though it crossed my mind that the dense carpet of treetops might be concealing a broken body or two.

'No,' I said aloud. I told myself, in Keith's voice, that I was being hysterical. Overanxious. That I was catastrophising. 'Nerine?' I called again.

No answer. I retraced my steps to the fire trail, where I turned left instead of right and made for the Huggetts' block.

I was pretty sure that Nerine wouldn't have headed in this direction. But there was no saying what Colette might have done if she was lost. I realised I'd have to search the whole property, and cursed myself for not bringing the car.

It took me about ten minutes to reach the Huggetts' fence, where I took a sharp right and struck out for Cox's Ridge Road. Esme, meanwhile, was mooching along without a care in the world. She barely lifted her head and didn't bark once. I stopped to pick up an old chip packet that must have blown in from somewhere else. I also found an apple core, brown with age and probably dropped by a bird.

As time went on, the images in my head grew more and more disturbing. I pictured bodies on the ground. Blood on tree trunks. Children in car boots.

I was parched and sweaty and exhausted when at last I arrived at the road.

It was empty. Not a vehicle in sight. I couldn't see any point checking the driveway, having already taken my car up to the house. So I ducked under the front fence, and walked along the verge for a while before plunging back into the bush not far from the Baumanns' fence line. Here another path led to the shallow gully that bisected my land.

Esme trotted along beside me. We hadn't gone very far before she gave an excited yap. At the same instant I heard something else: the distant sound of a child's cry.

Or was it a crow calling?

'Nerine?' I exclaimed. 'Colette?'

Esme bounded forward and I stumbled after her. Branches slapped at my knees as she led me down a narrow path to a slight hollow masked by the spreading leaves of two tree ferns. Esme slid beneath the leaves almost without disturbing them. I had to crouch and push them aside.

The sight that greeted me sent the blood rushing to my head. Nestled on a bed of leaf litter, Analiese was trying to fend off Esme's eager kisses.

'Ana! Are you all right?'

Her lips were clamped together because Esme was trying to lick her face. So I grabbed the dog and pulled her back, relieved to see that Ana's clothes weren't ripped, though they were covered in dirt and dead leaves. There was no blood anywhere. The girl hadn't been injured; her easy, supple movements told me that.

'Ana? What happened?'

'...hiding,' she mumbled. Then Esme barked.

'Hiding? Why?'

Ana's eyes flickered, alerting me.

I started to swing around as a hand came down hard on my shoulder. '*Gotcha!*' It was Nerine.

I jumped up. Colette was perched on her mother's hip, grubby and tousled. One of her feet was bare, but she didn't look upset. In fact her delight at seeing Esme was only too obvious.

Nerine was grinning. 'I win!' she told Ana. To me she said, 'I didn't expect you back so soon.'

I was stunned. Adrift. 'What's going on? What's all this about?'

'Hide-and-seek,' Nerine replied.

'Hide-and-seek?'

'They have to learn how to hide.' Nerine suddenly noticed the shoe I was clutching. 'Oh! You found it. Good.'

Then Ana slipped her hand into mine. Her smile, as she gazed up at me, was anxiously hopeful.

'She's been asking about her present,' Nerine observed. 'I guess we'd better head back.' Then she looked around, her forehead creasing. 'Which way *is* back? I get a bit lost out here.'

I pointed. She nodded. Then she plucked the shoe from my grip, pushed it onto Colette's foot and set off in the direction of the house, adding over her shoulder, 'That was very good, Big Bug. That was half an hour. You did well.'

On our way back home, Nerine explained to me that she herself had managed to lie low for nearly an hour before Ana had found her. It was quite a skill, keeping quiet for long periods of time. But with proper training, Analiese had been getting better and better.

'One of these days,' Nerine said, within earshot of both girls, 'it might save her life.'

I didn't respond. I couldn't.

The whole episode had left me speechless.

That night Keith called.

I was scrubbing an oven tray, trying to work out what I should tell Nerine. The sticker books had helped fill the afternoon. The Freddo frogs had added a celebratory twist to dinner. I'd had no trouble dealing with the kids, but talking to their mother was difficult. My experience out in the bush had shaken me; I was jumpy, distracted and acutely conscious of knowing something Nerine didn't: namely, that her husband was missing. I realised I would have to tell her at some point, but wasn't looking forward to it.

Had I made the right decision, waiting until the children were asleep? I didn't want to discuss their father in front of them, but I also didn't want Nerine dragging them out of bed in a panic. There didn't seem to be a solution. I was stymied.

Then the landline rang. It took me a few seconds to pull off my wet rubber gloves; I picked up on the fifth ring.

'Hello?' I said.

'You must be very pleased with yourself.'

I recognised Keith's voice instantly—in fact my body reacted before my brain did. A wave of nausea washed through me as I stiffened.

'What do you want?' I asked.

'Justice.'

'What?'

'She was my mother. And you turned her against me when she couldn't think for herself.' His tone was hectoring.

Intense. 'Now I know why you were always hanging around that nursing home. You wanted to worm your way into her finances—'

I cut him off. 'I know you've been making those anonymous calls, Keith. I could take out an AVO.'

'What are you talking about?' he spluttered. 'You're crazy.'

'You're the one who's crazy.' I'd recovered a little; the nausea had receded and I'd been gulping down air. But my voice quivered as I said, 'This is harassment. If you set *foot* on my land again, I'll have you arrested for trespassing.'

'*Trespassing?* Are you making false accusations?'

I cringed, holding the phone away from my ear. 'Listen—'

'Because it won't work. You won't win. I'm going to appeal against this injustice, and no smear campaign is going to stop me.'

'I've seen you, Keith.'

'What?'

'You drive a dark grey Mazda, don't you?'

There was a moment's silence at the other end of the line. Then he hissed, 'You're insane. You're sick.'

'And you're a stalker.'

'*Me?* Stalk *you?*' His laugh was jagged. 'You're delusional.'

'If you come here again I'll call the police.'

'You do that,' he yammered. 'You do that and they'll see you're a crazy woman making false reports. It will only help my case.'

'You don't have a case.'

'Prove it! Go on!' He lowered his voice. 'If you keep

fighting me, you're going to lose every cent along the way. So you might as well give up now and save yourself the stress.'

'Is that why you called? To threaten me?' My throat felt tight. My hands were shaking. I could hardly breathe.

'You'll never get that money. It's mine. You drove my daughter out of the country, you poisoned my mother's mind, and now you want to steal my inheritance—'

'Don't come here again.' I wasn't about to listen to him venting anymore. I'd done it for years and I'd had enough. 'Don't call. Don't write.' Then, because my anxiety levels were through the roof, I blurted out, 'I can defend myself, you know. I live on a farm.'

'What? *What*? Are you threatening me?'

'You threatened me.'

'That's it. I'm calling the police. I'm taking out an AVO.'

'Keith—'

'You're a public menace. You're unstable. I'm going to drag you through the courts until you don't even have a roof over your head.' Before I could argue, he finished, 'I wanted to discuss this like civilised human beings, but it's impossible with you. You're paranoid. You can't be reasoned with. No wonder Emily left.'

He hung up.

My hand was so unsteady I had a hard time fitting the handset back onto its cradle. I felt as if I'd been hit by a car. It was so long since I'd been exposed to one of Keith's rants that I'd forgotten how to defend myself.

Turning, I gave a start. Nerine was staring at me from the kitchen doorway.

'Keith?' she said.

I nodded.

'Have a drink,' she advised me. 'That's what I always do.' She handed me a glass of pinot—and as I took it, I decided not to tell her about Duncan.

After the stoush with Keith, I couldn't face any more stress.

SUNDAY LUNCH

SALLY AND DINAH lived on a proper farm. It wasn't a scrubby, ridge-top acreage like mine; it was in a lush valley, and the house itself was built halfway up a hill, overlooking a creek. Tall stands of mountain timber ringed the valley, but Dinah insisted it wasn't a firetrap because there were two ways out. Besides, there was a very large dam on the property and half-a-dozen concrete tanks attached to an emergency watering system. Dinah said that if a fire came over the hill, she'd stay and fight.

Sally didn't seem quite so sure.

They came down the front steps to greet me when I pulled up outside their sprawling, nineteenth-century homestead. It was made of timber and tin and had everything I'd ever wanted: French doors, stone fireplaces, a bullnose veranda. The rooms inside were a little dark, and hard to heat because of their high ceilings, but Dinah had painted them in pale, airy colours, and hung linen curtains the colour of buttermilk, and laid sturdy kilims on the stripped-pine floors. I'd learnt not to compliment Sally on her new fixtures and fittings because it was Dinah who cared for the house and outbuildings, as well as the animals and the garden. Sally invested so much energy in her medical practice that she liked to spend her weekends reading books and listening to podcasts. Lately, she'd also been in charge of their battle to adopt—and that had consumed a lot of time.

Sally's main hobby, however, was cooking. When I entered the big country kitchen at the back of the house, it was full of peelings and spice jars and luscious smells; she told me that she would be serving lamb pilaf and roast pumpkin salad, then produced a platter covered with dips and cheese and olives and lavash. I accepted a glass of sparkling mineral water, sampled the bread and cheese, admired the new oven, and secretly wished I was home in bed.

I'd had another fitful night's sleep followed by an early awakening. Colette had started screaming like a banshee at ten past five, rousing the whole house and making me worry that the Huggetts might hear. Nerine had been unable to explain why her younger daughter was throwing a blue-faced, head-banging tantrum. 'It's probably PTSD,' she'd said glumly.

Even Esme's warmth hadn't been enough to quiet Colette. Eventually Nerine had been forced to dump the poor little girl in a cold bath, which had shocked her into silence.

All of us had been completely wrung out after that, though Ana had still felt energetic enough to hang off me when I'd tried to walk out the door. 'Don't go,' she'd begged.

'I want you to stay. Stay, Meg, stay.'

I don't think I've ever set off for a Sunday lunch with less enthusiasm.

'Keith rang last night,' I told Sally, after she'd observed that I looked tired. She looked pretty tired herself, and thinner than ever; there were dark smudges under her eyes.

'You're kidding,' said Dinah.

'He had a go at me.'

'What did he say?' Sally demanded.

My account of Keith's phone call made Dinah fume and Sally shake her head. They had so much to say that at first I didn't notice the place settings. It wasn't until we'd thoroughly dissected Keith's possible motives and future tactics that I realised the dining table had been set for four instead of three.

'Are we expecting someone else?' I asked, with a nod at the nearest empty chair.

Dinah and Sally exchanged a furtive glance. Then Sally said, 'Tearle Godwin.'

My jaw dropped.

'Don't look at me.' Sally raised a defensive hand. 'It was Dinah.'

'These things are always easier in a group,' Dinah argued. 'It means you can socialise without any kind of pressure.'

Sally snorted. 'Yeah, right.'

'It's true,' Dinah insisted.

'No pressure? With you sitting there?' Sally turned to me. 'She can't help herself. She's a born matchmaker.'

'It's stockbreeding that does it,' Dinah said with a wink.

'Oh, please.' Sally pulled a disgusted face as she sautéed a handful of diced carrots. 'Poor Meg's going to walk out of here if you don't stop.'

'She doesn't mind. Do you, Meg?' Dinah threw an arm across my shoulders. I had to brace myself; her arm was amazingly heavy.

'Of course not,' I said, squinting up at her. 'Tearle's a friend. But that's all he is, Di. A friend.'

'I keep telling her that,' Sally complained.

'And I keep telling *her* it's a good start.' Dinah began to steer me towards the French doors at the back of the house. 'Come and see your pullets. Did you bring any carry cages?'

'I've only got one.'

'You can borrow some of ours if you want.' Pausing on the threshold, she asked Sally, 'Ten minutes?'

Sally nodded. 'Off you go.'

'Tearle will keep you company.' Dinah winked again as she hustled me out.

I'd always been envious of Dinah's chicken run. It was a very large shed attached to a fully fenced area the size of a small paddock. Some of her chickens were inside the run, but many were roaming about the farmyard, watched over by her white maremma sheepdog, Stanley.

Stanley barked when he saw us and eyed me with obvious misgiving. Dinah ignored him and ushered me into the poultry shed where, among all the roost bars and dropping boards, three young chickens were scratching in a corner pen. One of the birds was black, the others brown. They were still at the scrawny stage, but bigger than I'd expected.

'The ISAs are three months old,' said Dinah. 'The Australorp's a week older.'

'Do they have names?'

'"Meg's pullets".'

'How much?'

She tapped her chin with one finger. 'Hmmm. Let's see, now. How much should I charge a wealthy woman for these magnificent girls...?' Before I could make an offer, she laughed and said, 'Twenty each?'

'Di, that's too low.'

'I know you'll look after 'em.'

'But—'

'Next thing: the gun.' Suddenly her expression changed. It became more serious as she looked me straight in the eye. 'To be honest, I've hunted with unlicensed shooters before, but this is a step beyond. You wouldn't need the gun for long, would you? I mean—you have your trap ready?'

I nodded, acutely conscious of the flush mantling my cheeks.

'It's humane, right? A cage trap?' she pressed.

Again I nodded.

'Then you can shoot through the bars. Shouldn't be a problem.' Seeing my surprise, Dinah lowered her voice and said, 'If the gun's properly stored and you know how to use it, I can live with a loan. Especially if you've only got the thing for a week. But you should apply for a licence, Meg.'

'I know. I will.' I felt so shamefaced that I could barely lift my gaze from the ground.

'You'd get one, no problem. That's why this doesn't bother me. For someone with chickens, though, you need to think long-term...' She trailed off, frowning; she seemed to sense my agitation. 'What's wrong?' she asked. 'There's nothing to be guilty about. Foxes are feral—it's not like you're shooting a kangaroo.' Gripping my arm, she nudged me towards the exit. 'Sally offered to get hold of some ether but I told her the fox would tear you apart if you tried anything like that. One shot to the head will be quick enough...'

She kept talking as she guided me across the farmyard, through the kitchen and into her office, which was a small, messy room with a security screen on the window and a gun safe fastened to the wall in one corner. I'd seen this safe many times, but I'd never seen it open.

I was surprised to discover that not one but two rifles were hanging inside.

'I'll lend you the Remington because it's a better fit in my rifle case,' Dinah said breezily. 'Plus there's not much recoil with this one, so you won't hurt yourself.' She straightened up, a gun in one hand and a cardboard box of ammunition in the other. 'Don't look so scared, Meg. I'll show you how to load and aim and shoot, and I guarantee you won't have any trouble.' To my surprise, she slung the rifle over her shoulder and beamed at me. 'Come on.'

'What—you mean *now*?'

'Why not? We won't bother anyone if we head up the hill.'

I hesitated, because it was all happening too fast. I'd been waiting for Dinah to turn me down; I couldn't believe that she'd actually decided to lend me her gun. Certainly I'd never expected that I would have to fire it. The only reason I'd asked for it in the first place was to reassure Nerine. I was hoping that if I waved it around enough, she would feel safer.

'Come on, Meg.' Dinah was emptying some of the bullets from the cardboard box into her hand. They looked like miniature missiles. 'We need to do this before Tearle shows up. I don't think he'd really approve, do you?'

'No,' I mumbled, though to be honest I wasn't sure.

Someone with a house full of pistols probably wasn't as gun-shy as he looked.

Before loading her rifle, Dinah showed me how to remove the scope and bolt. Something about the whole process reminded me of my flute—how I used to pull the headjoint and footjoint off the body and pack all the pieces away in a velvet-lined case after shaking out the spit.

I started playing the flute in fourth grade, and took it with me to university. Despite years of piano lessons, and a lingering fondness for the accordion, I was only really serious about the flute—until I met Keith. I was working at a bar in Paddington when he walked up to me and said, 'I know you. You're that busker from the markets.' Then he asked me out on our first date.

I went because he told me we'd be eating at Rockpool, which in those days was like eating at the Ritz. I'd never been there, but I'd heard about it. The elegance of the decor, the size of the plates, the suaveness of the waiters—all of it took my breath away. At the time I was living in a mouldy share house with five other people; sometimes all we had to eat was baked beans on a bed of spaghetti. No wonder I was starry-eyed as I strolled along the harbour with Keith, who looked beautiful in his midnight-blue dinner jacket.

None of the men I knew in Sydney even owned a jacket.

That first date was magic. Keith made me feel part of a new world—vibrant, moneyed, downtown Sydney. Over the next few weeks he took me to clubs, to galleries, to fancy hotels. He told me I had the looks and talent to play in a band, though he said I should concentrate on keyboards. There wasn't room in rock music for more than one Jethro Tull, he said.

It wasn't long before I'd dropped the flute and thrown myself into mastering synths and electric piano.

Keith was managing two bands at the time, and I joined one of them: Sneaky Feelings, it was called. We were together for about three years. At one point we were getting quite a few gigs, though they tended to be around Kings Cross instead of Newtown and Annandale. It made me wonder about the kind of people Keith mixed with. I never saw any evidence that he actually broke the law, but he seemed to enjoy the company of people who did: dodgy lawyers, bent cops and the kind of restaurateurs who dealt drugs out the back door. He was always looking for loopholes, shortcuts, grey areas. It made me anxious, but I turned a blind eye because I'd grown up with a man who didn't mind bending the law when it came to helping his friends or harassing his enemies. I'd come to realise that the law isn't immutable, or beyond reproach. I'd learnt that sometimes, in individual cases, it's harsh, crude, one-eyed—even immoral.

That was why I'd agreed to help Nerine. I thought it was immoral to give her abusive ex-partner free access to her children.

Dinah Hodges probably didn't think it was immoral to withhold a gun from an unlicensed shooter. But she would have spent so much of her life feeling marginal that I wasn't so very surprised to learn she had a fairly pragmatic attitude towards lending firearms. It must have annoyed her that a highly respectable middle-aged citizen had to shell out hard-earnt money for permission to kill one measly fox. She must have felt that the safety of my new pullets was more important than filling in a form.

At least, that's how I assume she felt. I don't really know. All I know is that she took me up the hill at the back of her farm and showed me how to use her .223 Remington Model Seven bolt-action rifle.

Dinah told me that transporting a rifle was safer if you removed the bolt, which was just like the bolt on a door; she opened it by lifting and pulling back the attached handle. Then she pressed a tiny button in front of the trigger and the bolt slid free. 'Now you do it,' she said, and I did. It wasn't hard.

Next she demonstrated how to load the gun. After opening the bolt, she pushed three shiny bullets into the magazine.

'This gun is now loaded,' she explained, 'but it can't be fired. Not until I close the bolt and push the first round into the chamber.' Having done that, she released the safety switch over by the trigger guard. 'When your safety's off, and there's a round in the chamber, you're good to go,' she announced.

Next she reversed the whole procedure, unloading the gun so I could repeat all the steps myself. It was surprisingly fiddly. The fact that I kept dropping the shells from sheer nervousness didn't help, either; I jumped like a frightened rabbit the first time *that* happened. 'Don't worry,' Dinah said. 'They won't explode.'

In the end we spent more time loading and unloading the rifle than we did actually shooting it. 'Never load a gun unless you're ready to fire,' Dinah told me, over and over again. She showed me how to hold the gun safely. She showed me what to do if a round failed to discharge. She didn't show me how to use the scope because, she said, I wouldn't be needing it—not while I was shooting at close range. But I would be needing goggles and earmuffs.

'You don't want any ricochet, so make sure the cage isn't on a hard surface,' she said, adding that I should stick the muzzle of the gun inside the cage and aim for the animal's forehead from a distance of about fifteen centimetres. 'You can do that, can't you? Is there enough space between the bars?'

I nodded glumly. Would I have to buy a trap in case Dinah ever asked to see it? Perhaps I could tell her that I'd thrown it out because I hadn't wanted to clean fox brains off the steel mesh.

'You might have to use a stool or a crate to get down low enough for a clean shot,' she continued, as she placed the stock of the gun against my right shoulder. Then she positioned my left hand directly in front of the trigger guard, adjusted my stance, pushed my head slightly to the right and told me to aim at a weathered, leaking sandbag on the ground about half a metre away. 'Just let me get clear first,' she said, slapping the muffs over my ears.

With Dinah chivvying me along like one of her wayward cows, I hadn't really had time to consider what I was doing. Now, staring down the barrel of a very large, very heavy rifle, I almost had to pinch myself. The gun had seemed like an extension of Dinah, who'd handled it with a crisp, capable efficiency that made me realise why Sally had fallen for her in the first place. But to arm someone like me, short and heavy and dressed in a pale pink cardigan...well, it just seemed ridiculous.

When I pulled the trigger, the noise and recoil nearly made me drop the gun.

'Good!' Suddenly Dinah was with me again. She helped me pull back the bolt, and the empty cartridge sprang from the chamber, landing at my feet. When I shoved the bolt forward, everything clicked smoothly back into place.

'Try again,' she said.

I tried again. And again. My shots all hit the sandbag; I would have been surprised if they hadn't, since they were fired from about one metre away. I was just pushing the next three rounds into the magazine, under Dinah's careful supervision, when out of the blue she said, 'Whoops! There he is!'

I raised my head, startled. Dinah pointed down the hill at the distant road that snaked through the valley. A silver sedan was smoothly negotiating one of the trickier bends.

'That's Tearle's car,' she went on. 'We'd better get back. When he's gone, we can give it another try.'

'Are you sure?' I didn't want to put her out.

'God, yes. You need more practice.' Seeing my downcast expression, she patted me with one hand as she relieved me of her rifle with the other. 'You were fine,' she said. 'But you want more confidence. Let me put this away while you distract Tearle.'

Obediently I shuffled back to the house, treading carefully because the slope was quite steep and scattered with loose pebbles. By the time I reached the farmyard, Dinah had already overtaken me. But instead of making for the back door, she ducked behind the chicken run.

I assumed she was going to sneak around to the front veranda so Tearle wouldn't see the rifle.

'There you are!' Sally beckoned to me from the kitchen.

Tearle was standing next to her, holding a glass of home-made lemonade. He looked stiff and formal in his linen jacket and silk cravat, but offered me an awkward little smile when I joined him.

'Hello, Meg,' he murmured. 'Sally was telling me about Keith.'

'Oh.' The phone call. 'Yes. That was no fun.'

'You could take out an AVO,' he said.

'Let's not talk about AVOs.' I didn't want to approach the police. Nor did I want Tearle to approach the police on my behalf. In fact I was eager to avoid the police at all costs. 'Sally and Dinah are selling me some hens,' I told him. 'A fox killed most of mine the other day.'

'I'm sorry.'

'It was my own stupid fault. I left the gate open.' I shook my head as Sally raised the lemonade jug. 'Wish I could, Sal. It's too acidic for my bladder.'

The words were hardly out of my mouth before I regretted them. But Tearle smiled again—a wider smile, this time—and said, 'At least now you'll have the funds to keep your new hens in luxury.'

Then Dinah entered from the hallway, empty-handed. She greeted Tearle like an old friend, though I was pretty sure they didn't know each other very well. Dinah rarely visited Bulwell. Sally, on the other hand, was there all the time. She and Tearle had been on some committee together. Chamber of Commerce? Tidy Town panel? Something like that.

'I hope you guys eat leeks,' Dinah said, 'because we have a glut and we need to offload.'

'Bumper crop,' Sally nodded. 'But you can only cook so many leeks for two people.' The shadow that crossed her face made me suddenly remember how much she wanted a bigger family. And as Tearle gravely thanked her, I wondered if I should ask about the adoption thing.

'I'll pack each of you a veggie box to take home,' Dinah declared. 'We need to get rid of some cabbage, as well.'

'You have such a green thumb, Di.' I couldn't help sounding envious. 'My garden's a mess. The grubs and possums get into everything.'

We discussed pest control for a while as Sally pointed us towards an arrangement of large bowls and told us to serve ourselves. I dished up generous portions of pilaf, salad and yoghurt, then sat down next to Dinah.

'This is delicious, Sal,' I said. It was a relief to eat something that wasn't very plain, very sweet or covered in ketchup.

For a while we talked about the work Sally and Tearle had done together on the local council's disability advisory board. Then we discussed my court win. Tearle told some barrister stories; his humour was very dry and a little creaky, but I appreciated the effort. We also touched on the adoption process, which had been long and painful for Dinah and Sally. 'We've signed up to foster a child,' Dinah said. 'It'll give us some practice.'

We were just hoeing into Sally's apricot custard flan when my mobile chirped, deep inside my handbag. Everyone looked at me. But I knew it would be Nerine, having another panic attack, and I wanted to avoid getting flustered in public. I was concerned that Dinah might have second thoughts about lending her gun to a flustered woman.

'It'll keep,' I said, and forgot all about it.

Three hours later, on my way home, I pulled over and tried to call Nerine. When she didn't pick up, I left a message: 'It's me. I'm sorry. I'll be there soon.' I'd already checked my mobile and confirmed that she'd tried to ring me twice. The second time I'd been up on the hill again, shooting at sandbags. After that, Dinah had kept me busy for over half an hour, caging the pullets and loading them into my car. Then she'd locked the Remington in a rifle case and the two bullets in a cash box ('You won't need more than two rounds') and we'd packed *them* into the boot along with a crate of vegetables and a jar of her neighbour's honey. Our goodbyes had been warm and protracted.

'If you have any trouble with Keith,' she'd said with a glint in her eye, 'just give me a call. You've seen my arsenal. I'll come straight over and scare the living daylights out of him.' I could tell she was serious.

I left the farm at half past three with my new chickens wedged into the back seat and Dinah's rifle sharing the boot with about four kilos of leeks, cabbages and broccoli. The chickens were very disturbed; I didn't want to stress them by extending their time in the car, so after making my call I hastily resumed my interrupted journey home—which took about half an hour. I barely noticed the drive because I was too busy reviewing the more peculiar aspects of my visit: Dinah's unexpected generosity, Sally's confession about foster care, Tearle's creaky charm as he dusted off various ancient legal stories. I had a feeling he was perplexed by the lunch invitation, though he hadn't asked me if I was behind it.

I was hoping he hadn't got the wrong idea when I bumped down the last stretch of driveway and saw my garden gate standing ajar. Not only that—Ruby was scratching around outside the fence, blocking my way.

'Oh, for...' I braked with a curse. Then I switched off the engine, telling myself that I couldn't blame the children for being careless. I would certainly have a word with Nerine, though. Had she gone for a walk again? Perhaps she was playing her paranoid version of hide-and-seek.

Knowing I wouldn't be able to catch the runaway hen, I tried to chase her back through the gate by running at her and flapping my arms. It worked; she was soon scurrying past the shed towards the house, all ruffled feathers and pedalling feet. I was about to head back to the car when I noticed something on the ground that brought me to a screeching halt.

Unfamiliar tyre tracks.

AN UNEXPECTED VISITOR

'NERINE?' I CALLED. But there was no answer.

I stood for a moment, undecided. Should I drive in and close the gate, or leave the gate open in case I needed to get out fast? My brain felt sluggish. Overwhelmed. I knew I had to decide but I couldn't think it through…

I headed for the front door, hoping that the pullets in the back of the car would be fine for a few minutes. After all, I'd left a window open. The older hens were nowhere in sight; Ruby had scooted around the side of the house and the others were either down the back or lost in the bush.

I was wondering why Esme hadn't barked when I climbed the front steps and saw her.

She lay sprawled on the veranda in a pool of blood. I must have heard the low hum of flies but it hadn't registered; I only became conscious of the noise when I saw her pale coat, covered in red smears.

The shock was like a punch in the ribs. I couldn't scream.

I couldn't even draw breath.

I still don't remember exactly what happened after that. Time froze. My mind stopped working. I couldn't process what was in front of me: Esme, the wound, the blood. Blood everywhere. Sprays of it, all over the wall. All over the cane furniture. All over her.

She was dead. I saw that instantly, but I couldn't believe it. I felt as if I was in a dream. My vision blurred, my throat closed up, my knees turned to cottonwool. I had to grab a post to keep myself upright.

Esme, I thought. *Esme.* I wanted to grab her and hug her and weep and wail and destroy the whole house with my bare hands. I wanted to beat my skull against the nearest wall. I wanted to kill. Shriek. Throw myself down and never get up again.

As my head cleared, however, something stopped me. An awareness—a sudden spurt of fear.

Esme had been slaughtered. Her throat was cut.

A jumble of words and images seemed to engulf me like a wave. Ana. Colette. Nerine speaking: '*He cut its throat.*'

Duncan had killed their dog. Had he killed mine too?

I spun around and stumbled down the front stairs. Then I rushed back to the car, where I yanked open the boot. The keys to Dinah's cash box and rifle case were hanging off my keyring; it didn't take more than a few seconds to retrieve the gun and two bullets. Loading took a little longer. My hands were shaking and I wasn't thinking straight. But at last I pushed a round into the chamber.

Next I banged the boot shut and made for the house

again, holding the rifle against my right shoulder with the barrel down and the safety on, as Dinah had shown me. The further I went, the heavier it felt.

I started to climb the veranda steps. 'Nerine?' My voice was a raw whisper.

No response. Just the buzzing of flies.

Opening the front door should have been the hardest thing I've ever done, but by that time I no longer felt afraid. I no longer felt anything, though my face was wet with tears. It was as if my fear had taken over, propelling me forward, snuffing out all emotion as I watched everything numbly, from a distance.

I raised the gun as I entered the vestibule. 'Nerine?'

'Meg?'

'*Nerine!*'

I staggered into the living room, which was a mess. The television had been smashed. A lamp had been knocked over. The phone lay on the floor, its cord hacked and its keypad crushed.

Then Nerine appeared, framed in the doorway. She had a scab on her lip, a lump on her forehead, bruises and scratches on her neck.

She'd spread iodine on the scratches.

'He came,' she whimpered. Her eyes welled.

I tried to speak but couldn't. My expression must have been enough.

Nerine gave a sob and threw herself across the room, straight at me. I had to step back, pivoting a little to shield her from the gun.

'Careful,' I squawked, but she hugged me anyway, mumbling into my shoulder. I couldn't make out what she was saying.

'The kids,' I said. 'Where are the kids?'

Her muffled answer told me nothing.

'Nerine! Where are they? Did he take them?'

She pulled back at last, shaking her head and wiping her nose. 'They're in the cupboard.'

'Are they all right?'

With a nod she said, 'Hiding.'

'What happened? Where is he?'

Tears spilled down her cheeks, which were smeared with mascara. 'I'm so sorry,' she snivelled. 'He killed your dog.'

'*Where is he, Nerine?*'

She pointed at the front door.

'What do you mean?' I didn't understand. 'He left?'

'Nnnn-nnn...' Again she shook her head, lips trembling. 'Oh, Meg...oh, Meg...'

'Did you call the police?'

'No!' She grabbed my arm, thrust her face into mine and hissed, 'He's still here.'

'What?'

'Out there. In the shed.' As I stared at her she gabbled, 'I had to do *something*. He was gunna take the kids!'

She started tugging me towards the front door, muttering disjointed sentences. She didn't know what to do...he'd killed the dog...she'd hit him pretty hard...

'He came at me,' she moaned. 'He came at me with a knife.'

The screen door slammed open. She hustled me across the veranda, down the stairs, towards my shed—a fibro building large enough to house a couple of tractors. I used it mainly for storing things like spare rolls of fence wire, star pickets and chicken feed, as well as a crateful of old appliances the previous owner had left behind: an iron, a kettle, a chainsaw I'd never tried out because it looked so dangerous. The kids' car seats were also in there, tucked behind a stack of paint cans.

But now something new was in the shed.

Nerine pushed the roller door up and slowly unveiled an unfamiliar vehicle: tyres, bumper bar, headlights, then the grille, bonnet, windscreen…In some distant corner of my brain I identified it as a blue Mitsubishi Lancer, dented and mud-flecked, but that information never really bobbed to the surface before it was swept away by a tide of shock.

A man was hanging behind the car, in the gloom down the back. His hands were bound over his head with a length of spare clothesline which had been threaded over a rafter tie, then knotted around a wall bracket. I couldn't see his face— just the top of his head.

Blood was streaked across his forearms from where the cord had cut into his wrists.

I've seen some horrible things in my life. A heaving pile of maggots shaped like a dead lizard. Emily's face, after Keith told her she was probably not his daughter. A severed arm lying on the road when my father pulled over to help with a car accident.

But nothing was ever as bad as that man in my shed, dangling from the roof like a side of beef. The details are stamped on my memory. He was small and neatly built, with curly dark hair and tattoos. He wore a black T-shirt over torn jeans. He was smeared with dirt and blood.

'Oh my God.' I shoved my gun into Nerine's hands and rushed forward.

'Wait! Meg!'

The man's mouth was covered in duct tape; I saw it when I pushed his chin up. His face was blue. His eyes were closed and didn't open when I started ripping the tape off.

'Cut him down! Are you mad? Cut him down!' I wailed.

'Meg, stop—he'll bite you—'

'*Cut him down.*'

I patted his cheek, which was scrubby and cool. The blood that drenched it had run down from a wound in his head. I couldn't feel his breath on my wrist. He kept swinging and turning like a pendant as I touched him.

It was horrendous. Unspeakable. He smelled of sweat and urine.

'If I cut him down, he'll kill us!' There was an edge of hysteria in Nerine's voice. 'Don't wake him—Meg, *don't.*'

There was no chance of waking him. The sharp tang of urine made me feel for a pulse in his neck, but no matter how hard I tried, I couldn't find one.

'He's dead,' I whispered.

'What?'

'Oh my God. Oh my God.' I stepped back and put a hand on each knee, doubled over. I heaved and retched but I couldn't vomit.

'He can't be dead.' Nerine sounded dazed. 'All I did was hit him.'

'Oh my God.'

'He was alive a minute ago. He was trying to kick me.'

'You killed him.'

'I did not!' She lurched forward, the rifle slung over her shoulder, and began to slap his face. 'Wake up, you fucker! Wake up!'

'Stop it!' I gave her such a shove that she staggered and nearly fell. Then I sat down on the nearest bale of straw, my head spinning. I'd wandered into a nightmare. 'We should call the police,' I said.

'No.'

'Nerine…' My voice cracked as tears began to drip down my nose. 'We can't do this anymore.'

'We have to. For the kids' sake.'

I stared at her. Was she delusional? 'It's over.'

'I'll go to jail, you moron! And the kids will go to foster care!'

'It was an accident. He was attacking you. It was self-defence.'

'Oh, yeah? How am I gunna prove that?'

'You've been hit, Nerine.' The proof was on her face. 'It's obvious.'

'For Chrissake, would you listen to yourself?' Her caustic, derisory tone made me cringe. 'Who cares if he hit me? I *killed* him. And you took me in, Meg—you'll go to jail too, if you call the cops.'

My jaw flapped, but I couldn't speak. She was right. I'd broken the law. I had helped her violate a court order.

Would I really go to jail, though?

'He killed your dog, for fuck's sake,' she went on. 'Don't you care about that?'

'Of course I do, but—'

'He fucking deserved it!' She started to prowl up and down in front of the corpse that revolved slowly at the end of the cord like a set of windchimes. 'He tried to kill me. He had a knife. He said he'd kill the kids first, to make me suffer, and then he'd slice me open—'

'We have to cut him down.' I couldn't bear to watch him dangle there.

'Yeah, let's do that.' Nerine stopped abruptly, her eyes narrowing. 'Then we can dump him in his car and push it over the cliff.' Hearing me gasp, she said, 'No one knows he's here. He told me. He had to make sure he wouldn't get blamed for anything that happened.'

'Oh, no.' I started shaking my head as I rose again, my hands fending off such a monstrous idea. 'No. No, no.'

'It'll work,' she insisted.

'Are you crazy?' She looked crazy. Her eyes were ringed by black smudges. Her chin was streaked with blood. Her hair was sticking to the sweat on her face.

'I saw that cliff, Meg. When we were out playing hide-and-seek. There's bush at the bottom—it'll hide anything we throw into it.' Before I could protest, she asked, 'Do you have a knife?'

'A *knife?*'

'We can't cut him down without a knife.' She pointed at the bit of cord knotted to the wall bracket.

'But—'

'You said you wanted him down.'

It was true. I did want him down. So I shuffled over to the wall bracket as Nerine headed for the car. 'What about the kids?' I muttered. 'What about Colette? We can't just leave her with Ana...'

'Wouldn't be the first time,' Nerine said grimly. I wasn't looking at her; I was examining the knots in the clothesline, which were pulled so tight I knew I couldn't possibly untie them. I was reaching for a pair of secateurs when the Lancer roared to life behind me.

I spun around and saw Nerine in the driver's seat, the gun across her lap, the door beside her hanging open.

'What are you doing?' I had to shout above the engine noise. Nerine didn't answer because she didn't have to: the car was already reversing towards the man on the rope. Even as I cried out, the rear bumper hit his legs.

'Wait!' Nerine yelled. She yanked at the handbrake, jumped out of the car and pushed the man aside like a curtain to reach the catch on the boot. When its lid sprang open, she positioned his swinging feet over the ropes and rags that were suddenly revealed. 'Now,' she ordered.

I gaped at her.

'*Now.*' She took a step back, fixing me with her fierce green glare. 'Let him down.'

Stunned, I did as I was told. The secateurs weren't as sharp as they could have been; I had to chomp away at the nylon cord with scissoring blades until it finally broke. The man on the other end of the line dropped into the boot of his car with a sickening crunch of bone hitting metal.

'Help me,' said Nerine. She pushed at one of his legs, which was draped over the numberplate.

I stood frozen. The impact of his fall was still reverberating through my body.

'Come on,' Nerine snapped. She tossed one floppy hand onto his chest like someone chucking an empty can into a bin. 'We have to get him inside.'

I swallowed and shook my head. Then I made for the door.

'Meg!' The boot slammed shut. 'Where are you going?'

'I'm calling the police.'

'Meg!'

My mobile was in my handbag. My handbag was in my car. I didn't know what the reception would be like—it was generally non-existent here—but with the landline cut, there was no choice. Maybe I could drive out to the road and try for a signal there.

'Meg, stop!'

'We can't do this. I'm sorry. We can't.' My head had cleared. I was thinking again, finding a logical path through the fear and the horror. 'It was self-defence. I know we'll face charges, but it's better than what we'll face if we try to cover this up. We need to think of the kids.'

'I *am* thinking of the kids.' She sounded frantic, but I didn't turn around to look. 'I'm keeping 'em out of foster care. I'm keeping 'em safe.'

'This isn't safe.' I hurried towards the garden gate, shaky and tearful; things would only get worse if I didn't take a stand.

Then I heard a faint, mechanical click.

'I said stop!' Nerine barked.

When I looked back she was aiming the rifle straight at me.

My father wore a Smith and Wesson revolver at work. He wasn't supposed to bring it home, but sometimes he did because Taree was a small town. Occasionally, on his way from one domestic crisis to another, he would drop by the house to change his bloodstained clothes or pick up something he'd forgotten. And if I wasn't at school, I would catch a glimpse of his gun as he strode past me with a frown on his face.

My brothers were fascinated by the revolver but I was afraid of it. So was my mum. Every time it appeared in the kitchen, however briefly, she would flinch and mutter something about 'scaring the children', taking care to shoo me away if I happened to be around. Dad would ignore her, as usual, but I got the message loud and clear: guns were dangerous, scary, sinister things.

For my brothers, the glamour outweighed the risk. Brian kept boasting to his mates that he'd actually used my dad's revolver—that Dad kept the weapon at home sometimes, in a safe he didn't always lock. Wild tales of shots fired at burglars and dingos finally found their way back to the chief inspector, who felt compelled to 'clear things up'.

I doubt the stories were taken very seriously except by my father, who came storming home and laid into Brian with a ping-pong bat. Dad's fit of rage seemed to underscore the gun's menace. For me, the deadly little weapon became imbued with an almost supernatural aura. That was why I'd been so nervous about handling Dinah's rifle. That was why, when Nerine pointed it in my direction, it did more than just paralyse me.

It turned me back into a helpless, pliant, frightened little girl.

'You'd be doing the same thing,' Nerine said. She was sitting in the back of the Lancer, not directly behind the driver's seat but a bit to my left, so she had room to aim the gun. 'If Emily'd been threatened with foster care, you'd have done anything to stop it. Anything. It's all about the kids, Meg. They come first.'

If the kids come first, I thought, *why have you left them alone?* I didn't say it aloud. I was too scared of her. She'd turned into an enemy. An armed threat.

Instead I mumbled, 'Could you please aim that thing away from me? This is a really bumpy track.'

'I've got the safety on.' Nerine's voice was flat and hoarse. 'My brother used to hunt. Pigs, goats, you name it. I know how guns work.' Without waiting for a response, she added, 'My brother was friends with those bikers I was telling you about—the ones that pay fishing boats to smuggle drugs. I reckon I could find 'em again if I had a few thousand dollars.'

We were rattling down the fire trail, the Baumanns' electric fence to our left. I was driving the unfamiliar car nervously. It was a manual, and had stickier brakes than I was used to. It also smelled of cigarette smoke.

'You know, Meg—once we dump this car, and I get out of your hair, it'll be like nothing ever happened. You can go back to your old life. No one has to know. And if I manage to leave the country, there's no way anyone'll find out we were here. Unless Jill talks.'

I winced as we hit a pothole and the Remington's barrel bounced off the roof.

'What I'm saying is, you can easily get rid of me,' Nerine went on. 'All I need is cash. And now you've won your court case, I can borrow the cash from you.'

I had to clear my throat before answering. 'It'll be months before I get that money.'

'Yeah, but it's on its way. So you're not gunna miss a few thousand bucks in the meantime, are you?'

I was past feeling shocked. All the same, her sheer audacity was unbelievable.

'I've got three thousand in the bank, Nerine. That's all.'

'You could get a loan.'

'I doubt it.'

'With two hundred thou heading your way? 'Course you could.' Her tone brightened. 'Or maybe a mortgage top-up. Do you still have a mortgage?'

We were discussing my financial situation with a dead

body in the boot. It was surreal. It was crazy.

'We're here,' I announced—because we'd reached the end of the Baumanns' fence, where the fire trail took a sharp right along the clifftop. As I braked, however, Nerine said, 'Keep going.'

'What?' I didn't understand.

'Up to the edge.' She sounded impatient. 'You know. Where that lookout is. With the track leading up to it.'

'You didn't bring your kids out here, did you?'

'Just *go.*' She waggled the gun at me, scowling. So I turned right and headed for the lookout, crawling along until I arrived at the spot where I'd dumped my dead chickens. Stopping just short of the rock shelf, gazing out at the view, I suddenly realised that the sun was low and the shadows were lengthening.

'Wait.' Nerine pushed open the rear door. 'Stick it in neutral.'

'What?'

'Stick it in neutral!' She was climbing out. 'Leave the handbrake down and turn off the ignition.' When I failed to absorb these instructions quickly enough, she snapped, 'Unless you wanna *drive* this car over the edge?'

I didn't. Nor did I want to push it. But I didn't have a choice: Nerine was already pointing her gun at the front passenger window. All I could do was shift gears, turn the ignition key and scramble out of the driver's door—hastily, because there was an almost imperceptible incline underfoot.

'Okay, push.' Nerine gestured with the rifle.

I stared at her, open-mouthed. I'd never pushed a car in my life. I didn't have the back for it.

'Go on,' she barked.

'But—'

'Hurry!'

I laid both hands on the boot, then hesitated, overwhelmed by a sickening sense of disbelief. *This can't be happening*, I thought. Was Nerine going to kill me as well? What if I ended up in the gorge with Duncan?

'Meg.' Her tight voice was creaking with barely controlled impatience. 'Just do it.'

On the other hand, Nerine wanted money—and she wouldn't get a cent from me if I was dead. *You're being paranoid*, I told myself, much as Keith would have. Then I gave the Lancer a shove.

To my surprise, it actually moved.

'It's gunna roll,' she said. 'There's a slope.'

Though it wasn't much of a slope, it made things easier. A second shove sent the car drifting forward a couple of metres before it ground to a halt. A third was enough to propel it over a bump and down the wide, smooth top of the boulder, while I fell to my knees and then heaved myself up again, brushing dirt from my hands.

'There she goes!' Nerine exclaimed.

The car was gathering speed, strangely quiet as it coasted down the gentle gradient, its passage marked by just a few clunks and rattles. Watching it, I started to sob uncontrollably. I felt such a wild sense of despair that I had to cover my eyes.

Soon I heard a grinding creak, a crunch, a clang and a huge, earth-shaking thud, followed by a cascade of crashes that ended with a jerky rustling noise.

'Damn,' said Nerine.

When I uncovered my eyes, I saw that she was on the edge of the cliff, peering down into the gorge.

'A door came off.' She turned to look at me. 'You can't see the car, but you can see the door. It's kind of hanging...'

I didn't move—and I wasn't going to. She must have sensed that, because she shrugged and said, 'I have to get back to the kids. We'll sort this out later. Maybe walk up from the bottom. Or use a rope, or something.'

A funny noise, halfway between a snort and a snicker, emerged from my mouth. A rope or something! I could just see us rappelling down the side of the cliff...

'It's for your sake,' she added, heading straight for me. 'I'll be long gone before anyone notices.'

'Someone's going to see it soon,' I mumbled.

'What?'

'It's not the bottom of the ocean, Nerine.' I knew that the base of the gorge was part of the Baumanns' vast spread. It wasn't a well-frequented spot, but someone was bound to come along eventually. 'We're not in the outback—one of these days a stockman or a shooter will find it and then what?'

'Then you'll have a story ready. We'll think of one, okay?' She came right up to me, slung the rifle over her shoulder and gripped my arm. Her fingers felt like little steel rods. 'We're in this together now, Meg. You've got something on me and I've got something on you. As long as we don't lose our nerve, we'll manage.' Releasing me, she paused for a moment, studying my face with her piercing, bloodshot eyes. Then she turned and began to walk away.

'Come on,' she said. 'We need to get back to the kids.'

TRAPPED

I FOUND MYSELF sleepwalking through the rest of the afternoon. Nerine took charge when we arrived back at the house. She drove my car into the yard while I closed the gate. She helped me unload the pullets, then bundled Esme into a drop sheet and dumped her in the boot of the Commodore. She had me show her where all the cleaning equipment was, explaining that she would get rid of the blood while I looked after the children.

Finally, she opened the vestibule cupboard and stuck her head around the side of the door. 'It's me,' she said. 'You can come out now.'

Colette was asleep. She hardly stirred as Ana crawled into the light, speechless, blinking, her grey eyes huge in her small, peaky face. The eczema near her mouth looked like a burn. Mr Snuffles was clamped to her chest.

'Meg's back,' Nerine went on. 'She'll cook tonight. Won't you, Meg?'

I nodded dumbly. I don't know what kind of expression I was wearing, but it didn't seem to reassure Ana. She shrank into herself as she studied me. Then she looked away.

'Everything's fine now. We're safe,' Nerine declared. The rifle was still slung over her shoulder, but that didn't stop her from leaning inside the closet to pick up Colette. 'I'm going out to look for Esme. I'll be back soon. You stay here with Meg, Big Bug. Meg will look after you.'

Ana didn't even nod. She just sat there, her gaze on the floor, listening to her mother's receding footsteps.

Silence fell. I couldn't speak. The sight of Ana's wispy hair and skinny legs filled me with an acute sense of shame and despair. I'd just thrown her father's body off a cliff. Thinking about it, I wanted to run and hide. I wanted to crawl into a hole, but I had to be strong for the children's sake. Nerine had been saying the same thing over and over again: for the children's sake we had to be cheerful. For the children's sake we had to be calm. We had to make them feel that everything was ticking over as usual, with no nasty threats or surprises waiting in the wings. As Nerine had pointed out, the last thing the girls needed was more drama in their lives.

If I told anyone about Duncan, she said, the upheaval that followed would change things forever.

'Right!' Nerine appeared in the vestibule again, dirty, sweat-stained, wild-eyed, speckled with blood and iodine. Her energy was unnerving; it sparked like a fallen powerline. She wasn't carrying Colette any longer. I could only assume she'd put the little girl to bed. 'Can you stay with the kids? Maybe go and feed the chickens?' Turning to her daughter, she added, 'Meg's got some new chooks. You'd like to see them, wouldn't you?'

Ana's nod was barely perceptible.

'Off you go, then. I'll look for Esme. And then I'll clean up around here.'

Nerine gestured towards the living room, where the TV was still lying on the floor in a puddle of broken glass. When Ana's gaze fell on it, she made a muffled sound—and I realised she hadn't seen the damage before. Her shock was written all over her face.

That reassured me. It meant she'd been tucked away in the closet while Duncan was trashing things.

'Come.' I took her hand. 'Let's go and choose some names for the new hens. I think we should call one of them Ana…'

The trip to the back door was terrible. We had to walk past the smashed lamp, the ripped phone cord and the overturned coffee table, then pick our way through the shards of crockery on the kitchen floor. Duncan had broken nearly all of my mugs and had thrown my toaster at the fridge. He must have stomped on the kitchen phone socket, which was hanging off the baseboard in a spray of snapped wires.

The backyard felt peaceful in comparison, even though Ruby was chasing a pullet.

'Look! There's a new chicken,' I said.

Ana didn't reply. I didn't expect her to. We crossed the mangy lawn to where I kept a bin of chicken feed next to the henhouse. Filling up the feeder brought the older hens running—and something about their fussy, focused greed took the edge off Ana's fear. She didn't smile when Perdita muscled Ruby aside, but her shoulders relaxed. Then she became interested in the pullets, which were hanging around at the edge of the melee, looking anxious.

'Do you want to call the black one Ana?' I asked.

She shook her head.

'What about that brown one?'

She whispered something.

'Pardon?' I leaned down.

'Sprinkles,' she said softly.

'Sprinkles? You want to call that one Sprinkles?'

She nodded.

'All right. And the black one can be…?'

'Bluebell.'

'Bluebell. That's a pretty name.'

'And Rudolph.' Ana pointed at the last of my recent purchases. I didn't remind her that it was female. I just smiled and said, 'Lovely.' Together we stood there, watching the hens go about their business. Then I realised I ought to be checking on Colette, so I ushered Ana out of the coop and closed its gate firmly behind us.

On our way back to the house, she took my hand.

'What would you like for dinner?' I asked, wondering how much she'd witnessed. Did she know her father had shown up? She must have heard him vandalising my TV, but did she suspect that something even worse had happened?

I was sure of one thing: she had no idea that he'd killed

Esme. Nerine had made that quite clear.

'Fish fingers or scrambled eggs?' I asked.

'Fish fingers.' Ana's voice was as faint as a mosquito's whine.

'With chips?'

'Yes.'

'And peas?'

'Yes.'

Returning to the kitchen, I gazed at the wreckage on the floor and realised I would have to clean up before I cooked anything. So I went to the cupboard for a broom, noting as I crossed the living room that Nerine was still on the front veranda. I could see her silhouette against the gauze curtain; she was sloshing around with a mop and bucket.

'Why don't you go and see if Colette's still asleep?' I said to Ana, hoping to distract her from what was happening outside. She shook her head, still gripping my left hand, and wouldn't let go until I gave her the dustpan and brush, which she used to sweep up pieces of crockery from the kitchen floor. We worked together without speaking, ignoring the thumps and scrapes from the veranda.

I was too cowardly to ask her what she knew or how she felt. I was afraid I might distress her by saying the wrong thing. And I couldn't bring myself to lie about Esme; the words would have stuck in my throat. The only thing I did say, after we'd cleaned up the debris, was 'There. That's better.'

It *was* better. Almost normal. Putting fish fingers on the grill, dragging frozen peas out of the fridge, filling a saucepan with water…each of those simple acts calmed me down. The fuzziness in my head began to dissipate. My hands stopped trembling.

Then I heard an engine roar.

'It's all right,' I told Ana, who had stiffened. 'It's your mum.' Nerine had said she was going to dump poor Esme off the cliff, and I hadn't tried to dissuade her. 'She'll be back soon, don't worry. And then we'll eat.'

Ana stared at me for a moment. I couldn't read her expression. Her eyes were blank, her lips pursed. She was gripping the brush and pan so tightly that her knuckles had gone white.

I took a deep breath, knowing I should try to break through the invisible wall between us. It was my responsibility as an adult to help Ana talk about the fear she must have felt while she was hiding in that closet. Sitting there in the dark, as doors banged and glass shattered and her parents screamed…it must have been horrible.

I was about to ask the poor little scrap if she had anything she wanted to tell me when her sister suddenly cried out.

'Oh dear,' I muttered. 'That sounds like Colette. We'd better make sure she's okay.' I shoved a tray of chips into the oven, then held out my hand. 'Let's go and give her a hug.'

Stiffly, Ana laid down the dustpan. But she kept a tight hold of the brush as we moved out of the kitchen together, down the hallway, into the spare room. Here two things became instantly apparent: the window had been smashed and Colette had been placed in the middle of the bed, which was strewn with dirty clothes.

I couldn't believe what I was seeing. Nerine had left a two-year-old on an elevated platform next to a floor covered in broken glass. What if Colette had rolled off the mattress?

'Come on, sweetie. Let's get you out of here.' I darted forward to grab Colette, who was lying on her back, rubbing her eyes and making grumpy noises. She wore a shrunken yellow T-shirt and soiled leggings. When I picked her up, she didn't crow or writhe or screech or kick, but slumped against my shoulder, her skull heavy as a cannon ball. Her sticky hand reached half-heartedly for my collar, then slid back down the front of my cardigan. Her eyes were glazed.

I felt her forehead. 'Are you sick?'

She didn't feel hot. Her cheeks weren't flushed. Yet she wasn't herself; her movements were sluggish. Normally she couldn't sit still.

I was heading out of the room again when it hit me. Sleepy. Slow. Fretful. No temperature.

Had she been *drugged*?

'I gave her some Phenergan,' Nerine said. 'I had to, or she wouldn't have stayed quiet.'

We were sitting at the kitchen table with a half-empty bottle of shiraz. I felt I deserved a drink after my busy evening: I'd nailed a piece of plywood over the broken window, made dinner for the kids while Nerine swept up the glass in the spare room, bathed the children as she went to throw more things off the cliff, and read the kids a couple of bedtime stories, fending off Colette's repeated cries of 'Dok! Dok!'

while I ached for my beautiful Esme. I'd also helped clean the living room.

A dinner of warmed-up bolognese sauce on butterfly pasta hadn't tempted me; my stomach was still knotted into a tight little ball. But when both girls were finally asleep, Nerine insisted I force down a glass of wine.

'To help you relax,' she said.

I certainly felt relaxed. In fact I was having a lot of trouble piecing things together. I had to force myself to concentrate as Nerine explained how she'd dosed Colette with Phenergan the minute Duncan's car started jolting down the drive. 'After that, I locked all the doors and put both kids in the cupboard,' she explained. 'But Duncan broke a window and climbed into the spare room while I was getting the axe.' They'd found themselves face to face in the hallway, where Duncan had wrenched the axe from Nerine and used it to smash the television, chop up the phone cord and sweep all the cups off the high shelf in the kitchen.

'He wanted me to tell him where the kids were,' she mumbled, staring listlessly into her glass. 'He punched me when I wouldn't. He was gunna use the axe.' Her eyes narrowed and a smile flickered across her face. 'Then he tripped on one of Ana's toys and I hit him with the cutting board.'

I followed her gaze to where my marble cutting board sat in the plate rack.

'Oh, Christ,' I whispered.

'I washed it off,' she assured me. 'Right after I tied him up. But we'll have to do something about that board. We can bleach it, but they might still be able to test it for blood. I dunno. Do you?'

I shook my head. It felt like a dead weight.

'And we can't throw it off the cliff because it's yours. We don't want anyone finding it next to the car.' Nerine seemed to be thinking aloud. 'We can't burn it either. And if we bury it around here, they might dig it up. We need to get it off the property. Maybe chuck it in a skip somewhere. That's gotta be high on our to-do list.'

I didn't answer. I couldn't. A physical reaction to the day's events seemed to be setting in; I could barely lift my glass.

'Tomorrow we'll have a bunch of things to do,' Nerine went on, with a driving intensity that seemed undimmed by pain, fatigue or tension. 'We have to sort out that car door. We have to get the cutting board out of the house. And you have to call your lawyer about the money.'

'The money,' I echoed.

'You have to find out when you'll be getting it. Or if you can use it as collateral for a bank loan.' As I stared at her blankly, she added, 'A lawyer's letter might be all the bank needs. You can tell him your daughter's desperate for cash.'

The words seemed to be coming from a great distance. 'Where's the gun?' I asked.

'Oh, I hid that. We don't want the kids getting hold of it.'

'We should give it back to Dinah,' I mumbled. 'We don't need it anymore.'

'I wish I'd had it when Duncan showed up.' Nerine drained her glass, then set it down with a click. 'He'd still be alive if I'd had a gun to wave at him. He wouldn't have dared come inside.'

'You think so?' I was having trouble expressing myself. The muscles of my mouth felt lazy. 'You don't think you would have just shot him?'

'Maybe.' Nerine pondered for a moment, then shrugged. 'I don't feel bad,' she admitted. 'I mean, I feel bad I killed him, but I don't feel bad he's dead.' There was a gleam in her eye as she fixed it on me. 'Would you feel bad if Keith died?'

I didn't have to think about that—not for one second. 'I'd feel bad if he was murdered.'

Nerine scowled. 'It wasn't murder, it was self-defence!' Before I could apologise, she flapped her hand. 'Anyway, it's not the same. I bet Keith never got you drunk and had his mates rape you. I bet Keith never tried to shove your kid in a freezer. Duncan was a psychopath. He deserved to die.'

I didn't know what to say. My brain had slowed to a crawl. Nerine picked up the wine bottle and poured herself another glass. 'You get some rest. I'll clean up.'

'I wanted to talk…'

'Tomorrow.'

'But not with the kids. I mean, around. With them around.'

'No.'

'We have to…' What did we have to do?

'Good night, Meg. And thanks.' She offered me a tremulous smile, her eyes pouchy and bloodshot. 'We make a great team, don't you think?'

On my way out of the kitchen, I bumped into the doorframe. Then I staggered down the hall, wondering why I was so exhausted. *Shock*, I thought. *Delayed shock*. I'd been hoping to escape to my room after dinner and think. Plan. Mourn Esme. Weigh up the situation in peace and quiet.

But I could barely find the energy to clean my teeth, let alone change into my pyjamas. And when at last I fell into bed, I was asleep almost before my head hit the pillow.

Once, when Emily was eight years old, I came home to find the kitchen floor covered in food. Keith had removed almost everything from the fridge and the pantry cupboard—the baked beans, the Coco Pops, the Tiny Teddies, the apple juice and tinned pears and cheese slices—and had smeared and splashed and crushed them all over the tiles. I stood for a moment, staring down at the chaos. Then I heard Keith padding up behind me.

'That stuff you've been feeding her is rubbish,' he growled. 'And rubbish doesn't belong in the fridge. Rubbish is what you dump.'

I ought to be stewing fresh fruit, he said. Making my own preservative-free biscuits. Exposing Emily to the strong taste of proper organic cheese and avoiding juice altogether, unless I squeezed it myself. 'I can't believe you brought that sugary cereal into the house,' he spat. 'No wonder her development's so slow. You're starving her of proper nutrients.'

I was used to letting Keith rant and rave, but the sight of that filthy floor lit a fuse in my head. I swung my fist and hit him bang on the nose. He lurched sideways a few steps, clutching his face. Then he straightened up, his eyes fixed on mine, and said with a hint of triumph, 'That's assault. I could have you charged for that.'

Later on, he took photographs of the bruises. I was in a panic for days, but he didn't go to the police. Instead he kept the photos and used them when we got divorced. They were proof I'd hit him.

I have to admit that Keith never hit me. Despite everything, he wasn't the one who had lashed out. I was. And although it would be easy enough to find excuses, I haven't tried.

There's no excuse, not ever. Everyone knows that.

When I woke I couldn't believe how late it was. I never slept till ten.

As soon as I sat up, I realised that something was amiss. After nearly twelve hours of sleep, I still felt groggy. My tongue was like sandpaper. My neck was a plank.

By the time I'd donned my Ugg boots and cardigan, I'd decided Nerine must have put some of Colette's Phenergan in my food. But why? To stop me from going to the police? From bearing witness? From getting in her way?

A pang of fright sent me scampering through the door and into the spare room. I was half-expecting to find it deserted, with all Nerine's possessions gone and the bed neatly made, but the place was a bombsite. Sheets in a knot, toys all over the floor, open bags strewn about, clothes piled on every surface.

Clearly Nerine hadn't done a runner during the night.

'Hi, Meg!' she trilled, when I finally stumbled into the kitchen. It took me a moment to understand what she'd done to herself. Her skin was very pale. Her lips were very dark. She was wearing one of my shirts, which gave her a heavier, friendlier look. Had she been rifling through my wardrobe?

Speaking of rifles...'Where's the gun?'

'Don't worry. It's safe.' She grinned at me and twirled, as if putting herself on display. 'What do you think? I look just like Emily, don't I? It's the lipstick; she uses that really dark lipstick. Bit of a mistake on someone so fair. Luckily I had ultra-pale foundation in my kit—that Pan Stik totally hides my scratches.'

It took me a while to process what she'd said. Gazing around, I saw that Colette was on the floor, playing with my plastic measuring cups. Ana sat at the table with her stuffed rabbit, drawing pictures. The whole room smelled of baking and bleach and artificial lemon. The dishes were washed. The table and benchtops had been wiped down. Everything sparkled in the morning sunshine.

'From now on I'm going to be your daughter,' Nerine explained. 'Just in case anyone sees me.' Before I could protest, she continued, 'The funny thing is, I kind of feel like I am your daughter. God knows, you're a better mum than mine ever was. Which is why I ended up in foster care.' She ruffled Ana's hair on her way to the oven. 'You're the first real granny these kids have had. No wonder they love you. And I know you love them.' Stooping to pull open the oven door, she glanced up at me and said, 'I don't suppose you fancy a chocolate chip cookie for breakfast?'

She's mad, I thought. I felt as if I was in a David Lynch film. Everything looked spick and span and warm and wonderful, yet a man lay dead outside. Nerine's reactions seemed positively bipolar. *Was* she bipolar? Or had fear and stress tipped her over the edge?

Whatever her problem was, it gave her the power to create her own little world wherever she happened to be: a world of playful whimsy or cosy comfort or intense paranoia. This morning's world was one of cheerful domesticity, and I couldn't stomach it. She had drugged me, she had killed her ex, she had concealed his corpse—and now she wanted to play happy families?

But I couldn't talk about any of these things in front of the kids.

'Did you let the hens out?' I said.

'Ana let the hens out. Didn't you, Big Bug?'

Ana nodded. She was watching me, blank-faced.

'Looks like the new ones are getting hammered by the old ones,' Nerine observed, wielding an oven glove. 'I guess that's why they call it a pecking order.'

I grunted.

'Once you've had breakfast,' Nerine went on, 'we can go for a drive and find a signal on your phone. We need to call that lawyer and ask about the money.'

'Just let me get dressed.' I turned and trudged back to my room, where I sat on my bed and tried to think.

I was in the middle of a nightmare. A psychopathic stalker had been killed. His body had been disposed of. I was implicated in the disposal and Nerine was using my involvement to extort money from me. No—that wasn't right. It was more nuanced than that. Nerine had to leave. She knew it. I knew it. Once she left, only Jill and Renee would ever realise she'd been here. And that would be a good thing if Duncan was found—or rather, *when* Duncan was found. I had no illusions; someone would stumble on him eventually.

But Nerine needed money to get away. If she had enough of it, the girls might somehow survive this disaster without ending up in foster care. I toyed for a moment with a rose-coloured dream—Nerine hitching a ride on a fishing boat to Indonesia or Chile and living an idyllic existence while her carefree children ran around barefoot. It was a calming, beguiling image, but it was a fantasy.

I thought about foster care. Was it really that bad? I thought about what would happen if I called the police. Then I wondered *how* I would call the police. My landline wasn't working. My mobile…where was that? It wasn't on the bedside table. I must have left it in my handbag, which I'd last seen in the car, along with my car keys. Nerine had obviously kept the keys after dumping Esme's corpse.

Esme. Remembering my precious girl, I felt a wave of grief surge through me and bent over, clutching my stomach. The loss was like a stab in the guts; it propelled me to my feet and sent me swaying across the room to Esme's bed, which sat in the corner, heaped with old towels and rugs and some of the odd things she'd brought back from her walks: a stick, a mouldering tennis ball, a sun-bleached bone. Kneeling beside the bed, I grabbed a rug, pressed it to my nose and inhaled.

The rug smelled of dog. Of Esme. My tears ran down to soak it as I rocked back and forth, trying to stifle my sobs for the sake of the children.

Then I noticed something strange. Dragging the rug out of Esme's bed, I'd dislodged a tangle of familiar objects. I recognised the squeaky pig and the rubber crocodile. I also recognised my own masticated bed sock, reduced to a crusty rag.

The shoe, however, was something I hadn't seen before. It was a loafer, caked with dirt—*filled* with dirt—and very large. A man's shoe, gnawed at the edges.

I knew the pattern on its corrugated sole.

CLUES

ESME LOVED SHOES. She loved tearing them apart. She also liked digging, as long as there was something worth digging for. Once she managed to excavate a dead chook that I buried near the fence. Even after she grew old and arthritic, she enjoyed trying to dig under the compost bin.

When I saw the dirt-encrusted shoe in her bed, I knew instantly that it had been dug up. But where? Had Nerine been letting Esme roam around in the bush? Or had the shoe been unearthed closer to home? Squatting like a frog, staring at the loafer, I wondered why on earth Duncan—or Keith or Fred Huggett, for that matter—had decided to bury it.

There was no doubt in my mind that this shoe had left the prints under my guestroom window. The patterns were identical, and it wasn't as if my immediate neighbourhood was awash with men's footwear. I forced myself to think back to the scene in my shed, flinching as I remembered Duncan crashing into the boot of his car. He'd had shoes on both feet, at the time—black trainers with white soles. He could have buried the loafer after messing with my windchimes, but why do something so risky? And why wear loafers at all? From what I could remember, he'd been dressed in a young man's outfit: jeans, T-shirt, trainers. Loafers were golfing shoes. Yachting shoes. Middle-aged shoes.

Tearle sometimes wore them. But his feet were much smaller than the size thirteen shoe in my hand.

Keith was a ten.

I closed my eyes, trying to picture Duncan's feet. They hadn't looked outstandingly large—not like this shoe. Then again, I hadn't been thinking straight when I'd first laid eyes on him. He could have been wearing hoop earrings and I might not have noticed.

'Meg?' Nerine suddenly rapped on the door. 'Do you want me to make you some toast?'

I jumped to my feet. My heart was hammering.

'Uh—no,' I said. 'That's okay.'

'Coffee?'

'I'll do it. Thanks.' Standing there, clutching the shoe, I realised I wasn't about to let Nerine make me anything. 'I'm not very hungry, to be honest.'

'Okay. But we need to get rolling.'

'Yes, I know. Sorry.'

I hid the shoe under my mattress and scrambled into my clothes, barely able to concentrate on buttons and laces because my head was buzzing. Maybe Fred Huggett *had* played a tune on my windchimes. But if he'd been tramping around under my guestroom window, why had he then taken off a shoe and buried it? Only someone with dementia would have trudged back home through the bush wearing a single shoe.

Or was it Keith? Perhaps he'd deliberately left prints with an outsized shoe—just to prove that he wasn't involved—and then buried it in my garden. He was the sort of person who would go to any lengths for revenge, though he was usually more straightforward. Shit, bills, broken plates, rotting food…

A buried shoe wasn't going to make me sick or cost me money. But it *had* left me feeling unnerved.

'Nerine?' I said, when I returned to the kitchen. 'Did you see anyone else around yesterday?'

She stared at me, chewing. There was a half-eaten cookie in her hand. 'No,' she replied, through a mouthful of chocolate chips. 'Why?'

'Nothing.' I didn't want to agitate her with my concerns about what Keith might have witnessed. I also didn't want to tell her about the shoe.

I needed more time to ponder that.

'Want one of these biscuits?' she asked. 'Or some fruit?'

'I'll have a banana.' It was all I could stomach.

'Good,' said Nerine. 'Breakfast's the most important meal of the day.' Then she whipped my mobile out of her pocket. 'We'll try to pick up a signal somewhere round the house. If that doesn't work we might have to hit the road.'

I nodded as I dropped my banana peel into the bin. Dinah's gun, I noticed, wasn't on top of the kitchen cupboards. The axe had gone too.

'We'll have to get the booster seats,' Nerine went on. Then she turned to Ana. 'Go and find a box. Something you can put your specimens in.' To me she said, 'Ana wants to make a nature museum. I told her we can collect stuff while we're driving around.'

'That's a good idea.' I smiled at Ana. She didn't smile back. Her face looked tight; if the museum really was her idea, it didn't seem to excite her anymore.

But she put down her crayon, slid off the chair and sloped into the living room.

Nerine picked up Colette. 'You stay with this one while I strap in the car seats. She's allowed one more biscuit.'

'Dok,' the toddler said mournfully.

'No dog. Doggie went on holiday.' Nerine said, rolling her eyes. Then she shoved her daughter into my arms. 'I'll be back in a second. I've got your keys.'

She bounded away, fizzing with energy, as Colette whined and wriggled and tried to get down. Once again, the demands of a small, struggling child drove nearly everything else out of my head. When I set her on her feet, she made straight for the open back door. When I shut it in her face, she began to cry. When I offered her a cookie, she snatched it from my hand, stomped across the room and started to make a fuss, waving her arms and craning her neck. I lifted her up to the benchtop and she reached over to drop her cookie into the toaster.

'Not the cookie,' I said. 'You can't toast a cookie.'

She began to howl.

'The bread. Look. You can toast the bread.' I was groping

around in the breadbin when I heard the creak of hinges behind me. Glancing over my shoulder, I saw that Ana had returned.

She was carrying a pillowslip.

'Look, Collie—there's Ana. What's she got? Is it a bag?'

Colette scowled at her big sister, who wore a sombre expression. At that instant I had a brainwave; I put the toddler down, pulled out a drawer full of Tupperware and dumped the whole thing on the floor. 'Why don't you stick these in Ana's bag?' I said. 'Why don't you see how many you can fit?'

Ana passed me her pillowslip without waiting to be asked. She stood mutely waiting as I dropped a rubbery lid into it. I'd just picked up a measuring jug when Colette snatched the jug from me, crowing with delight, and thrust it into the pillowslip.

After that I was able to sit back on my heels, holding open the cloth pouch while Colette filled it with harmless bits of plastic.

'How were the hens?' I asked Ana, conscious of how tense she was. 'Are the old ones being mean to the new ones?'

She nodded.

'We'll have to distract them. If we hang a lettuce in the coop, it'll keep them so busy that they won't have time to bully each other.' Seeing her sceptical look, I sighed and said, 'Or maybe you can help me build a separate pen for the new ones. Just until they settle in.'

Which would be a hell of a job. I saw myself pounding star pickets into the rocky ground. Digging a narrow trench between the pickets so the wire would be deep enough to repel foxes. Using a pick as well as a spade…

Then I realised: if the size-thirteen shoe had been buried inside the garden, someone would have heard. My yard wasn't carpeted with loam. It was an uneven expanse of stony, compacted dirt like crumbling concrete. If someone had been digging it up at night, Esme would have noticed. *I* would have noticed. There would have been a lot of noise.

'What a pity Esme isn't here,' I said, watching Ana. 'I don't think the chickens would have been so mean if Esme was around.' When her shoulders drooped, I added, 'Maybe she went for a walk and got lost. She used to go for walks all the time, didn't she? In the bush? While I was away?'

Startled, Ana blinked. She shook her head firmly.

'Oh. Okay.' I tried to sound puzzled. 'So where did she dig up that old shoe? In the garden?'

Ana opened her mouth and lifted her hand to point. Then she stiffened, her face fell and her arm flipped back as if pulled by a rubber band. She clapped her two clenched fists to her chest and stared at me with eyes full of fear.

The whole process didn't take more than a second, but it told me everything I needed to know. It told me that Ana was aware of the buried shoe, that she was afraid to admit it—and that something was very, very wrong.

I thought about the footprints. The flyscreen. I thought about the guestroom window, which wasn't far off the ground. And I thought about how Nerine had once shown the kids how to play tunes on my windchimes.

'Did your mum ask you to climb out your bedroom window?' I asked in my calmest, friendliest voice, because I didn't want to scare Ana. I didn't want her to think I was angry or frightened.

Her eyes filled with tears. She began to gnaw at her knuckles.

Then Nerine called to us from the front yard.

'I'm done, Meg! You can bring 'em out now!'

'Stop,' said Nerine.

She was sitting beside me in the front passenger seat. We'd been crawling along the fire trail, looking for a signal; my mobile phone was in her hand and she'd been waving it about, her eyes on the screen, her arm out the window. Now, at last, she wrenched her gaze away from the device and fixed it on me.

'Couple of bars,' she announced as I braked. 'We should give it a go.' Then she pushed open the door next to her. 'Away from the car, so he can't hear Colette.'

I switched off the ignition and glanced back at the kids. Colette was moaning and writhing. Ana sat like a little statue, her empty pillowcase in one hand, Mr Snuffles in the other. She wouldn't look at me.

'Come on.' Nerine sounded impatient. She was already outside. 'Leave the keys where they are.'

'But the kids—'

'It won't take long. We'll leave the door open.' Thrusting her head back into the car, she added, 'Kids! If you're really quiet, we'll go for a walk. But you have to be quiet first.'

Without waiting for an answer, she moved away. By this time Colette was thrashing about like someone in a strait-jacket, red-faced and scowling. It was obvious that Nerine's instructions had meant absolutely nothing to her.

'If you start getting hot, you should tell us,' I warned Ana, who didn't so much as glance in my direction. I don't like leaving children in cars, so I opened my own door reluctantly. But then Nerine grabbed my arm and hustled me down the trail.

'Here,' she said, pushing the mobile into my hand. 'Call your lawyer. Ask him about the money.'

One look at the screen showed me that I'd missed five calls. But I went straight to my contact list and scrolled down until I reached David's number, which I selected with a tap before raising the phone to my ear.

I wasn't surprised when I heard a recorded voice saying, 'You've reached David Blazek. I'm not available right now, so please leave a message.'

'Hi, David.' I cleared my throat and took a deep breath. 'It's Meg Lowry. I just want to ask you something. Could you call me back? Thank you.'

Nerine frowned as I broke the connection. 'Damn,' she said.

'He could be in court.'

'I guess we'll have to hang around here for a few minutes.' She scanned the surrounding scrub, looking disgruntled. 'What about that other lawyer?'

'Tearle?'

'Would he know the score?'

Before I could reply, the phone rang.

'That'll be David,' said Nerine.

But it wasn't. I could see from the screen that Dinah was calling.

'Hello?'

'Meg?'

'Oh—hi, Dinah.'

'Are you okay? I've been trying to get hold of you.'

'My landline's down.' I turned away from Nerine, who was dragging a finger across her throat. 'I had to go looking for a signal—the reception's shocking at my place.'

'Well, that's a relief.' The tension seemed to drain from Dinah's voice, leaving it light and airy. 'I was wondering if it had something to do with your daughter. I thought maybe you'd battened down the hatches.' She paused for a moment. When I didn't respond, she said, 'You should have told us Emily was visiting. You could have brought her along yesterday.'

I felt a burning sensation in my chest that might have been gastric reflux. My jaw dropped. I folded at the waist, like someone punched in the stomach.

'Hello? Meg?'

Nerine mouthed, 'What is it?'

I was staring at her: at her dyed hair, her heavy fringe, her muddy lipstick, her cosmetic pallor. She was trying to look like Emily, but she wasn't the same at all. My daughter's energy was cautious. Sad. Withdrawn. Nerine's was hard, bright and unpredictable. She moved like a lizard, darting and twitching. Her pale eyes had no depth.

I thought to myself, *Be careful*. And I felt a chill seep into my bones.

'Meg? Are you there?' Dinah was still piping away. 'Can you hear me? Hello?'

'I'm here.' My creaky tone made Nerine frown. 'Sorry. Like I said, the reception's appalling.'

'I'll be quick, then. I just wanted to say you can bring Emily over any time. Especially if there's a problem...' She trailed off, signalling a question without actually asking it.

The question was: why hadn't I told her about my daughter?

'Did someone *say* Emily was here?' I asked, and Nerine's whole body clenched.

'Sal heard it from Gail Kerr,' Dinah revealed. 'Barry was the one who gave Emily a lift back to your place on Saturday. It was pouring, he said, and she wasn't far from home. Must have been around the same time we were chatting in Bathurst.'

'And she told him what, exactly?' I was trying to ignore Nerine, whose throat-cutting gestures were getting fiercer.

'Well—when he heard where she was going, he asked if you were a friend. And then she mentioned who she was.' With a little laugh Dinah added, 'He tore strips off her for hitch-hiking. It wasn't a smart thing to do, even if she *was* drenched. Out here...well, it's not like England.'

'No. It's not.' I was trying to dodge Nerine, who had decided to take the phone away. 'Listen,' I said quickly, 'could you just—'

But I wasn't allowed to finish. Nerine wrenched the mobile from my hand and broke the connection. Then she gave me a shove.

'What the fuck are you doing?' she spat.

'What the fuck are *you* doing?' I didn't recognise my own voice; it was weak and wobbly. 'You went out? On the road?'

'For about ten minutes...'

'You *hitchhiked*?'

'I had to! I would have drowned out there!' Seeing the look on my face, she bared her teeth and snarled, 'I've been shut up in that fucking house all week. I was stir-crazy. You dunno what it's like.'

I couldn't believe what I was hearing. 'Did you take the kids?'

'Of course not! Christ!'

The way I was retreating from her, step by step, must have triggered something in Nerine. Suddenly she seemed aware that she was making a bad impression. She took a deep breath. Her face smoothed out. 'The kids were having a nap,' she muttered.

'You left them?'

'For about ten fucking minutes.'

'But you told me Duncan was around.' I was trying to make sense of it all. 'You told me he was closing in. And you left your kids alone?'

By this time Nerine was almost unnaturally calm. 'Esme was with them,' she reminded me.

'Esme?' My laugh was like the noise made by someone

being stabbed. 'He *cut her throat*, Nerine.'

Before she could answer, the phone trilled. When she glanced at the screen, I could tell from her face that it wasn't David calling.

Dinah, I thought, as we both stood listening to the rings go on and on. At last the unanswered call went to voicemail. Silence fell.

'All right. I admit it. I made a mistake,' Nerine said at last. 'I thought if I stayed in that house a minute longer, I might do something crazy. So I went for a walk.'

'But…' I gestured at the bush that encircled us, indicating that she had plenty of open space in which to roam unseen.

'I'm not a nature person, Meg. I wanted to find out if there was—I dunno—a truck stop nearby. I had cabin fever.'

I didn't know whether to believe her. Was she really that stupid? She'd lied to me before, about the windchimes; I was sure of that now. She had removed the flyscreen from the guestroom window, then told her own daughter to climb out, play with the windchimes and scamper back to bed before she was caught.

But why would anyone devise such an elaborate hoax? What was the pay-off for making me panic?

And where had Nerine found the shoe?

My mobile sounded again, making me jump. This time she handed it straight over, flicking it onto speaker mode because David's name had appeared on the screen.

'Hello?' I said.

'Hello, Meg. It's David.'

'Hi, David.'

'You have a question for me?'

'Uh—yeah.' Conscious of Nerine's fixed glare, I stammered, 'It's about—it's the—you know, the...um...payout.'

'Yes?'

'I was just wondering when I'll be getting it.' For a moment I couldn't understand why Nerine was frantically pointing at herself, but then I grasped what she was trying to say. 'My daughter needs money,' I added.

'Hmmm. I see. Well, as I told you before, these things take time.'

'Weeks?' I asked. 'Or months?'

'Months. Definitely months.'

Nerine started miming her next question, but I didn't need her help. I knew what to say. 'What about borrowing against it? Could I do that?'

'Possibly. I don't know. How much do you want to borrow?'

I searched my memory for a sum—and found one. Nerine had mentioned it a few days earlier. 'Ten thousand dollars.'

She nodded eagerly.

David said, 'I don't see why not. It's called a pending settlement loan. But I'm no expert. You're better off talking to a bank...'

'Oh.'

'Though I doubt many banks would offer it. But there are organisations that specialise in that kind of...shall we say, unconventional lending?' His tone became distracted, as if someone had just handed him a contract to sign. 'I'd be happy to provide any documentation you might need,' he went on. 'My advice, though, is to wait. Unconventional lenders sometimes charge very high interest.'

Nerine mouthed, 'Who?' She wanted names.

I cleared my throat. 'Um…what lenders are you talking about?'

'I'm not sure,' said David. 'If I were you, I'd start with the bank, then move on from there.' A low background murmur told me that he was with other people. 'Is that all, Meg? Can I help you with anything else?'

He could have helped me with a lot, as it happened, but Nerine didn't let him. Without warning, she plucked the phone from my hand and yelped, 'Nup!' before cutting him off.

I knew I was in deep trouble. Nerine had some kind of crazy scheme in her head and she wasn't about to let me interfere with it. That was probably why she had me trapped on my own property—because I couldn't just walk away from her kids. How could I, when there was no telling what she might do? She'd already killed someone; she was volatile, capricious, desperate, unhinged. Manipulative, too—I realised that, now. She'd always been a handful, but killing her ex had flipped an emotional switch that seemed to have left her without any impulse control.

And she had my phone. She was tapping away at it while she marched towards the car, her attention divided between the screen and her kids. 'Okay, girls,' she said, pausing to lean through the driver's door. 'Out you get. Meg's gunna help you find some things for your museum.'

When she straightened up again, I realised that she'd swiped the keys from the ignition.

'I'll just ring a bank and find out about those settlement loans,' she informed me. 'Can you look after the kids for five minutes?'

I nodded. Then I went to unstrap poor Colette, who was flailing and screeching and arching her back. But she shut up as soon as her feet hit the ground. She even let me take her hand as she stomped along the fire trail, dropping to her haunches occasionally to pick up a leaf, a gumnut or a dead insect.

We put all these things in Ana's bag, which Ana proffered listlessly, going through the motions. She was acutely anxious—I could tell by the stiffness of her posture and the way her gaze jumped about—and I suddenly noticed how she angled herself so she never had her back to Nerine. I realised with growing dismay that this was something she did all the time. How had I not seen it before? What had blinded me to the obvious?

Why had I always assumed that her pervasive fear was triggered by a person *who wasn't even there*?

I wondered how much she knew about her mother's games. It occurred to me, as I watched Colette throwing herself around, that Nerine might have used Phenergan on both girls. Maybe Ana hadn't crawled into the chicken coop that night. Maybe Nerine had drugged her, carried her to the henhouse and left her there. It would explain why the poor little scrap hadn't been roused by all the slaughter.

But why would Nerine have dreamed up such a weird scenario in the first place?

'Baif,' said Colette. She pounced on a feather and waved it triumphantly.

'Wow!' My smile felt pasted on. 'Put it in the bag. That's it. Good girl...'

Ana seemed slightly distracted, perhaps because she was listening to her mother's voice as it rose and fell in the distance. Nerine was talking on the phone. I couldn't make out exactly what she was saying, but I could tell from her tone that she was asking question after question.

'Lit!' Colette squealed. She pointed at a skink that was sunning itself ahead of us. But when she galloped towards it, dragging me with her, the skink vanished under a log.

'Lee! Bah!' Colette protested.

'It's a lizard. Can you say lizard? Li-zard.' Quailing at the thought of what her meaty little fist might do to a defence-less reptile, I said quickly, 'But we don't want a lizard for our museum. Lizards belong in a zoo.'

'Zoo!' Colette knew exactly what that meant. Her face lit up. 'Zoo!'

'You like zoos?' My thoughts drifted vaguely towards the problem of how we might cobble together a makeshift zoo with chickens and caterpillars. But then Ana spoke.

'Mum won't let us have a zoo,' she reminded her sister in a lifeless voice.

I looked at her. She looked at me. Her eyes were as deep as the ocean; they held secrets. Stories. Hopes and fears.

They were blue, not green. I thought about her father, dangling from a rope like a fish on a line. His eyes had been closed. I hadn't seen their colour. But his hair was black and crisp, his skin swarthy, his nose broad.

All at once a horrific notion surfaced inside my head like a snapping crocodile. It made me gasp. It was like having a rug pulled out from under me.

I had to steady my voice as I said, 'Hey, Ana? Does your dad have fair hair like you?'

She shook her head.

'Is it black?'

She glanced over at her mother, as if calculating her chances of being heard. But Nerine was still busy, pacing about near my car and firing questions into my phone.

Ana must have found this reassuring, because she mumbled, 'Orange.'

'Orange? Your dad has orange hair?'

Again she nodded.

This news sucked the breath out of me. I wanted to scoop the kids up and run. Throw them in my car. Drive away.

But Nerine had my keys. She had my phone. She had the gun.

I wasn't just in trouble. I was in danger.

CORNERED

MY FATHER REFUSED to pay for my wedding.

I never thought he would, but Keith was devastated. Traditionally, the bride's parents are always stuck with the bill, and Keith was expecting my dad to help fund a lavish reception at Boronia House, a Mosman establishment that offered the works: manicured grounds, an elegant mansion, gourmet food, classy table settings. Keith felt that we deserved the best, even if we couldn't afford it. He was shattered when Dad wouldn't step up.

Instead our reception took place at a beachside restaurant that Carol paid for. It was lovely, but Keith kept obsessing over Boronia House. He talked about Boronia House so much that I can still remember the name after all these years. He said that he was disappointed for my sake—that I deserved better than the 'scungy' restaurant I'd chosen so carefully, with its salt-smeared plate glass, its unfashionable menu, its grubby toilets and its unprofessional staff. Most of the speech he gave during the toasts consisted of apologies for the restaurant in which we were being served.

It was embarrassing, but at the time I felt for him. I figured he was a perfectionist and accustomed to nice things, so naturally he took it hard when one of the guests didn't get her vegetarian meal or when the PA system broke down halfway through the bridal waltz. I didn't blame him for sulking. With a few glasses of champagne inside me, I thought it was cute. He looked just like a little boy with his twisted bow tie and adorable pout. I was all over him for most of the evening, though he didn't offer much encouragement. 'What a fiasco,' he kept saying mournfully. 'What a bloody fiasco.'

The bouquet-tossing was a fiasco too, because I pitched the bouquet so high that it landed in a gutter and the staff had to bring a ladder to get it down. Everyone laughed about my wrist spin—everyone, that is, except Keith. He just stood with his hand over his eyes, shaking his head in despair.

For our wedding night I'd booked the bridal suite at a reasonably priced place in Terrey Hills that called itself a resort. It meant a long drive back to Sydney on the F3, but Keith hadn't wanted to stay anywhere on the northern peninsula. Luckily he hadn't drunk too much; the quality of the booze at our reception had also failed to impress him. I was in a giggly mood when we set off, but it wasn't long before my high spirits evaporated. Keith took the bends on Woy Woy Road too fast and by the time he hit the F3 he was way over the speed limit.

'Slow down.' I was gripping the dashboard. 'Please slow down.'

But he wouldn't: his disappointment was fuelling his road rage. I don't know how fast we were going by the time we hit Berowra, but if the highway had been any busier, we would have died for sure.

That was the first time I ever felt really scared of Keith. That was when I realised his anger could have very serious consequences. I remember how sick and shocked I felt in the aftermath—how my whole perspective on the world shifted slightly, as if I had vertigo. I remember how little I enjoyed my wedding night as a result.

But I also remember how eagerly I thought up excuses for him. All weddings were stressful, and Keith had very high standards—in clothes, food, holidays, vehicles, technology, interior design…even accessories like cufflinks. Everything had to be perfect, especially when it came to the big milestones. Of course he'd reacted badly when our big day hadn't lived up to expectations. It was only fair to cut him a little slack.

I ignored the pang of unease that I felt when Keith first showed me what he was capable of. But I wasn't about to do the same thing with Nerine. This time I was going to follow my gut and get the hell out of her way, as soon as possible.

The trouble was, I didn't know how.

Nerine drove back to my place. She talked about loans the whole way, but I wasn't listening. I was too busy working out what to do next. It was obvious that I had to keep her onside, since there was no telling how she might react if she became suspicious of me. And I didn't rate my chances very high if I tried to wrench the keys or the mobile away from her. She was about half my age and nearly six inches taller; I'd probably end up with my face smashed in.

As for the landline, it was dead: handset destroyed, cord cut. The socket in the kitchen was also damaged. The one in the living room might still be working but it was no use to me without a phone.

And then I remembered: there was a phone in the shed.

'...something called an irrevocable authority, signed by your solicitor,' Nerine was saying. 'But if you apply online, they won't lend you more than five thousand bucks. So you'd have to visit an agency, and the nearest one is in Bathurst— some kind of pawn shop.' Pulling into my front yard, she braked and turned off the engine. 'Maybe it would be easier to top up your mortgage. Unless you wanna sell something. Not the car, though—you wouldn't get a thousand bucks for this heap of shit.'

I could have told Nerine that a mortgage top-up was out of the question on my income. But I stayed silent, thinking furiously as I climbed out of the car and closed the gate.

'I already texted David to send that irrevocable authority,' Nerine went on, unstrapping Colette. 'Figured I might as well. One way or another, I'll have the money by the end of the week.' She hoisted the toddler onto her hip, then began shepherding Ana towards the house. 'What we should do now, though,' she added, 'is sort out that whole car-door business. Got any ideas?'

It took me a moment to understand what she was saying. 'To get down the cliff?' I asked numbly. 'No, of course not.'

'Okay, well—you wanna hide those seats for me?'

'Huh?'

'The car seats. So no one spots 'em.' By this time Nerine was at the foot of the front stairs. 'I'll just give the kids some lunch while we figure out how to tackle that cliff.'

'Okay. Sure.' I couldn't believe it. She was actually leaving me alone! Before she could change her mind, I unbuckled Ana's car seat, carried it over to the shed and ducked under the roller door.

I hadn't set foot inside the shed since driving out of it in Duncan's Lancer. Nerine had cleaned up every trace of what had happened there. The old clothesline was gone. No tyre tracks were visible. If there were any threads or scuff marks or drops of blood, I couldn't see them—and I certainly didn't stop to look.

Instead I shoved Ana's seat behind a pile of paint cans and rushed over to the shelves along the back wall. Here, stacked up in clumsy rows, were at least a dozen battered cardboard boxes containing toys, books, board games, photo albums and junk left by the old man who'd sold me the house. Luckily his stuff was on a high shelf. If I hadn't been struggling to dislodge it, standing on tiptoe with my nose pressed against the shelf underneath, I wouldn't have seen the thin cream cable running along the wall behind the boxes.

It took me a few seconds to realise that this particular cable was attached to a phone socket. All at once the words of the real estate agent came back to me: 'It's very well serviced, this shed. There's enough voltage for power tools, there's a tap, there's a phone connection, and if you want to install a toilet, the sewer pipe's just outside…'

'God!' I heaved my chosen box onto the floor and started frantically rummaging through vintage appliances—kettle, toaster, iron, sandwich maker—until I found the old phone, a sticky, dusty, cream-coloured wedge of obsolete technology about the size of a large paperback. It had a keypad and a cable, so I grabbed the plug and hunkered down to find its matching wall socket, which for some reason was hidden away under the lowest shelf. I nearly dislocated my shoulder trying to push in that plug. And as soon as I did, the phone rang.

Alarmed, I swung around to answer it. The last thing I wanted was for Nerine to hear the damn thing.

'Yes? Hello?'

'Meg?'

'*Jill?* Oh my God—'

'Listen.'

'Jill—'

'Duncan's dead!'

I nearly choked on my gasp of alarm.

'Nicole just called. They found him in the roof of his house. Meg, he'd been there for *weeks*. You've got to get away from that woman.'

'Jill—'

'I'm so sorry. This is my fault, I didn't—'

All at once the handset was jerked away. I saw it slam back

into its cradle. Then I looked up.

Nerine was looming over me. She seized the phone and yanked the line out.

'Who was that?' she hissed, her expression hard.

'No one.'

She smashed the phone straight into my face. The pain was like a bolt of lightning. I fell back, too shocked to cry out. Tears spurted from my eyes.

'Who *was* that?' she repeated.

Uncovering my nose, I looked down and saw that my fingers were covered with blood. When I spoke, I sounded as if I had a head cold.

'More to the point, who was *that*?' I pointed at the rafter tie where her victim had been hanging. 'I know it wasn't your ex. Your ex is dead in your attic.'

Something shifted behind her eyes. She retreated a step, still holding the phone. It had a smear of blood on it. 'What? What are you talking about?'

By this time I was staggering to my feet, though I didn't know if I'd be able to run.

'Who did we push off the cliff?' I was blowing tiny bubbles through the blood in my mouth. 'Who did you kill?'

She stood for a moment, completely still, her blank gaze fixed on me. Then she said, 'A rapist.'

I blinked.

'I was out walking,' she continued flatly. 'I went too far, he gave me a lift home, then he tried to feel me up and when I got out of the car and ran into the house, he tried to follow me—'

'Bullshit.'

I didn't normally swear like that. She was speechless for a moment, her mouth agape. In the sudden silence I heard something.

An approaching vehicle.

Nerine heard it too. Her head swivelled. 'What the fuck?' she said. Then she rounded on me again. 'Who the fuck is that?'

'I don't know.'

She raised the phone threateningly. '*Who were you talking to?*'

'To Jill. She's up north. This can't be her.'

Nerine froze again for half a second. I could almost hear the cogs whirring inside her head. Then she reached out and grabbed my wrist.

'We're in this together, Meg,' she reminded me in a low voice. 'If I get caught, so do you. If we stay cool, nobody gets caught. And nobody gets hurt, either.'

Nobody gets hurt? I stared at her, astonished, the blood still trickling from my nose.

'Come on.' She began to haul me outside. I went because I was scared. If I tried to break free she could easily club me to death with that phone. And I knew she wouldn't hesitate to do it because I'd seen her face: flinty, savage and clenched like a fist. She was beyond reason now. Something strange and dark had flowered inside her.

As I stumbled towards the house I tried to slow my pace so the driver heading in our direction would reach the gate before

I reached the front door. It was no good, though; Nerine dug her nails into my arm, forcing me to speed up. Together we mounted the steps and banged into the vestibule, where she locked the door behind her and said, 'Get the kids. They're in the kitchen.'

I was surprised when she released me; she had to know there was a risk that I would escape through the back. But when I reached the kitchen and saw Ana patiently helping Colette put the Tupperware back in its drawer, I knew I couldn't just walk out on them. If I was leaving, I would have to take the kids.

'Hello, girls.' I was about to swoop on Colette when Ana turned to look at me. Her mouth crumpled. Her arms coiled around her little sister, who began to cry.

I suddenly remembered the blood all over my face.

'It's all right,' I said. 'You don't have to worry. I fell over and hit my nose, that's all.'

'Nah!' moaned Colette. She started crawling away. When I tried to pick her up, she hit out at me, squealing.

'Give her some Phenergan.'

I spun around. Nerine was standing in the doorway with Dinah's rifle. She must have hidden it in the cupboard.

'Check the Earl Grey,' she said.

As I stood there gawking, Ana sprang to her feet, hurried over to the pantry cupboard and produced a small brown bottle from the tea canister. She unscrewed the lid and poured some medicine into it.

Her hands were shaking.

'One cap,' Nerine told her.

Appalled, I watched Ana pour the Phenergan down her sister's throat. 'Nerine—'

'Shut up.' The rifle swung in my direction. 'It's the only way to keep her quiet.'

'Please. Put the gun down.' I was trying to stay calm for the sake of the children. It's amazing what you can do when children are involved. I would have screamed my head off, otherwise. 'This isn't necessary. You're making things worse. Think of the kids.'

'I am,' Nerine snarled.

There was a sudden knock on the front door. 'Meg?' a familiar voice said loudly. 'I know you're in there. Open up.'

It was Keith.

For a moment I couldn't speak, let alone call for help. I clapped my hand over my mouth.

'Who is it?' Nerine whispered.

'Your car's out the front,' Keith continued from the veranda. 'And you've left your shed open. Are you going to let me in?'

He knocked again, then jiggled the doorknob. Nerine beckoned urgently to Ana, hissing, 'Get in your cupboard.'

Ana darted out of the kitchen. I grabbed Colette, who was groping for the brown bottle on the floor, and lifted her onto my hip. Nerine motioned me into the living room with a twitch of her gun.

'Who is it?' she repeated.

'My ex.'

She pulled a bemused face. I could hear Keith's footsteps retreating down the front stairs.

'We should be very quiet, then.' Nerine spoke softly. She followed me almost as far as the vestibule, but paused at the living-room window to peer through its gauzy curtain. By this time Ana had plunged into her hideaway; I was down on my knees, laying Colette beside her sister in a fluffy nest of pillows, when Nerine growled, 'I can't see him. Where's he gone?'

I didn't answer. Instead I put my mouth to Ana's ear. 'Look up,' I breathed, jerking my chin at the dim shape of the manhole overhead.

She obeyed.

'You can hide up there and no one will find you. Not even your mum.' My voice was so muted, I could barely hear it myself.

Ana frowned. She glanced at me with a question in her eyes—which I answered by gently touching the ladder that was leaning against the wall next to us.

'Oh, fuck,' said Nerine. 'Meg! Come here!'

She kicked my ankle. Reluctantly I crawled backwards out of the closet. There was a popping and cracking of joints as I climbed to my feet.

'He's heading round the side,' Nerine growled, her gun still aimed in my direction. 'What's he doing?'

'I don't know.' I didn't care, either. I was beyond that. 'Maybe he just wants to have a go at me.'

'Did you lock the back door?'

We stared at each other. A doorknob rattled, and Nerine swore under her breath. It crossed my mind that I ought to shout a warning but I didn't want to get shot. Not on Keith's account.

Nerine nudged me into the living room with the barrel of the gun. It was too late, though; by the time we reached the kitchen, Keith was already inside.

He jumped when he spotted me.

'Jesus!' he spluttered. 'What the hell have you done to your—' He stopped suddenly as his gaze settled on Nerine. '*Emily?*'

Being in the same room with Keith was always difficult. He seemed to change the atmosphere, filling every space he occupied with prickly vibrations. He was one of those people who triggered the need to placate, distract and soothe. It was something to do with his tone, I think—and his expression. Years of petulance had moulded his face into a permanently aggrieved expression.

He hadn't changed much since our last meeting. His hair was still dyed—something that infuriated me after all the shit I'd copped for dyeing my own. Then again, he probably didn't have a choice. The small patch of jet-black implants on his scalp would have looked pretty odd in a sea of grey.

Despite the implants, he cut an impressive figure: tall, sleek, well groomed, broad-shouldered. He smelled good, too, because his cologne was always expensive. I'm sure someone with a fashion sense could have identified the brand of every item he was wearing, but I've never had much of a fashion sense. It was one of my many failings, according to him.

'No, wait. You're not Emily.' His attention shifted to the rifle. 'What the hell is going on?'

'You're trespassing,' Nerine said.

'Who the fuck is this?' Keith demanded, turning to me.

Nerine raised the barrel of the Remington. 'None of your business.'

'Is that a threat?' Keith stood with his hands on his hips, his feet squarely planted. I could tell from his heightened colour and tight jaw that he was building up to one of his tantrums. It wasn't surprising; he always felt so superior to me that I could never intimidate him. And he tended to dismiss women as drama queens anyway. 'Great. Fantastic,' he barked. 'I bloody knew it—you're shacked up with a dyke who breaks your nose and looks like your own daughter. Wait till I tell Emily about this. You're perverted. Sick.'

He certainly knew how to push my buttons. I must have turned white under the bloodstains, but before I could ask him how he proposed to talk to Emily when she refused to talk to him, Nerine said, 'What do you want?'

'I want to settle this,' he replied, before addressing me again. 'I don't care what kind of warped stuff you're getting up to out here in the boondocks. It's no skin off my nose. But I want my fair share of the money or I'll go straight to the Supreme Court. It's up to you. Either you lose everything on lawyers or we split it fifty-fifty. I'm being more than generous—by rights I should be getting at least seventy-five per cent, since I'm her fucking *son*.'

I completely forgot about Nerine, the gun, the children and the dead man at the bottom of the cliff. Suddenly the only thing in my heart was the desire to make Keith suffer. I couldn't bear it that he was standing in my kitchen trying to boss me around again. I couldn't bear his fancy clothes, or his fruity cologne, or the way he was sneering at everything around him.

'You had your chance to negotiate,' I spat. 'You were offered a fifty-fifty split right at the start and you turned it down.'

'Then why are we arguing?' He reached inside his pea coat and pulled out a folded document. 'I've got a legal agreement right here. It's been signed and witnessed. If you sign it yourself, this whole thing will go away. And you'll still have more than a hundred thousand dollars in your pocket.'

I gave a snort. 'Are you serious?'

'Would you rather lose the money? Would you rather it all went to lawyers just so you can get your own back?' He rolled his eyes and shook his head, condescension oozing from every pore. 'Grow up, Megan. This is the real world.'

'I'm not signing anything unless David sees it first.'

'Meaning you still can't think for yourself?'

He was trying to needle me into making a mistake, but I just folded my arms and said, 'None of my share's going into my own pocket. Emily's getting the lot. So why don't you give her your share as well? Or don't you love her enough?'

Hah, I thought, watching my words hit home. I'd finally outmanoeuvred him; his eye twitched and his lips compressed as his face turned crimson. But before I could say anything else, Nerine interrupted.

'Meg will sign that form if you agree to hand over half her share right now.'

I gave a start and shook my head. 'Oh, no,' I mumbled. 'No, no...'

Keith looked confused. 'What?'

'Transfer fifty thousand dollars into her account right now and she'll sign anything. You can do it electronically.'

Keith's lip curled as he studied Nerine. 'You're mad,' he scoffed, his tone so contemptuous that it set off warning bells in my brain. 'I don't have fifty thousand dollars.'

'How much do you have, then?'

But he'd lost patience. 'Who is this?' he asked me.

'*How much do you have?*' Nerine repeated.

'That's none of your business.' It was as if he couldn't see the gun. 'Why don't you step out, whoever you are, and let Meg do her own talking?'

'Shut. The. Fuck. *Up.*' Nerine hoisted the rifle to her shoulder and aimed it straight at him. 'I know all about you. You're a whining, greedy, dickless waste of space. But for once you're gunna be useful.' She took a step forward, squinting down the barrel. 'Gimme your phone.'

I was still frantically shaking my head because I could see the whole disaster unfolding in front of me and I couldn't stop it. Nerine's voice was icy. Every one of her muscles was coiled like a spring. But if Keith was picking up the signals that were so alarmingly obvious to me, he seemed determined to ignore them. Perhaps he was too angry to notice. Perhaps he was bluffing. Or perhaps he still couldn't take a woman seriously.

'You know what? This is pointless.' He flapped his hands in disgust. 'I came here to negotiate, but there's no reasoning with people who are unhinged.' As he passed me on his way out, he thrust his face into mine and added, 'You'll be hearing from my lawyer. *And* from the police. I hope you've got a licence for that firearm because—'

The room exploded.

I screamed as splinters flew in every direction. The noise almost split my eardrums. I dropped to my haunches, shielding my eyes and wondering frantically how to get out. Then I remembered the children.

'Fuck!' Keith bellowed—and I realised he was cowering beside me. 'For fuck's sake! What are you—?'

'Don't move,' said Nerine. When I glanced up, I saw that the muzzle of her gun was just grazing the top of Keith's head.

'Nerine, don't.'

She ignored me. The shot, I noticed, had left a great gouge in my doorframe.

'This is what we're gunna do,' she told Keith. 'First you're gunna gimme your phone. Then we'll drive out to where we can actually get a fucking signal in this godforsaken dump. Then I'll check the balance in your account. And then you're gunna transfer fifty grand over to Meg. After which…'

She yanked back the bolt of her rifle with a ratcheting noise, releasing an empty cartridge that clinked to the floor.

'After which, Meg will sign your fucking contract. Okay?

Are we clear? Is everyone on board?'

Keith was squatting next to me, both hands raised. Panting and wild-eyed, he looked ready to erupt. But when he glanced at me, seeking help with some suicidal act of resistance, I gave my head an almost imperceptible shake.

'Yes? No? What's it gunna be?' Nerine demanded, prodding Keith with her rifle.

'Okay. Yes,' he croaked.

'Good. Great. Let's go, then.' She stepped back, gesturing with the gun. But as Keith slowly straightened, she said, 'Just to be clear, though—if you try anything stupid, I'll blow your balls off. Got that?'

Keith nodded.

It was a bittersweet moment. On the one hand, I was almost catatonic with fear and absolutely frantic about the children.

On the other hand, it was good to see my narcissistic ex-husband get slammed.

SIGNATURE

IT WAS THE cloudbank that reminded me. Heavy and slate-coloured, with a wispy white trim, it was rolling in from the west, straight towards us, as I made for the Baumanns' fence line.

The instant I spotted those clouds, I knew there was rain coming. And I also remembered the spring-loaded umbrella that I kept under the driver's seat.

I'd put it there for emergencies.

'Stop!' Nerine snapped. She was sitting directly behind me, her gun aimed at Keith's head. He was hunched in the front passenger seat, his knees pressed firmly against the glove box. Nerine had insisted on ramming the seat forward as far as it would go.

'Right,' she said. 'I've got a signal. Turn off the engine.'

I did as I was told. Something prodded me in the back of the neck.

'Here.' She pushed Keith's phone into my hand. 'You do

this. Remember what he said? Tap the dollar icon…'

Keith had already told us how to use his banking app. He'd also surrendered his car keys and his password, though not without encouragement. It had taken a while, but he'd finally got the message: Nerine was dangerous.

He'd probably decided to cooperate because he knew me so well. Having seen the look on my face as I watched Nerine, he must have realised I was more scared of her than I was of him. And that would have made him nervous.

The gunshot might have had an impact, too.

Now he sat huddled in the next seat, a fine sheen of sweat on his jaw. Though silent, he was thinking furiously; I could tell by his expression. It was the same expression I'd seen on his face when he was plotting to con a client or get even with a boss. The narrowed eyes, the pursed lips, the pounding vein in his forehead…they'd always signalled trouble in the past, and they always made my heart sink.

I hoped he wasn't about to do something that would get us both killed.

'Good. All right.' Nerine was murmuring into my ear as she peered over my shoulder. 'So next you enter the password…'

Keith's password was written on my arm, along with my own account details, which weren't recorded on my phone because I didn't have a banking app. The signal at my house was so useless, there was no point.

'Just copy all the details from your chequebook,' Nerine had said impatiently, back in the kitchen—at which point it dawned on me that she'd been through my things. How else would she have known I still had a chequebook? Not many people do now.

'There. That's it,' Nerine said. I could feel her breath grazing my cheek as a list of accounts appeared on the screen in my hand—five of them. Four were almost empty and one had a balance of forty-eight thousand dollars.

I couldn't help glowering at Keith. He'd claimed in court that he was skint.

'That's all earmarked,' he mumbled. 'I've got debts.'

Nerine wasn't listening. 'Hoo boy! The mother lode!' she said happily. 'I reckon forty thou will do me. You wanna enter your account, Meg?'

I didn't want to do anything of the sort. For one thing, I wasn't a thief—and for another, I could sense Keith's mounting fury. Reading his moods had once dominated my waking moments and I hadn't lost the skill.

Nerine wasn't giving me much of a choice, though. She had a gun and I didn't. She'd lost her mind and I hadn't.

So after keying in my account details, I transferred forty thousand with a single flick of my finger.

'Done,' I said.

Keith hissed.

'Ok-*a-ay*.' Nerine leaned back. I could hear the vinyl squeaking under her backside. 'Now Meg'll sign that contract. Got it there, Mr Wonderful?'

She was addressing Keith, who muttered under his breath as he produced the document again. He seemed reluctant to let it go. Perhaps he was afraid I'd tear it up.

'Give it to Meg,' Nerine told him. To me she said, 'Sign it.'

'With what?' I asked.

'Jesus.' She sounded ready to hit me. 'Anyone got a pen?'

Keith didn't respond.

'Come on, guys, we need a signature!' The growing urgency in Nerine's tone was making me anxious. And when I'm anxious, I appease.

'There's one in the glove box,' I told her, just as an idea flashed into my head. I knew I needed a back-up plan because Nerine was getting increasingly wired. Why the desperate need for a signature when it shouldn't even matter to her?

As Keith leaned forward, she jabbed the muzzle of her gun into his spine.

'Take it slow,' she warned.

Keith opened the glove box with a trembling hand. There was nothing inside that could have been used as a weapon—apart from the pen, of course, which he pulled out after rummaging through a pile of papers, wet wipes, spilled mints and screwed-up tissues. When he passed me the black ballpoint, I dropped it into the footwell. 'Sorry.' I quavered, though it wasn't really an accident.

'For fuck's sake.' Nerine sounded tetchy but not suspicious. She'd got into the habit of regarding me the way Keith did, I realised—as slow, clumsy, docile, gullible. A herbivore. So she didn't pay much attention as I groped around under my seat to retrieve the pen. By the time I'd straightened up, I also had the umbrella, which was tucked between my knees.

'Okay. Gimme the phone.' Nerine's fingers fluttered

briefly beside my left ear before clamping onto Keith's mobile. 'Now—sign the bloody contract and then we'll go and do something about that car door.'

I stiffened. 'What?'

'We've got a man with us,' Nerine said. 'I reckon this big boy could get down that cliff, don't you?'

My heart rate began to climb. Sweat broke out on my forehead. 'I don't think that's a good idea.'

'No? I do.' She was actually smirking. 'Go on, Meg. Sign the form.'

Keith was already offering it to me. His eyes narrowed when they focused on my face, which must have been putty-coloured. If Nerine was about to risk showing him the wreck of Duncan's car, it was because she had no intention of letting him talk about it afterwards. I was pretty sure that once we reached the clifftop, she would push him over the edge. And despite hating Keith with every fibre of my being, I couldn't just stand by while someone killed him.

If nothing else, he was Emily's father.

'We've got to go back,' I protested feebly, turning in my seat. 'What about the kids?'

'Shut up.' Nerine's voice was as cold as her glare. 'Sign the form.'

'But they'll be frightened.'

'No they won't. Colette will be fast asleep by now.'

'What about Ana, though?'

'Sign the fucking form, Meg.'

Sensing how close she was to an explosion, I snatched the

contract from Keith. And as I scribbled my name, a chilling thought crossed my mind. Did Nerine want my signature because she had my chequebook?

If she could forge a cheque, she wouldn't be needing me anymore…

'Thanks.' She whisked the contract away before I could stop her. 'Now let's get going.'

'Wait—hang on—that's mine,' Keith protested.

'You'll get it back when we're done,' said Nerine. Aware that her gaze had shifted towards him, I plucked the umbrella from where it had been resting, acutely conscious that there was only one more bullet in the gun. Without that threat hanging over us, Keith and I would be much better off.

'Can't we go back for the kids first?' I pleaded.

She scowled. 'Don't be a fool.'

'But I could keep them busy. On a bushwalk, say.'

'Drive.' Nerine shifted the gun slightly. Its muzzle swung in my direction, away from Keith, towards the windscreen. I immediately shoved my umbrella up at the gun and pressed the button on its handle. The umbrella sprang open like a parachute, pushing the gun-barrel skywards as a shot pierced the roof.

Keith hurled himself out of the car. I grappled for the gun. If Nerine was yelling at me, I couldn't hear; my ears were ringing.

Then she disappeared. I was still frantically trying to extricate the rifle from the spokes of the umbrella when she hauled open my door and yanked at my hair.

The pain was excruciating. I hit out reflexively but didn't connect. She dragged me from the driver's seat by my collar, tightening it around my throat like a noose as I kicked and clawed. For one horrifying moment I thought I was going to black out. Then I hit the ground and she let go. The air poured into my lungs again.

I rolled onto my stomach. She stamped on my arm. In fact she trampled all over my body to reach the driver's seat, where she briefly wrestled with the gun. Next thing I knew, I was staring straight down the muzzle.

'If you'd only got me out of this fucking place,' she spat, her eyes wide and hot and utterly insane, 'I wouldn't be doing this.' She pulled the trigger. Twice.

Nothing happened.

Snarling, she spun the weapon around and swung it at my head like a club. I moved just in time; my shoulder took a glancing blow hard enough to make me scream. Still, I managed to grab the rifle stock and hang on, using my weight to jerk it from her grasp. As I tumbled backwards she started to kick me in the ribs. So I hit her with the gun, making her bellow.

I thought she was going to lunge at me again but she retreated, throwing herself behind the steering wheel. The driver's door slammed shut. The engine roared.

'Shit!' I started crawling out of the way, terrified she was going to run me over. I knew I'd be safe once I was off the trail; the bush on either side was too rugged for my old Commodore. But the car was already reversing as she lined it up to ram me.

I dropped the gun, scrambled to my feet and stumbled towards the nearest tree trunk, which was thick enough to stop anything smaller than a semitrailer. I only realised I was limping when I tried to run. At first I didn't look back; I knew the slightest delay could be fatal.

It wasn't long, however, before I realised that the car behind me wasn't crashing through the undergrowth in pursuit. So I glanced over my shoulder—and saw, to my surprise, that the Commodore was completing a jagged three-point turn.

Next thing I knew, Nerine was heading back towards the house.

I didn't understand it. What the hell was she up to? Was she leaving? Was she pretending to leave? If I was lured out onto the trail again, would she be lying in wait somewhere up ahead?

I remembered Keith, who had disappeared into the bush. It didn't surprise me that he'd headed back to his car. Keith only ever worried about Keith; it wouldn't have crossed his mind to stay and help. Perhaps Nerine had gone to chase him down. Perhaps she was more worried about him than me because he was big and angry and had a head start. She obviously didn't realise that I had one major advantage over Keith: I knew the terrain. This was my land—my home—and I was familiar with every gully, thicket, path and boulder. Keith might get lost, but I wouldn't. I could easily find my way to the Huggetts' house, despite my bum knee, my bruises, my swollen nose and aching ribs.

The trouble was, I couldn't leave Ana and Colette. They

wouldn't be safe with Nerine. I was pretty sure she would drive off with the pair of them once she'd run over Keith and pocketed my chequebook.

I didn't know how I was going to stop her, but I had to try. I wouldn't be able to live with myself if I walked away. So rather than make a beeline for the Huggetts' fence, I retraced my steps to the fire trail, hoping to retrieve Dinah's gun. I thought it would be better if I hid it, since you can still threaten people with an unloaded firearm.

But the only thing left on the trail was a tangle of freshly churned tyre tracks.

My escape from Keith was planned very carefully. Before I left, I opened a new bank account. I cancelled my credit cards. I packed up birth certificates, prescriptions, passports, immunisation records. I made copies of Keith's various documents. I even sent some of Emily's toys ahead by mail.

Then, on the day of our departure, I shoved everything I could into a mismatched set of suitcases, stuffed Emily into a rental car and drove off to stay with my brother Brian, in Albury. Brian put me up for a month. We weren't close; he was seven years older and had much more in common with our brother Geoff. The pair of them had always regarded me as a spoiled brat because my father never hit me. He hit them all the time, until they finally left home when they were still in their teens and I was in primary school. I rarely saw them again.

Brian was an electrical engineer, dour and undemonstrative. Though he came to my wedding, he wasn't impressed with Keith. His own wife, Adele, was cheerful and competent and a great mother. Brian could have been more outwardly affectionate with his kids, in my opinion, but at least he didn't beat them. And he'd softened a little over the years.

'You're stronger than I thought,' he told me while I was living with him. 'I'm surprised you stuck with Keith for as long as you did.' He also told me, during a quiet moment on his front veranda, that I had done the right thing by running away. 'Sometimes escaping is the only smart option,' he said—and I knew he was thinking about Dad.

Escaping from Nerine was very much the smart option, but I couldn't do it. Not yet. Not till I knew her kids were safe.

The scrub on my property was crisscrossed with narrow tracks. One of them wandered north from the fire trail, then swooped around and made its way back towards my house, through a stand of mountain ash, over a dry creek bed and past the rear wall of my chicken coop. I decided to take that path instead of the road to the Huggetts' boundary line, just in case I ran into Nerine.

Thanks to the indirect route and my twisted knee, it took me so long to reach my destination that I was concerned I might have missed her. She was driving, after all, and if she hadn't gone looking for Keith, she would have been back at the house within five or six minutes. Her packing wouldn't have taken long, since she hadn't brought much. And I knew that the kids wouldn't have slowed her down. They wouldn't have dared.

I had a feeling that I'd get to the house and find the spare room stripped and my car gone. So I was surprised to hear Nerine's voice as I sidled up to the backyard, bent double behind a screen of native mint. She was shouting angrily about fifty metres away, somewhere near the chicken coop.

'Ana!' she bellowed. 'Analiese! You'd better come out now, you little shit!'

My heart rate shot up. I crept forward, holding my breath and wincing at every snap and shuffle. I don't think I've ever been so frightened—except once, after my divorce, when Keith dropped Emily off late and I thought he might have taken her out of the country. I remember how desperately I tried to stifle my growing sense of panic as I watched the minutes tick by, not knowing whether I should call the police or not.

This was the same kind of fear because I had no idea where Ana had got to. I'd shown her the manhole, the ladder. But climbing into the roof would be a big deal for such a little kid. She was more likely to have made a run for the henhouse.

'Fuck it!' Nerine yelped. There was a sharp bang; it sounded to me like the gate on the coop. 'Ana?' she screeched. 'Where are you? You'd better move your arse right now or I'll gut your fucking rabbit!'

A cold trickle of rage gave me the courage to keep moving, though I was afraid Nerine might hear the crackle of leaf litter under my feet. It was as if every tree and bird and insect was holding its breath at the approach of the storm on the horizon. The hush in the air seemed to magnify every little noise I made.

But Nerine was too busy yelling at her daughter to notice my rustling and crunching.

'Ana? If you don't come out, I'm gunna burn this whole place down!'

Her voice was fading slightly as she headed away from the coop. By this time I could actually see the wall of the henhouse just a few metres ahead, so I used it as cover, creeping up to the fence with my head down and my ears pricked.

I was about to peer over the tin roof in front of me when Nerine bawled, 'Don't make me come find you! Don't make me mad!' Then in a low tone she added, 'Fuck it, you better not have run away.'

I wondered if Ana had run away. It seemed unlikely, though. She didn't know the area. I'd shown her a secure hiding place—the manhole, the ladder—*surely* she would have used it.

'I'm coming to get you, Ana!' roared Nerine. 'If you're in that fucking shed, you'd better watch it!'

This was my chance. I raised my head and there she was—Nerine, stalking around the side of the house. Dinah's rifle was slung over her shoulder, and she moved with a jerky vehemence that boded ill for anyone standing in her way. I didn't move a muscle until she'd completely disappeared. Then I slipped between the strands of fence wire and hurried over to the back door, which was standing wide open.

The screen door squeaked a little but I knew Nerine wouldn't hear it—not from where she was. I also knew she wouldn't hear the sound of my footsteps as I crossed the living room, keeping well away from the window. The front door was shut, and since there was no glass in it, I wasn't visible from the yard.

Nerine must have searched the vestibule cupboard. All the blankets and pillows and stuffed animals had been yanked out of it and scattered all over the floor. But as far as I could tell, the manhole hadn't been disturbed.

She obviously hadn't looked up.

'Ana?' I said softly. 'It's me. Meg.'

I listened hard but couldn't hear anything. So I gripped the ladder with both hands and cautiously placed a foot on the bottom rung.

'I can take you away, if you want,' I murmured. 'But we'll have to hurry.'

There was a small clunk overhead, followed by a scraping noise. The manhole cover shifted slightly, exposing a triangle of darkness.

'Colette's asleep,' Ana announced.

At that instant I knew I'd been right to come back. A small bloom of happiness flowered in my heart.

She didn't trust her mother, but she trusted me.

'I'll carry her down.' As I climbed towards the manhole, Ana uncovered it. I was able to stick my head into the attic above—and saw with relief that she wasn't sitting in the dark. Light was seeping beneath the eaves and through the roof vent.

All the same, I could imagine now frightening it must have been, crouched in that stuffy, dismal space, surrounded by cobwebs and rat baits and crumbling insulation batts. No wonder she looked so pale.

Her sister was lying on one of the batts, eyes closed, mouth open.

'How did you get her up here?' I asked, mounting a few more rungs so I could reach for the motionless toddler.

'She wasn't asleep then,' Ana mumbled.

I slid my arms beneath Colette's limp form and pulled her towards me. Getting her through the hole was difficult—I had to descend the ladder, then drag her after me headfirst, my left arm clamped around her chest. She squirmed and muttered, but didn't open her eyes until her foot banged against the top rung.

At that point she began to whimper.

'Shh. It's okay. Shh.' Back on solid ground, I wrapped her in my arms and stroked her head as it settled onto my shoulder. She seemed to find comfort in my touch; the heavy rasp of her breathing was the only sound I heard while I waited in the vestibule.

On joining me, Ana whispered, 'Where's Mummy gone?'

I put a finger to my lips. Then I cocked my thumb at the front door before heading towards the kitchen, confident that Ana would follow me. If I'd had a spare key for the car, I would have tried to drive away. But the old Commodore hadn't come with a spare key. It hadn't even come with a spare tyre.

My best bet would be to fade into the bush again, heading for the Huggetts' and keeping well away from the drive out front. All I had to do was sneak across the backyard without being seen. A glance through the screen door told me the coast was clear. So with Colette balanced on my hip and Ana's hand tucked into mine, I crept down the stairs as quickly and quietly as I could, praying that Colette wouldn't notice Ruby or Perdita over by the henhouse. If she did, I knew, she would make some kind of noise.

At the bottom of the steps I turned right. Then I sidled along the wall of the house until it ended. The distance from there to the garden fence was only about twelve metres, but those twelve metres were pretty much devoid of cover. The viburnum along the fence was struggling. The maple I'd planted in the middle of the lawn was a scraggy little thing. The bed of hydrangea and jasmine and tree ferns along the eastern wall was only about forty centimetres wide.

Peeping around the corner, I could see the clump of grevillea near the gate. I could see the remains of a sawn-up tree that I'd never used for firewood because the pieces were as big as car tyres. I could see a tap and a watering can and the rear wheel of Keith's Audi, which was parked on the grass. But I couldn't see Nerine.

'This way,' I hissed and took a step forward as thunder rumbled in the distance.

'Hey!' A voice rang out behind us. *'Hey!'*

Nerine had come around the other side of the house.

FLIGHT

IF I'D BEEN ALONE, I might have given up. I might have tried to argue or plead. But the tightening of Ana's grip on my hand seemed to goose every neuron in my brain.

I knew we wouldn't reach the Huggetts' house. The path that led there was too rough for running; I'd been hoping we could pick our way along it unseen. With Nerine behind us we didn't stand a chance.

So I turned and galloped towards the garden gate. Cox's Ridge Road was closer than the Huggetts', and my driveway was easy to navigate on foot. I figured that on a Monday afternoon there had to be *some* passing traffic—enough, at least, to stop Nerine from pounding my skull to bits with her rifle stock.

'Stop right there!' she yelled. 'Ana! Stop!'

She sounded as if she was right behind me. I couldn't look back, though. I couldn't risk the delay.

'Go! Run!' I told Ana, as soon as we were through the gate

posts. Then I released her hand, hoping to see her streak ahead like a whippet. Instead she whimpered with distress, glancing over her shoulder. Tears were running down her cheeks.

'Come here, Big Bug.' Nerine's voice almost clanged with suppressed rage.

I wasn't thinking clearly, or I would have realised she had the advantage, even though we were the ones with the head start. She was younger than me, with longer legs. She wasn't limping or carrying a toddler. If she'd decided to run after us, she would have caught up long before we reached the cattle grid.

But she didn't run. I was jogging along clumsily behind Ana, with Colette banging against my hip, when I heard an engine revving.

Nerine was in my car.

'Shit!' An image leaped into my head like a signpost and I told myself, *You know this area. Nerine doesn't.* So I swerved. 'Ana! This way!'

She followed my lead, changing course towards a trail-head that was just a metre-wide gap in the wall of bush to our right. I was hoping that this narrow trail would force Nerine out of the Commodore. I was also hoping that, where the trail hit a T-junction about twenty metres ahead, I would be able to lie in wait for her with a branch or a rock.

I didn't understand how angry she was. When the car crashed onto the track behind us, toppling shrubs and crushing undergrowth, Ana screamed. She started sobbing loudly, clutching my shirt tails.

'Meg! Meg!' she wailed. 'Mummy's so mad!'

I didn't have the breath to reassure her, but I knew just what to do. The solution had come to me suddenly: a vision of the terrain up ahead. The left-hand turn. The sandy track. The slight rise leading up to the deepest stretch of watercourse on my block. A dry depression wound its way from the sou'-western corner to the eastern boundary, but only in one spot was it more than a shallow ditch. And at this very point, where puddles spread and lingered after heavy rain, a plank had been laid across the gully, forming a bridge between two paths.

Thanks to the lie of the land, this gully—about as wide as it was deep—couldn't be seen until you were almost on top of it.

'She wants us back,' Ana snivelled. Her weight was dragging on me. Colette was bawling. But I could barely hear either of them over the noise their mother was making in my car, which she was flogging along like a four-wheel drive. The desperate snarl of the engine mingled with the thud of rocks hitting metal and the crack of breaking boughs. Splinters sprayed everywhere as the vehicle headed straight for us.

I pulled Ana around the next bend. 'It's okay,' I panted. 'We'll be okay.' I was picturing the net of paths spread across my property while I calculated how to use them. I had the key to the maze and Nerine didn't. I could lose her in the laby-rinth. But first we had to get over the bridge.

'Maybe we should stop,' Ana moaned. 'Mummy's too mad. She's too mad.'

'Just a little bit further.' I was coughing and gasping,

winded, slowing down. But that didn't matter, because the path was beginning to rise. Scrambling up a gentle slope laced with tree roots, I heard the Commodore squeal like a buzz saw. The sound made me wince, and not just because it was so loud.

I knew my old car would never recover. I was mentally saying goodbye to it, just as I'd said goodbye to Esme.

'Watch your feet,' I warned Ana. We'd hit the top of the incline and the plank in front of me looked very narrow as I shuffled across it, trying not to break my stride in case the change of pace alerted Nerine. I found it helped if I focused on the plank and not on the gully beneath it. I had to let go of Ana's hand.

'Are you all right?' I asked, raising my voice over the furious howling and revving of my poor car. She didn't answer; she was too busy glancing back at the cloud of dust being churned up behind us. Then, just as we reached solid ground again, the Commodore's front grille and headlights lurched into view above a pair of furiously spinning tyres. For a split second everything seemed to hang there: the lights, the grille, the tyres, the bumper. Then, with a throaty roar, the front of the car almost sprang into the air before it toppled down into the gully, dragging the rest of the vehicle with it.

Frozen, I watched the plank snap like a toothpick. I ducked as the windscreen flashed by. I flinched at all the rending and screeching and banging. There was a thud that shook the ground and made me stumble backwards. A gush of steam jetted up.

Ana shrieked.

'It's okay.' I embraced her with my free arm. From where I stood, I couldn't see Nerine; I was looking at the tilted roof of my car through a veil of dust. The back wheels were still on the trail but the front ones were deep in the ditch below me. The engine was still running.

I suddenly realised that Colette was screaming in my ear.

'Stay here, okay?' I told Ana. Releasing her, I took one, two, three steps forward until the Commodore's cracked windscreen became visible. Through the crazed glass I spotted Nerine's silhouette, struggling furiously.

'You bitch!' she cried. Then, with a grinding rattle, the driver's door popped open. The engine clicked off. An arm appeared.

I didn't hang around to watch her climb out of the car. I figured if she was well enough to shout, she was well enough to come after me with her gun.

'She's fine,' I said to Ana. 'Let's go.' Seizing her hand again, I charged down the path on my bad knee, struggling with Colette, who was now well and truly out of her Phenergan stupor. She yelled. She flailed. She scratched and snivelled.

'Shh. It's all right. We'll be there in a minute…' I spoke mechanically, preoccupied with the route ahead. I needed to reach the road before Nerine did. A shorter path drifted back towards the drive; a longer one went all the way to the Baumanns' fence before turning south.

But the shorter path was badly overgrown, blocked by prickly branches and fallen tree-limbs. I had to edge along sideways like a crab, shielding Colette from the clawing, slashing scrub. She wouldn't stop crying no matter what I did. After about ten minutes of very slow progress I was amazed that Nerine hadn't caught up. God knows, we were easy enough to track.

'Look, Colly—poo!' I said at last, in sheer desperation. I eased down to a squat, puffing and blowing and straining my poor knees, to pick up a couple of wallaby scats. As I gave them to Colette, I told myself that wallabies were herbivores—that the scats were old and dry—that a few encounters with healthy garden dirt sometimes helped to boost a child's immune system. 'It's kangaroo poo, look.'

'Ooo-pooo,' she murmured, her sobs miraculously silenced. I straightened up and set off again, hurrying towards the road. Then a strange cry from the west made me stop and listen. A man's voice? It sounded a bit like Keith.

'What's that?' Ana whined.

'I don't know.' It occurred to me that Keith might have tried to climb through the Baumanns' electric fence, but I didn't want to alarm Ana. 'Maybe it's a cockatoo.'

'No, not that. *That.*' Her tone was impatient. She tugged at my arm.

I frowned, then caught my breath as the sound reached me too. It was the rumble of an engine. For a moment I thought it was coming from the road. I was picking up my pace, hoping to intercept whatever vehicle might be passing, when I realised that the low purr was somewhere behind us.

A car was rolling down my driveway.

*

When I think about it now, I realise that Emily has spent her whole life trying to escape.

It all began with her father's tantrums. If they were noisy and explosive, she would hide under the bed or climb into the laundry basket. If they were ominously silent, she would sit at the dinner table willing herself to disappear. I remember the deafening clank of forks on plates as we mutely ate our food. I remember the aggressive way Keith would bite off a mouthful, or shake the saltcellar, or set down his glass with a ringing *snap*. I also remember how Emily did everything right. She never ate with her elbows on the table or laid a dirty knife on the cloth. She was trying not to become the focus of his free-ranging temper.

As she grew up, she learned the art of distancing herself. When he came through the front door, she would go out the back. When the phone rang, she let it: she wouldn't pick up in case it was Keith. She found welcoming boltholes at the homes of neighbours and schoolfriends. Later, she spent a lot of time at the library, or at after-school drama and sports clubs. She didn't particularly enjoy netball or scene-shifting, but she liked Keith's scorn even less. 'You're just like your mother,' he'd say, and it wasn't meant as a compliment.

That criticism hit home, even though she ended up despising him. The one thing she didn't want was to be like me. She wasn't interested in music. She hated my taste in movies and clothes. She grew increasingly dismissive of my opinions on anything more controversial than laundry powder.

When she was twelve years old I left Keith, but I didn't really escape. I had vague ideas of teaching music in the country somewhere; it never occurred to me that he would set the police on us. After failing to have me charged with kidnapping, he finally managed to get a court order that stopped me from 'relocating' with my child. I was dragged back to Sydney—where I found it very hard to make ends meet—and for the next four years, Emily had to spend holidays and most weekends with her father. She didn't want to. Sometimes she would run away from him. Sometimes she would run away from me when I tried to take her to him.

I know she still blames me for not winning the endless custody battle.

When she turned sixteen she refused to visit him anymore. I copped a lot of flak from Keith over that, but it was Emily's decision. That same year, she insisted on learning how to drive. I couldn't afford driving lessons so I attempted to teach her myself, with predictable results. I was putting her off with my 'insane anxiety', she said, and went to visit my brother Brian, who taught her how to drive his ute. That was also her decision. I didn't have any say in it.

She finished school at eighteen, then immediately moved out. Nothing I said could dissuade her. She told me she'd found herself a waitressing job and would be renting a room in a share house because she wanted her independence. University wasn't going to give her that. 'Don't tell Dad where I am,' she said as we traded goodbyes on the doorstep of her new home. 'I don't want him sniffing around looking for money.'

'He won't,' I assured her with a crooked grin. 'For one thing, you don't have enough.'

Emily snorted. Then she told me how he'd once borrowed the birthday money his mother had given her. 'He never repaid it,' she said. 'Just like he didn't give back the change he stole from my piggybank when I was six.' Seeing my face, she sighed and shrugged. 'Come on. You didn't figure it out?'

'You should have told me.'

'Oh, yeah,' she drawled. 'That would have worked.'

All things considered, I shouldn't have been surprised five years later when she rang to say she was moving to England with her boyfriend Nick. I was living near Bulwell by that time, and never saw her unless I visited Sydney. She had no interest in the bush. No interest in Esme. No interest in me, really, though she approved of my job at the Women's Health Collective.

The only thing I could do for her was to keep her address hidden from Keith, and I even failed at that. He must have hired a private detective; I know she paid good money to keep her number unlisted.

'I'm lucky Gran was born in Scotland,' she said, referring to Carol—who was still alive then, and always eager to see Emily. 'Means I can get an ancestry visa.'

'But—I mean—how long are you planning to stay there?'

'Dunno. We'll see what happens. Gran's given me some money, so that'll help.' She gave a sudden honk of laughter. 'Dad heard about that money, did you know? He actually bailed me up on the street outside Gran's and told me I should invest it instead of "pissing it away". Can you believe that?'

'Oh, dear.'

'I said to him, "You mean pissing it away on one of your dodgy businesses?" Nick had to threaten him with a guitar case.' Her tone became pensive. 'You should keep an eye on Gran while I'm gone, in case he tries to kill her. I wouldn't put it past him. He'd do anything for cash.'

Three weeks later, I said goodbye to her at the airport. I was blinking back tears, but her eyes remained dry. Though excited and scared, she wasn't regretful. She kept rummaging in her bag for a tube of lip balm while I offered up a few sad little bits of advice.

She did kiss me. That was something. And Nick gave me a sympathetic hug.

Watching them head for the departure gates, I waited for Emily to glance back. When she didn't, I knew I'd lost her. All I could do was hope she'd be happy, though I had my doubts. She wanted to escape from her father, and from me, and from the country where the family court had failed her so egregiously. But I had a sneaking suspicion she also wanted to escape from Emily Delgado. And that wasn't going to happen. It never happens. You might try to leave your old self behind, but it always comes with you.

The only thing you can do is fight it with every weapon at your disposal.

'Is it Mummy?' Ana squeaked, as we listened to the grumble of the engine closing in on us.

I didn't see how it could be anyone else. The only

functioning car left on my property was Keith's, and Nerine had taken his keys. She must have staggered back to the house for the Audi. But did this mean she was on the run?

I doubted it. She'd brought her children all this way; I couldn't see her abandoning them now.

'Shhh,' I whispered. 'Be very quiet.'

Somewhere beyond a screen of grey-green foliage, the car was drawing level with us. I held my breath, hunkering down to hide. There was no wind, so I had to be careful. I didn't want to make any branches sway.

The car didn't stop. It didn't even slow. Plotting its course as it passed us, I smelled a whiff of exhaust. Then I heard the thump and whir of wheels hitting the cattle grid at my front gate.

I couldn't believe it. Was Nerine actually leaving?

'Meg—' Ana began.

'Shh! Wait!'

I was straining my ears. The car had braked at Cox's Ridge Road. Would it turn left or right? *Right*, I thought.

It was turning right, towards Bulwell.

But the crackle of tyres wasn't followed by a change in the pitch of the Audi's low, idling growl. Instead the engine was switched off. A few clicks told me the car was sitting by the side of the road, no more than twenty-five metres away, with Nerine inside it.

She was lying in wait.

Colette muttered something, still engrossed in her handful of poo.

'Shh...' I was thinking hard. There were two ways out of this. We could head for the Huggetts' house and hope Nerine didn't have the same idea. Or we could make for a spot further to the west, just beyond the edge of my property, where Cox's Ridge Road hit a sweeping bend. It was impossible to see the road past that bend if you were anywhere near my front gate. All I had to do was climb through the Baumanns' fence and keep going.

I began to retreat cautiously, hoping that Nerine couldn't see the bushes nod and dip as I brushed past them. Ana was wiping her face, which was wet with tears and snot. I could feel her hand trembling in mine.

Colette was getting heavier and heavier.

'Poo,' she said, as the last of the crushed droppings trickled through her fingers.

'Yes. Poo,' I replied in a low voice. 'Do you want some more?'

'Poo!'

'Shh. Let's look for some more.' I had to keep her occupied. If I didn't, she would start to get noisy. 'Watch the ground. Can you see? Is there poo on the ground?'

For the next few metres Colette kept her gaze pinned to the track ahead of us, which became wide and straight once we hit the first junction. By that time I was switching her from hip to hip every couple of minutes because my arms were so tired. My knee was aching too, and I was very thirsty. 'Not far now,' I assured Ana. 'We're nearly there.' I couldn't tell if she was listening; her expression was dazed. Preoccupied.

At one point we encountered a half-eaten chew toy—a rubbery red mouse that had once been Esme's. When I picked it up, I was relieved to find the squeaker was missing.

Colette was very excited by this headless mouse. She squeezed it and sucked it and shook the dirt out of it, clucking to herself but never raising her voice. I didn't try to stop her. Whatever kept her quiet was okay by me.

At last we reached the Baumanns' fence, which was fitted with cut-off switches at regular intervals. I found one and slammed the lever down.

Then I turned to Ana. 'We can climb through now,' I said. 'The electricity's turned off.'

Ana fixed me with a blank look. I demonstrated what I meant by manoeuvring Colette between the fence wires, stamping on one while I lifted the other. After placing Colette on the Baumanns' land—where she sat down abruptly and began to fill the red mouse with dirt—I climbed through the fence myself. Then I offered Ana an encouraging smile, which prompted her to follow me.

'Dah!' Colette cried, when I picked her up again. She rammed the red mouse into my swollen nose so hard that my eyes watered.

'Lovely,' I mumbled, weighing my options.

I had no mental map of the Baumanns' place. I didn't know where to find their paths. I didn't even know if there *were* any paths, since the house itself was miles away, at the bottom of a steep hill where the gorge opened out onto prime riverside grazing. The last thing I wanted to do was blunder about in the bush until I fell off a cliff.

The only visible way out was the cleared strip along the Baumanns' fence. I could see almost as far as the road when I stared down that straight, empty ribbon of dirt, which was kept free of grass and vines to stop the fence from shorting. But my eyes weren't good enough to pick out any intersecting paths up ahead. I just had to hope I would hit one.

'Come on,' I said, taking Ana's hand. I was hobbling by this time. My shoulders ached, my damaged nose throbbed and spasms of pain kept shooting through my right knee. I was starting to worry that I wouldn't make it.

You have to, I told myself fiercely. *For the children.*

Thunder rumbled overhead. The light seemed almost subterranean.

'Gorloff,' said Colette, shaking dirt out of the mouse. Some of the dirt landed on me. Some hit Ana, who seemed to snap out of her trance.

'Stop it,' she hissed.

Then I noticed a fork in the trail. It was about five metres in front of us and exactly what I'd been looking for. While the main track followed the fence, another path peeled off to the right, in a sou'-westerly direction. Narrow, poorly defined and pinched between outbreaks of Christmas bush, this side-path looked more like a wallaby pad than anything else. But it was our only option.

Ana began to complain almost as soon as we turned down it. 'Ow!' she whined. 'It's scratchy.'

'Sorry, sweetheart. Not much longer.'

'You said that before.'

'I know, but it's true. Look.' I pointed at a cleared patch beyond a band of roadside trees. I knew that the road itself was swinging around to meet us—that we'd reached the bend where it drifted north. Soon, I decided, the path and road would intersect. And then we'd be able to flag someone down without being spotted by Nerine.

I was wrong, though. We'd been walking for a few more minutes when the trail under our feet began to veer off to the right, and I realised that we would have to have to cut our own path to the road. It wouldn't be a long path, but it was going to hurt. So I let go of Ana's hand.

'Get behind me, sweetie,' I said. 'Close your eyes and hold onto my cardigan. Collie? Sweetheart? I'm going to give you a piggyback.'

That last stretch was the hardest. I put my head down and slammed through the scrub like a bulldozer, cutting my hands, scratching my face, tearing my clothes. I jarred my bad knee flattening the carpet of twigs underfoot. Thunder rolled overhead and Colette mewed in my ear. When she dropped her red mouse, I had to stop and pick it up.

But at last there was no more bush. I stumbled out onto the roadside gravel just as the sound of an engine reached us.

I froze. Was it Nerine?

Then I realised the vehicle was coming from Bulwell.

'Here we are.' My voice was hoarse and ragged. 'Here's someone.'

I turned my face to the west and began to wave my arms

like a drowning swimmer, waiting for the unseen car to round the bend down the hill. When a vehicle finally appeared, I nearly cried with joy—because it was an old silver Mercedes.

I recognised Tearle Godwin's car.

BETRAYAL

'OH MY GOD.' I was about to yell for help when I remembered. No noise. We had to be very quiet.

So I let my arms do the screaming, swinging them about like a semaphore signal tower.

The Mercedes was already losing speed. As it approached us, I caught a glimpse of Tearle's face beneath the patches of light and shade sliding over the glass in front of him. His mouth had fallen open.

'Cah,' Colette cheeped, pointing.

'Shh.' I dredged up a tattered smile for Tearle, who was easing the Mercedes onto the wide gravel shoulder. By the time he came to a halt a step or two away from me, he was already lowering the passenger window.

I leaned down to address him, but he spoke first.

'For Christ's sake, Meg, what happened?'

At that instant I caught sight of my reflection in a side mirror. My face was smeared with dried blood. My hair was a bird's nest, stabbed with twigs and leaves. My clothes were filthy and dishevelled.

'Thank God you're here.' There was a lump in my throat. 'What a stroke of luck.'

'It wasn't luck. David Blazek called.' Craning his neck, Tearle stared up at me. I'd never seen him look so shaken. 'He was worried because you sounded strange on the phone, so when I couldn't get through, I thought I'd come and make sure you were all right.'

'We have to go. Right now.'

'Meg, who are these kids?'

'They're with me.' To Ana I said, 'Get in.'

'No! Wait!' Tearle was aghast. 'I don't have legal child restraints!'

Ana froze in the act of pulling open the rear door. I couldn't believe what I was hearing. 'We're in *danger*, Tearle.'

At that instant Colette began to cry. The urgency in my voice must have set her off.

I hastily shoved her into the back seat, ignoring Tearle's splutter of reproof.

'We're going for a drive,' I told her, with a forced cheeriness that didn't sound the least bit convincing. 'Look at Tearle's lovely car. Isn't it nice?' I was struggling to belt her in when someone shouted.

It wasn't Analiese. It wasn't Tearle, either—he was still behind the wheel, twisting around to see what I was doing.

It took me a moment to realise that Keith had burst out of the bush a few metres down the road.

'Stop!' he screeched. 'She's dangerous!'

I backed out of the car so quickly that I thumped my head. Ana was clutching my sleeve in terror. 'Get in,' I croaked.

I felt like murdering Keith.

He was stumbling towards us, all scratched and bedraggled. 'Don't listen to her. She tried to kill me—they both did.'

'Shhh.' I flapped my hands at him. 'Shut up, you fool, she'll hear you.'

He didn't listen. He never listened.

By this time Tearle had pushed open his door and was climbing out of the car. If Keith recognised him from our visit to court, he gave no sign of it.

'I'm the victim, not her,' Keith insisted. 'This woman and her girlfriend—they tried to shoot me—'

'Girlfriend?' Tearle echoed.

'For God's sake, get in!' I'd yanked open the front passenger door. 'Both of you get in.'

Tearle hesitated. 'What are you doing here?' he asked Keith, his voice hardening. 'Were you invited?'

'Of course not.' Safely tucked inside the Mercedes, I fumbled for my seatbelt. The girls were now cowering in the back; I peered around to smile at them. 'Shh. It's okay. This is Tearle. He's a friend of mine.' To Tearle I said, 'Will you please get us out of here?'

'If you've been harassing this woman, Mr Delgado—'

'Come on, will you?' Leaning across the gearstick, trying to attract his attention, I grabbed the door next to me and yanked it shut. I didn't realise Keith was reaching into the car with one hand.

His scream of pain nearly burst my eardrum. I reacted automatically, shoving the door open again as Colette raised her own voice as well. The commotion was deafening. Nerine was bound to hear it.

'Shh. Get in,' I pleaded.

But Keith was now tottering about, howling and clutching his fingers.

'You stupid bitch!' he wailed. 'You stupid fucking bitch!'

From the back seat, Colette was screaming like a power tool. Tearle said, 'Oh, God.' I searched the footwell in front of me for a rag, but saw only a familiar strongbox.

'Jesus, Tearle. Were you planning to shoot someone?' Stripping off my cardigan, I thrust it at Keith. 'Here,' I said breathlessly. 'Is it bleeding?' He didn't seem to hear.

By this time Tearle had stuck his head back in the car. 'I wasn't intending to use the gun,' he told me. 'I was on my way to a dealer when David called.' His voice was barely audible through the racket that Colette was making.

I swivelled in my seat to address her.

'Sweetie—Collie—where's the mouse? Eh? Where's the red mouse?' But I couldn't see Esme's chew toy. Ana was no help, either; curled up in a grubby little ball, she'd shut her eyes and was sucking her thumb. It was as if she wanted to block out the whole world.

Then suddenly Keith cried, 'Shit! Fuck! She's got my car!'

When I glanced through the windscreen, I saw his Audi coming round the bend up ahead.

'Drive, Tearle! Drive!' I was vaguely aware of Keith scrambling into the seat behind me. A door slammed. Colette squawked like a cockatoo. I could hear Ana whimpering, 'I'm sorry, Mummy. I'm sorry, Mummy.'

But Tearle just stood there, staring at the Audi as it barrelled along the road. He might have been in shock. *I* was in shock. For one fleeting moment I thought that Nerine was going to plough straight into us, since she was speeding down the wrong lane.

Instead she braked and yanked at the wheel, skidding sideways until she screeched to a halt just in front of the Mercedes. I didn't see any of this; I'd instinctively covered my eyes to shield myself from the coming crash. It was the squeal of tyres and the smell of burning rubber that made me lift my head.

When I did, I realised that the Audi was angled across the road, blocking the eastward lane and part of the shoulder. For a split second nobody moved. Tearle was standing frozen, one foot in his car and one foot outside it. Keith had grabbed my headrest with his uninjured hand. Even Colette was silent.

Then Nerine pushed open her door and climbed out of Keith's car. She looked almost as bad as I did. There was blood in her hair. Dirt on her clothes. She moved stiffly, her face set in a grimace of pain.

'Oh, shit,' said Keith. Then he yelled at Tearle, 'Get the fuck inside!'

But Tearle was in lawyer mode. He straightened, addressing Nerine in a crisp, dry, official voice.

'You'll have to move that vehicle. You're endangering people's lives.'

Nerine pointed straight at me and snarled, 'She stole my kids.'

'And *she* tried to kill me!' Keith suddenly bawled, right in my ear. 'She's a fucking maniac!'

'Okay, listen,' said Tearle. 'First that car has to be moved. Then we can discuss this in a civilised way—'

'She stole my fucking kids,' Nerine snapped. 'Is that civilised?'

'*She* stole my fucking car,' Keith countered. He'd stuck his unscathed hand out the window to point at her.

'Tearle, she's killed people.' I found my voice, at last, though it was hoarse and broken. 'She's not in her right mind.'

I don't know if he heard me. Nerine certainly didn't. 'Gimme my kids and I'll go,' she said. 'Those are *my kids*.'

'I'm not disputing that,' Tearle replied. 'I'm also not doing anything until you move your car. It's a hazard where it is.'

'Gimme the kids first.'

But Tearle held his ground. 'If you don't move your car, the children might be injured. Please—this is a blind corner. Move your car.'

I couldn't help being impressed by his calm and careful attitude, though it obviously infuriated Keith, who yelped, 'It's not her car, it's mine. Oh, for fuck's sake.'

Everyone ignored him. Nerine thrust an arm back into

the Audi. Tearle said, 'Maybe we should call the police.' He was reaching into his own vehicle for his phone when Nerine suddenly jerked upright, cradling Dinah's gun.

'Don't move.' She was aiming straight at him.

'Oh, shit.' Keith must have ducked down into the foot-well behind me because my seat started to shake beneath the impact of his knees and shoulders. Hearing Colette's wordless protest, I wondered if he'd pushed her out of the way.

'Tearle, that gun's not loaded.' I had already grabbed Tearle's mobile, but it was a fancy new iPhone with face ID. It wouldn't unlock.

'Step away from the car,' Nerine said. I glanced up to see that she was closing in on Tearle, chin lowered, eyes blazing. 'Ana!' she yelled. 'Get outta there! Now!'

A squeak and a shuffle told me that Ana had decided to obey. I turned my head and saw the defeated slump of her shoulders. She wouldn't look at me.

'Don't,' I begged her. 'Wait.' And I snatched at Tearle's keys, which were still sitting in the ignition.

I was only vaguely aware of Colette, who had shoved her whole fist into her mouth. Tearle seemed to be moving away from the Mercedes. Down on the floor, Keith was hissing, 'How do you *know* it's not loaded?'

I ignored him and scooped up the steel strongbox from its place under my feet. Then I examined Tearle's keys with trembling fingers. It was the same set he'd used on our tour of his house. I knew the key to the strongbox was in there some-where. I even knew what to look for.

Outside, Tearle was saying, 'Please. Someone could come around that bend at any moment.' His voice sounded higher than usual, but still calm. 'Think of the children—'

'Shut up.' Nerine's voice was calm too. 'Ana? I'll count to three. One…two…'

I heard the click of a rear doorhandle. A gust of cool air wafted into the car just as I found the right key.

'That gun's not loaded,' I cried, unlocking the strongbox, 'but this one is!'

Then I whisked Tearle's suicide special from its blue-velvet nest and scrambled out of the Mercedes.

'Oh, Christ,' moaned Tearle. He was staring at his pistol, which I'd pointed straight at Nerine. I'm sure she could see its barrel shaking.

'Drop that gun. Now,' I said to her. 'And put your hands on your head.'

I was quoting from some long-forgotten movie. Nerine must have sensed it, because she sneered as she let the rifle fall to the ground with a crash. Ana, by this time, was standing on the road near Tearle, her whole body quivering like a cobweb. My heart bled for her.

Tearle's hands were in the air.

'Pick that up,' I told him, nodding at the rifle.

He lowered his arms. 'Meg—'

'*Pick it up.*' I was so sick of people second-guessing me. I was so sick of coaxing and deferring and being ignored. Even Tearle seemed to think I was a halfwit. Why couldn't he just pick up the bloody gun?

'You'd better do it,' Nerine suddenly blurted out. 'She's crazy.'

I was glaring at her when a Land Rover came roaring around the bend. It was heading west, in the other lane, so it didn't plough into us. But as it whizzed past I caught a flash of someone's startled face framed in the driver's window. A mouth dropped open. A pair of dark eyes focused on my revolver.

Then the vehicle shot off down the hill, gathering speed. I wondered if someone inside was already reaching for a phone.

'She stole my kids,' Nerine went on, attempting to sound reasonable. 'She killed a guy and pushed him off a cliff in his car.'

I almost laughed out loud. The gall of the woman! 'No, that's what *she* did.'

'We've been trapped in her house for a week. She made me dye my hair so I'd look like her daughter.' Nerine's voice suddenly caught on a sob. 'It's been a nightmare. I'm sorry, I guess I lost it for a moment, but what was I supposed to do when she drove off with my kids?'

'Shut up.' I jerked the pistol at her. 'She's lying,' I assured Tearle, who was looking confused. 'Keith—tell him what really happened.'

Keith was now halfway out of the Mercedes, with Tearle's phone in his good hand. The other was hanging limp, red and swollen. 'Don't ask me,' he growled. 'I don't know what the fuck is going on.'

An old, entrenched rage bubbled up inside me like stomach

acid. 'Keith,' I barked, 'you were *there*. You *saw*.'

'Saw what? A couple of crazy bitches with a gun?' Ignoring my gasp of outrage, he added, 'And one of 'em's done up like my daughter, which is sick. What's that about, for God's sake?'

He wasn't going to help me. He was going to destroy me if he could. I turned back to Tearle and said, 'He's trying to get even. You know what he's like.'

But Tearle just extended his open palm, grim-faced. The rifle was in his other hand. 'Give me that gun, please.'

'Be careful.' Nerine spoke in a shaky voice, pretending to be scared. 'She's already killed one person.'

'That's a lie!' As I rounded on her, she stepped back and put her hands on her head. It suddenly occurred to me that I wasn't cutting a very impressive figure. So I lowered the pistol and passed it to Tearle—just as a screech of brakes made everyone jump and cringe.

Neville Huggett's white ute had appeared round the bend behind us. If it had been going any faster, it would have cleaned up the Audi. Instead it fishtailed into the oncoming lane, swerved onto the opposite shoulder and bounced to a halt.

Neville sprang out of the cabin, almost incandescent with fury. He slammed his door shut.

'What the fuck is going on?' he shouted. Then he spotted the pistol. 'What the fuck is that?'

'She stole my kids.' Nerine jabbed a finger in my direction. 'She tried to kill me.'

Neville wasn't listening. He stormed across the road.

'Get that fucking car outta the way! Jesus! You're gunna kill someone!'

'She already has,' said Nerine.

'That's a lie,' I protested. '*She* did it. And she forced me to help her get rid of the body.' Even as the words tumbled from my lips, I could see the impact they had on Tearle. He blanched. He swallowed. His whole frame sagged.

'Hey, mate.' Keith was talking to Neville, who had reached the patch of roadside gravel where the Mercedes was parked. 'Have you got a phone? Can you call the cops for us? Or an ambulance?'

'Not from here. The signal's shit.' Neville jerked a thumb at the Audi. 'Is that your car?'

'Yeah, but—'

'Then move it. Now.'

'I can't,' Keith retorted. 'Because *she's* got the fucking keys.'

He nodded at Nerine, who turned towards the Audi, saying, 'They're still inside. But I'll move it if you want—'

'No!' I wanted to grab the pistol back. 'Tearle, stop her. She'll run us over.'

Tearle winced. So did Ana, who was staring at the ground.

Nerine froze, then shrugged. She put her hands back on her head. 'Fine,' she said. 'Whatever. Don't argue with her. She's crazy.'

'I'm not.'

'You bloody are,' said Neville in tones of disgust. 'You're bloody paranoid. Accusing my poor old dad of stealing eggs, when you've been over ours stealing his shoes.' Before I could even process that, he called out to Keith, who was staggering towards the Audi. 'Are you moving yer car, mate?'

'Yep.'

'Good.' Neville was calming down. There was a gleam of genuine interest in his eyes as he peered at Tearle. 'What's with all the guns?'

'The rifle belongs to Meg,' Nerine piped up. 'She used it to stop us from leaving.'

'It's not mine,' I began, then remembered I'd borrowed it. Illegally.

'She made me dye my hair and wear makeup and put on clothes that didn't belong to me.' Nerine flicked a finger at the shirt she was wearing. 'Then one day a guy came to the door and I asked for his help and Meg killed him.'

'*She* killed him,' I cried, with mounting alarm. Tearle was actually listening to her—as was Neville. Neville looked absorbed. Tearle looked as if he was going to be sick.

'She killed her husband too,' I added quickly. 'Then she killed another bloke—I don't know why.' Had he attacked her? Had he asked too many questions? Or had he killed him so I would be irrevocably sucked into the chaos she'd created? None of these reasons seemed sufficient for murder, but I couldn't think of a reason that was. 'She's on the run from the police. She told me her husband was abusive. I'm not even sure that's true. She's been lying and lying. She slaughtered my dog.'

'She made my kids call her "Granny",' Nerine broke in. Behind her, the Audi roared as Keith circled around and pulled onto the shoulder up ahead. 'She called me "Emily". I kept saying I wasn't her daughter, but she wouldn't listen.'

'Tearle, for God's sake.' I was beginning to panic; Tearle's expression was remote. Stony. He seemed to be weighing up everything I told him. 'You know I'm not crazy. I took her in, and that was wrong, but I wouldn't kill someone.' Seeing him glance down at the rifle, I said urgently, 'She dyed her own hair because she's hiding out. It wasn't my idea. I was trying to help her, not hurt her.'

'Okay, I was hiding out,' Nerine admitted. 'I was running away from my husband. But she took advantage of that—she said she'd call the cops if I tried to leave. And when I did try, she locked me up. At gunpoint.' Warming to her subject, Nerine gestured vaguely towards the roadside bush. 'You should see her house. Everywhere you look, she's got pictures of her daughter. She's obsessed.'

'That doesn't surprise me.' Keith had switched off his car and climbed out. As he moved towards Nerine, he added, 'Emily left Australia because Meg wouldn't leave her alone.'

'Oh, you shit.' A flash of white-hot anger engulfed me. '*You're* the reason she went, you bastard!'

Keith didn't even glance in my direction. 'Where's my phone?' he asked Nerine, stopping beside her. 'I want it back.'

Nerine handed it straight to him. I couldn't believe my eyes. After all that had happened, was Keith really going to support her, just so he could mess with me?

'Tearle, Nerine's husband was found dead. In their home.'

I was trying to keep my voice steady. 'She must have killed him. Call the police—they'll tell you.'

'I didn't kill anyone,' Nerine protested. 'If Duncan really is dead, then some of his biker friends must have done it. But I bet he isn't. I bet she's making it up. She's always making things up.' Nerine's gaze wandered from Tearle's shuttered face to Ana's teary one. 'Ask my daughter. She'll tell you.'

I caught my breath. 'No,' I bleated.

'Isn't that right, Big Bug? Remember how you told Meg not to call me Emily? "That's not Mummy's name," you said.'

'No.' I moved to intercede. 'For God's sake, Tearle, don't let her drag Ana into it.'

But Neville grabbed me as I tried to pass. 'Leave the kid alone,' he growled.

I wrenched my arm away. Tearle gave a hiss and said, 'There's no need for that. Let's all keep calm.'

Meanwhile, Nerine was approaching Ana with a big, eager smile. 'Remember how Meg locked you in the cupboard? Remember how she threatened Mummy with that gun?'

Ana shrank away, all liquid eyes and eczema. There were red welts on her wrists, now. And on her neck. And on her shins.

I felt a pity so intense that it shook me to the bone. 'Don't,' I begged. 'Nerine. Leave her. The police will sort this out.'

'Remember how you had to call Meg "Granny"? Remember that?' Nerine was closing in on the poor kid like a lion stalking its prey. I was poised to yank her back when a stealthy movement caught my eye.

Colette had climbed out of the Mercedes and was toddling down the road.

'Oh, shit.' I charged after her, knocking Neville aside. Tearle had to step back, startled, as I pounced on the toddler and swept her into my arms. 'It's okay,' I crooned. 'Shh. Where's your mouse? Let's find your mouse.'

'Look. See? She wants my kids.' Nerine stood with her hands on her hips, looming over Analiese, who was rocking from foot to foot. I didn't have a clear view of Ana's expression, but her quailing posture filled me with despair. 'You tell the man, Big Bug. Meg locked us up, didn't she? Tell him.'

'Sweetie? Ana?' I looked at her and spoke as gently as I could. I wished I could hug her fear away. 'You say what you have to. I don't care. Whatever you say is fine.'

I meant it, from the bottom of my heart. Nothing Ana said would make any difference in the long run, and I didn't want her to feel guilty or unsafe or responsible for anything.

But when her head swung around, and she stared up at me, I was startled by the look on her face. It wasn't wretched. It wasn't remorseful. It was defiant. Resolute. Full of grim determination.

'Mummy's lying,' she said firmly.

Then she came over and took my hand.

EPILOGUE

I USED TO tell Emily bedtime stories. Once-upon-a-time stories.

Once upon a time there was a little blonde girl...

Once upon a time there was a sad little girl who had no front teeth...

Once upon a time there was an old woman living happily in a little green house in a big dark forest. But then a wolf came along, disguised as a mother, and she huffed and she puffed and she blew the house down.

I lost almost everything because of Nerine—though I could have lost more. The maximum penalty for child stealing is ten years. The maximum for conspiracy to defeat justice is seven. And then there's the unlicensed use of a firearm, which carries a penalty of up to five. I could have been imprisoned for twenty years or more, but I wasn't. My sentence was four years, and I was released on parole after eighteen months.

Renee picked me up from the Emu Plains Correctional Centre and drove me back to Taree. At least I didn't lose *her*;

there was no way of proving that we'd talked about Nerine, since we talked regularly about all kinds of things. But I lost my other friends: Jill Muzatti, who went to jail and whose family insisted we break off all contact. Bridget from work, who was disgusted with me. Sally Kristensen, who blamed me for what happened to Dinah and wasn't remotely appeased when I claimed in court that I'd told Dinah I had a gun licence. The lie might have helped; I don't really know. All I know is that Dinah had her own licence suspended.

But I think the shame of being my friend was worse punishment than anything. I was out on bail before the trial, so I know what it was like in Bulwell. People stared and pointed. People spat at me in the street. People refused to visit the Women's Health Collective while I was on the front desk, so I was taken off it. In the end I quit because I couldn't stand the strain. Sally didn't want me there. Bridget didn't want me there either.

Everyone hated me because I'd brought Nerine Ariel Sullivan into town, and Nerine had killed one of its favourite sons.

His name was Archie Foenander. He'd worked at Clenins coalmine with his brother Dave. He had a pregnant girl-friend, two dogs, a sister, an auntie and a whole lot of friends. According to the police he'd picked up Nerine on Cox's Ridge Road and taken her back to my house, where she'd killed him.

I don't know exactly what happened, or why. Perhaps he did try to rape her, though I doubt it.

I think she was looking for someone to kill. I think she

wanted me bound to her with chains of guilt and fear, and she needed someone the same age as Duncan, so she patrolled the road that ran past my place until she found the right man. That's certainly what the police think. It's also what Bulwell thinks.

No one there likes living in a Murder Town. A Mystery Town. For weeks after the news broke, Bulwell was crawling with reporters. People had to lock their doors and draw their curtains. A men's rights activist turned up and filmed himself making speeches in front of the town cenotaph. Everyone hated that.

And it was all my fault. In breaking the law, I had opened my door to a monster. Nerine had killed her husband with one of his own hunting knives. Then she'd come down to Bulwell and hit Archie on the head with a rock. He hadn't died immediately. He might have been saved if she'd called the hospital, though he would have suffered permanent brain damage.

I wrote a letter to his family because I couldn't think of anything else to do, but I don't suppose they read it. They probably threw it away unopened.

No one wanted to hear from me in Bulwell. Before I went to trial, while I was still living at the Bolt Hole, some drunken hoons came one night on dirt bikes, yelling and swearing and splashing kerosene around. By the time they left, my shed was on fire. I sat and watched until the building was reduced to smouldering embers. Then I put out the embers with a hose. In the end I didn't go to the cops. Not long afterwards, I sold the house.

I knew I wouldn't be able to live there any longer, no matter what happened in court. For one thing, the Bolt Hole no longer felt like home. Not with Esme's blood staining its veranda. Not with Archie's ghost haunting its front yard. And I had nothing to keep me in Bulwell. No job. No friends. No lawyer.

Tearle didn't want to represent me. Apart from being retired, he was a witness. I'd used his gun, after all. That was another charge I forgot to mention—common assault. I can't remember what the maximum penalty was for threatening Nerine with an unloaded firearm, but I do remember how complicated everything got, since Nerine had been threatening *me* with an unloaded firearm at the same time. The lawyers had a lot of fun trying to untangle that mess, but Tearle didn't think it was fun—not any of it. He loathed having to testify. He loathed being questioned about transporting an antique gun, even though he'd done nothing illegal.

What he loathed most of all, though, was the way I'd fooled him. He'd thought I was a quirky, harmless, endearing middle-aged woman who should have made him feel even more organised and discriminating than he already did. Instead I'd turned out to be a liar. A criminal. A lowlife. And he hadn't sensed it, despite all his legal experience.

So I lost Tearle, too, within days of the incident. I lost him, I lost Esme, I lost Jill and Sally and Dinah and Bridget and my house and both my jobs and I'm also in the process of losing my inheritance, because the Foenanders are suing me. And on top of all that I've lost my family, who didn't exactly step up. Keith, of course, couldn't have been happier. He even tried to have me charged for hurting his hand, though the charges didn't stick. Brian kept his head down, hoping no one in Albury would make the connection. As for Geoff, he's in Dubai. If he's heard about my problems, he's never bothered to call.

Emily kept her distance. I'm glad of it. I'm glad she's in England, where no one pays much attention to Australian news stories. I'm glad she was spared the guilt and the shame and the lack of privacy. She phoned me a couple of times in the early stages. She also sent me a few letters while I was at Emu Plains: breezy accounts of her daily life, so I wouldn't worry about her. As a matter of fact, I *wasn't* worrying about her; I was worrying about me. Emu Plains might be a minimum-security jail, but it's not the kind of place where you can sleep at night. I ended up on anti-anxiety meds while I was there, because of my hair loss and ectopic heartbeats and immune problems. That was something else I lost, thanks to Nerine— my health. I'm not a well person anymore. I have arthritis and irritable bowel syndrome and very bad dreams.

One thing I don't have is Emily's phone number. Or her email address. She doesn't want me intruding, and I can respect that. When I feel a desperate need for connection, I trawl her Instagram posts: all the candid photos of her smiling and clowning and having a ball. I know I can't help her—that she doesn't want my help—so I've bowed out. For her sake.

There was one big question still hanging over me when I left Emu Plains, though. There was one person whose state of mind was still a mystery. That was why, two weeks after arriving in Taree, I borrowed Renee's car and drove back towards Sydney, promising to return the next day.

I didn't drive all the way to Silverwater. I wasn't visiting Nerine; there was no point. I'd spent months and months thinking about her, racking my brain, trying to work out why she'd done it, how she felt, who she was.

Then I testified at her trial. I saw her there, all dolled up in a pearl necklace and pants suit, looking more like a lawyer than most of the other lawyers in that courtroom with her neat blonde ponytail, straight back, subtle makeup and grave, preoccupied expression. But when we locked eyes, there was nothing in her gaze—nothing at all. A black emptiness. It was as if we'd never met.

I realised that I would never understand Nerine because she functioned differently. The person I'd known at Bulwell was an image—a mirage—which she'd constructed out of my expectations to meet her own needs. At trial, the prosecutors identified her motivation as being profoundly, almost childishly primitive: she wanted the freedom to do whatever she liked. She wanted to leave her husband, leave my house, leave the country. And since she regarded her children as an extension of herself, with no rights, requirements or abilities of their own, she wanted the same for them.

Personally, I'm not even sure that the inside of Nerine's head is as well organised as those lawyers seem to think. I wonder sometimes if she's just a loose collection of shifting desires that occasionally coalesce around an object or purpose.

For that reason I've come to regard her less as a human being and more as a wild animal, or a natural disaster, or an act of God. You can't hate a natural disaster the same way you can hate a person—and hate is something you should try to avoid if you want to stay sane.

So I didn't visit Silverwater jail. I went to Bulwell instead. More specifically, I went to a farm outside Bulwell—a farm in a lush valley surrounded by trees. I was familiar with the place so I knew where to stand for a decent view of the homestead, but I didn't park anywhere near that spot. I didn't want to be seen.

I left my car in a shady rest area beyond a bend in the road that ran through the valley. Then I shouldered a pack full of water and muesli bars and hiked to a casuarina thicket where I could watch the house unnoticed even by Stanley the maremma, who was around the back, guarding the chickens.

I was trespassing, of course, but I figured it was the best way. Sally and Dinah wouldn't have wanted me there. They probably wouldn't have run me off the property if I'd walked up and knocked at the door, but my sudden appearance would have ruined their day. And I didn't want to upset anyone. I just wanted a quick look. I wanted to make sure that someone, somewhere had been saved.

I arrived early to make sure I didn't miss the school run. Dinah wasn't at home when I reached my little hideaway, but she soon returned, driving a brand new people mover instead of her old black truck. I couldn't watch her unload because she parked in the garage. But it wasn't long before I heard piping voices. Then a small bright figure ran out into the sunshine.

It was Colette: a four-year-old Colette. She was taller than Ana had been when I first laid eyes on them both, and much more sturdy; she had a round face and a solid little torso and thick blonde hair tied into bunches. She wore a blue patterned dress and yellow socks, and she was talking—properly talking —in a clear, high, happy voice.

'Can I show Stanley?' she asked, as Dinah emerged from the garage carrying a bright pink backpack.

'You can show Stanley once you've gone to the toilet,' said Dinah. When she paused to reach up for the catch on the roller door, I studied her hungrily, thinking that she looked a bit tired. Then my gaze slipped to the figure walking past her, out of the shadows.

Analiese.

'Okay.' Dinah yanked at the door, which rumbled down until it kissed the concrete. 'Who's hungry?'

'Me!' Colette cried. 'Me, me, me!'

'What about you, Ana? Bran muffin?'

Ana nodded. She'd filled out a little, though she hadn't grown much taller. Her school uniform looked too big for her. She wore her hair in two short plaits and there was a mark on her knee, but it was just a scab. There was no eczema anywhere on her skin;. it was clear and bright and dusted with a scatter- ing of new freckles.

I wanted to weep with happiness.

'Could you close the gate, hon?' Dinah said, steering Colette towards the house while Ana turned on her heel, her thumbs tucked into the straps of her flowered backpack. I kept an eye on Dinah until she and Colette had disappeared through the front door. Then I gave all my attention to Ana, who was closing the gate very carefully as she hummed to herself.

Her colour was good. Her posture was good. Her face wasn't pinched and her shoulders weren't tense. I could see for myself, just from the way she moved, that she felt safer.

But there was still something of the old Ana in her eyes. Turning to retrace her steps, she scanned the vicinity with an alert, restless gaze, looking up, around, behind, until she spotted me.

For what seemed like a hundred years, we stared at each other. Eventually I waved and smiled.

She lifted her hand. It was a slow, uncertain movement. But just before I moved away, she smiled back—freely and fondly, if a little sadly—and I realised I hadn't lost quite everything.

Then I walked back to the car, leaving her behind.

ACKNOWLEDGMENTS

The author would like to thank Janine Bavin, Margaret Connolly, Peter Dockrill and Mandy Brett for their help with this book.